AN ACCIDENT OR MURDER?

"What the hell..." I muttered, and stood up to see out the window.

It seemed to be one of those things that happen all too often but always to someone else. A man came running out of the hotel across the street as though the devil were at his heels. Following him was a nut with a gun. The man with the gun stopped and grasped the pistol in a two-handed grip. With horrified fascination, I watched as he carefully sighted and squeezed the trigger. It almost appeared as though he were aiming at us. The plate-glass window fell in sheets to the floor in front of me with a shattering and tinkling that made me jump. I dimly heard screams from people on the street and the sound of sirens not too far off. I was riveted by the scene. I could not turn away to look at Jessica, to see if she had been hurt. I knew I must, but it took all my effort. I did not want to see.....

MICHAEL W. SHERER

An Option On Death

HarperPaperbacks
A Division of HarperCollinsPublishers

This is a work of fiction. The characters, incidents, and dialogues are products of the author's imagination and are not to be construed as real. Any resemblance to actual events or persons, living or dead, is entirely coincidental.

HarperPaperbacks *A Division of* HarperCollins*Publishers*
10 East 53rd Street, New York, N.Y. 10022

A hardcover edition of this book was published in 1988 by Dodd, Mead & Company, Inc.

Cover illustration by Earl Keleny

First HarperPaperbacks printing: September 1991

Printed in the United States of America

HarperPaperbacks and colophon are trademarks of HarperCollins*Publishers*

10 9 8 7 6 5 4 3 2 1

To the believers, especially Mel, C.H.K.v.R., and Cecile:
Thank you.

Prologue

THE CHILD faced water. Some primitive instinct told him he faced east, but there was no way to know for sure. There was only hope that from some direction light would come soon. The child stood trembling, unable to move. Hardly anything was discernible—flat vastness of desert behind, mirrored in front by the sea, all shrouded in velvet, starless night. The only break in that black continuum was the line of ocean froth gently breaking on shore. The only sound came from there, too. The child was alone, and as that realization crept into his consciousness, the sound of the water became the hissing from the maw of some huge, otherworldly monster; the froth on the beach became hunger-induced saliva from the same maw. The child emitted a low animal moan, softly at first, which built into an uncontrollable yowl of sheer terror.

I was that child, and my own howling brought me out of the nightmare into the light of day. I could not let my hopes be crushed, so I had none. The fears threatened to reduce me to helplessness and I could sense my sanity slipping into the darkness. Desperately, my mind latched on to an emotion that had been tucked in a corner, buried under the weight of all the rest—rage. I nurtured it, let it build and grow, then considered it, analyzed it, determined its source. The mind became attentive, focused on the feeling and its causes, and there was calm. Cold, icy calm. I held it there, fueling it occasionally with flashes of remembrance until the mind

1

was clear and in control and working the problem.

I was on a small damn island in a big damn ocean, and I had to get off without the wrong people knowing, without getting killed.

I

SHE WAS SLEEPING comfortably when I left her, and I thought she would be all right for an hour or so. I tucked her into the double bed and left a number where I could be reached in case she woke up. I locked her in and went in search of dinner. I had gotten a drink, finished it, and was starting on a second when the steak arrived. It was sixteen ounces of prime sirloin, but it might as well have been cardboard. After two bites I pushed it away and sat back with my drink.

I had known Jessica Pearson Johnston for a long time, since her graduation from college, in fact. We'd had a fierce but friendly competition for promotions in the same stock brokerage firm for a couple years. We both worked our way up and then began competing for commissions. We grew to understand each other and so had spent a lot of time together—drinking, partying, skiing, laughing—until I quit the job.

We'd shared a lot, and had become close friends. So close, in fact, that on a few of the occasions that her father had come to visit, he'd taken me aside to ask me if I had intentions of marriage. Perhaps we'd grown too close, or maybe we'd never let ourselves get close enough. Romance just never sparked between us, and I would shrug off John Pearson's queries with a laugh and a "someday."

Shortly after I left the firm, Jessica was transferred, and I lost track of her for about two years. Then I received a short note from her announcing her marriage to Vince Johnston. It

took me by surprise and even though we'd never been ro-
mantically involved, I felt a vague sense of jealousy, as though
I had been all that time harboring some notion that she would
eventually become a permanent fixture in my life, one that
held all too few things of permanence. Some piece of me had
believed in "someday." But she did not need, nor had she
asked for, my approval.

I left Denver. There was nothing to hold me there. I'd hated
the brokerage business and hadn't been that good at it. I'd
known enough, though, to save a client's ass. He'd bought a
large stake in a mining concern and had ridden it up during
a rise in gold prices. When gold prices suddenly began to
fall, my client had been on vacation and inaccessible by
phone. I'd sold his holdings, even though his last instructions
had been to do nothing until he got back. The stock had
nose-dived. By selling, I'd made him a tidy profit and saved
him three quarters of a million in losses.

He'd been grateful and had insisted on giving me something
in addition to the commissions I'd made on his account. He
had an old GMC motor home that I'd had my eyes on. I knew
he didn't use it, and it was in disrepair. We dickered some—
I insisted on paying something for it—and finally arrived at
an agreement satisfactory to both of us.

A friend and I had overseen its refurbishment, and I took
to the road, working as a freelance writer. It had been fun,
and I'd done fairly well, managing to cover my expenses with
a little left over. After six months on the road, I'd ended up
in Chicago, and had settled down, finding lots of opportunities
and a few close friends.

The next time I'd seen Jess must have been three or four
years after she married. Some friends had lured me away
from a blustery and cold winter, tempting me with visions of
warm, turquoise waters and pink-sand beaches. I had spent
some time with them cruising the Caymans, then the Bahamian Out Islands on a fifty-foot trimaran. We lolled in the

doldrums, soaking up the sun and floating with the current, and sailed on days when a white froth was whipped up on wavy, deep blue water by a Hamilton Beach wind that whistled through stays, tautened nylon until it thrummed, and lifted the windward hull out of water. After three weeks, we arrived in Governor's Harbour on Eleuthera and put down anchor for a couple of days. And one afternoon on shore, I stumbled across Jessica in a hotel bar.

I almost didn't recognize her. The Jessica Pearson I'd known had been strong and vibrant. She'd had the type of elegance that is acquired at an early age at one of those small schools they go to before going on to Barnard or Smith, a sensual grace well suited to her tall slenderness. The woman I found in the bar was a shrunken, withered, listless husk containing the barest spark of life, blond hair tangled and dirty, gray eyes dulled and sunken in a face that had grown old and thin, the skin stretched tightly over cheekbones and jaw but loose around the throat. And she was drunk.

"Dat one, she's a lady, mon," the bartender noted in island singsong when he saw me staring at her, "but someone done her powerful wrong."

"She needs help," I said unable to take my eyes off her.

"And it's your help she needs, eh, mon?" The bartender looked with suspicion over my six-foot-four frame. My size tends to intimidate, and the five-day stubble on my face probably didn't do much to enhance my image. For a moment I wasn't sure what I should do. I looked back at Jessica before answering, and absentmindedly pulled on the end of my mustache. It would have to be trimmed when I shaved off the stubble, I thought.

"I know her," I said haltingly, not knowing how to explain. "She's an old friend. How the hell did she get here?"

The bartender knew little about her, but watched her carefully whenever she came in, which, he said, was not often. I finally convinced him that I was trustworthy by asking him to recommend a doctor. I brought the doctor back to the bar to help me get Jessie back to the villa the bartender said was hers. We half carried her out and eased her into the doctor's car. She passed out on the way, and when we found the place, I carried her inside. She weighed nothing in my arms, a bundle of dried sticks loosely wrapped in parchment.

When we undressed her to put her to bed, it hurt me to see how she had dwindled. She was painfully thin, ribs protruding, meatiness of hips and breasts and flanks all burned away, butt flattened as though it had been struck with a one-by-ten plank, belly round under tight skin indicating starvation. I left her alone with the doctor and wandered around the villa. It was a mess, clothes and dirty dishes strewn everywhere, a broken lamp lying on the living-room floor. A postcard lay in the midst of the shards, and I picked it up curiously. "Dear Martha, having a wonderful time, wish you were here (ha-ha!)." There was no address, no date. I wondered with sadness when she had stopped having a wonderful time.

I found a large tray in the kitchen and went around collecting the dirties, scraped stale, untouched food off them, and set the dishwasher to humming. Then I picked up the soiled clothing and found a laundry bag to put it in. I had started to sweep and polish when the doctor emerged.

His name was Roland Gilbert, and he looked like an English country gentleman, tallish but stocky, with silver hair brushed neatly back, steely blue eyes under bushy eyebrows, a clipped white mustache, and ruddy complexion that would never tan, only burn under the tropic sun. He sat on a kitchen stool and drank some of the coffee I'd made, and what I had thought was an immutable facade of genteel refinement was gone. He scowled darkly into his coffee mug.

"How is she?"

He looked up and slowly focused on me as though he'd momentarily forgotten my presence. "Suffering from malnutrition and an oversaturation of alcohol," he said after a moment's hesitation. "She seems to be on the brink of an emotional breakdown. And I would say she's been physically abused, badly, but I don't know to what extent. There are some horrible bruises still healing, but no recent ones."

"What should be done?"

He eyed me speculatively. "Do you know her fairly well?"

"I haven't seen her for years, but I've known her a long time."

"Or you could be the one who did this to her," he said evenly. His comment took me by surprise; I could think of no reply.

"Blast it all!" he burst out suddenly. "That's a damn waste of an exquisite creature in there. It's a bloody shame. What's happened to her shouldn't happen to anybody."

His vehemence startled me. "You knew her?"

"Yes, yes, I met her—months ago," he said impatiently. "Charming woman. Vibrant, full of life. There's no reason she should have come to this."

"Can she be helped?"

"She needs a lot of attention, both physical and psychological, and we don't have the facilities here. She needs more care than I can give her, and I don't even know if she's strong enough to pull through."

"She's hurt that badly?"

"Oh, physically she'll be fine. Mentally . . ." He shrugged.

"I could help," I offered hesitantly. Medical men make us feel so helpless. Our instinct is to assume they, and they alone, have the power to heal, to diagnose, to pass judgment on whether a patient will live or die. Too often we feel impotent around the sick; a doctor's presence simply amplifies the feeling because of the knowledge and power he wields. Gilbert did not disappoint me.

"Who the bloody hell are you? You say you know this woman, but I certainly don't know you. You could be a drug-runner, or a sex fiend, or a bloody pirate for all I know!"

"Look," I said soothingly, trying to placate him, "we used to work together. I should have married her—then she wouldn't be here. By sheerest coincidence I ran into her in a bar on one of the hundreds of islands in the Caribbean. She's in trouble. I want to help."

I tried to look innocent, and he stared at me curiously for a long moment.

"She hasn't seen you for a while," he said finally. "Would she trust you?"

"I think so."

He frowned. "I just don't know how far gone she is. A little nerve, a spot of pride—that's all she has left. Build her up with rich soups, keep her tranquilized, let her sleep, and she might come along." He seemed to be thinking aloud, convincing himself of the best prescription. "You can stay with her?"

I nodded. He looked at me again, then smiled faintly, appearing to have made a decision about me.

"Good. She might want to talk it out—I could make a good guess at some of it—but I warn you, if she does, she may become emotionally dependent on you. She probably should be hospitalized, but if you're willing, I think this would be a better arrangement for her."

I rode back into town with him and got my gear off the boat, explaining to my friends what had happened. They were sorry to lose my company, but didn't question my self-imposed obligation to stay. I rented a little Austin jeep, bought supplies, dropped off the dirty clothes, and went back to the villa. She was in a deep sleep, breathing evenly. I finished putting the house in order, occasionally looking in on her, and when she finally awoke, I had a can of soup heated for her.

It was two days before she recognized me. She simply accepted my presence like an obedient child. She slept, ate, then slept some more. At night when she would start out of sleep from some nightmare, I was there to hold her hand. I would stroke and soothe her like one would a terrified animal, in a gentle yet impersonal way. At first she would buck at the slightest touch, but eventually her trembling would stop and she would slide back into sleep. I helped her out of bed and into a shower the second morning, and while she was getting clean, I changed her sweat-soaked bedding. Dr. Gilbert stopped in that day and marked her improvement. As he was leaving, he hesitated at the door.

"I would advise against letting anyone see her in this condition. And I would certainly advise keeping her away from whoever drove her to this state. Someone did things to her that she could not accept, could not live with."

"Couldn't live with?"

"Just so, Mr. Ward. Some part of her is blocking out some terrible events; she is slowly killing herself to avoid confronting the memory. But I think she'll be all right if she learns to trust you and talks to you. We shall see."

Jessica stared at me wide-eyed and startled when I came into her bedroom on the morning of the third day.

"Emerson," she said in a choked little voice, and her hand went to her mouth. She made a fist and gnawed on a knuckle, and then it all broke loose, starting with a soft wail that built until she couldn't hold it back anymore. I felt an empathetic hurt that seared my heart, and I sat on the edge of the bed and held her tightly while she cried the hell out of it with whooping sobs and wails and shuddery inhalations.

It started to come out then. Vince Johnston had tried to destroy her. He had approached her—a big, handsome, smiling man—and had wooed her and married her. Then he had taken control of her life, abusing her, humiliating her, taking her cruelly and forcefully when, and as often as, he pleased. He kept her drunk most of the time so she would be easier to handle, keeping her dazed and confused. She had not minded the booze so much; it was a small escape from the brutal sex and constant demands. When she had almost reached the breaking point, she had started to come out of it, to regain her strength in spite of him. He had seen it happening and so had arranged for the final destruction of Jessica Pearson Johnston. They had come to the secluded villa on Eleuthera, and Vince had combed the resort hotels to find the swingers, a continuous succession of lovers for Jessica, both male and female. And still he had smiled, always the genial and well-mannered host, out for a few of life's kinkier pleasures. When she finally broke, he forced her to sign her holdings over to him—the stocks, the trust fund—leaving her with next to nothing.

Most of us give a resigned shrug and apathetically turn the page of the paper when confronted with such a story. And therein lies the shame, for we are all potential victims of the beast. Hiding behind suburban doors does not rid the world of those people who are compelled to ravage and destroy. The Beatitudes are wrong; the strong will inherit the earth—the meek will lie broken and silently screaming in the wake of the beasts.

When Jessica was all talked out, she slid exhausted into sleep. I bent to kiss her sweaty forehead, hoping I was wrong. Perhaps the evolutionary process that had produced this elegant and cultured woman would eventually weed out the ugliness she had fallen prey to.

She mended slowly but steadily. I was in charge of a gelatinous creature—apathetic, unquestioning, innocently trusting, softly remote, touchingly childlike, an eater and a sleeper. She had slipped into a protective fantasy, assuming she was finally and forever safe from all harm, removing herself from the explosive and fragmentary images Vince had left her with. I finally suggested that perhaps it was time to think about what she wanted to do, to think about leaving that place. She absently murmured agreement, readily accepting any decision I might make. If I'd suggested we try skydiving without chutes she would have agreed with a calm assurance that I knew what was best for her.

I made her pack the things she wanted to take with her, settled the rental of the villa with the real estate office in town, and paid off Gilbert, who offered no ideas as to what the future might hold. Then I made reservations for two to Chicago. Finally, I pulled the door to the villa shut behind us, bundled the lady and her belongings into the Austin, and went to pick up a man from the rental garage who would drive us to the airport.

I took Jessica home with me to my cozy brownstone on Chicago's near north side. I fixed up the guest room for her, airing it out and putting fresh linens and a down comforter on the bed. I unpacked her things and arranged them neatly in drawers and the closet. I ran a hot bath for her. As I moved around the room I chattered incessantly, inanely while she sat unmoving in a chair, dull eyes following my movements but registering nothing. I finally helped her out of the chair and led her to the bath. She sank into the water up to her chin, and I saw a faint smile form on her face. When I was sure she wouldn't sink any lower and drown, I went downstairs to make a list of what I needed to restock the pantry.

I could think of no safer place for her than my house. I lived a fairly solitary and inconspicuous existence; no one would bother her. And I could think of no better therapy for her than exposure to my few close friends who would accept her as they accepted me, with warmth and kindness, especially Brandt. I made a mental note to call him as soon as I came back from shopping.

Upstairs, I checked on Jessica, and she nodded when I asked her if she was ready to get out of the bath. I toweled her off and wrapped a robe around her. She accepted my ministrations as calmly as a child, with no hint of modesty at being naked in front of me. She had been through so much that she was beyond shame. I helped her to bed, explaining that I was going out to get groceries, assuring her that she would be safe. I wouldn't be gone long. She nodded again, yawned, closed her eyes, and was asleep within moments.

She was still sleeping when I returned. I remembered to call Brandt, and invited him over for cocktails, then puttered around the house. I went upstairs and unpacked my own bags, then came back down and spent some time in the little den off the kitchen going through the mail. I called Greg Edwards's office and patiently fought through the screens of receptionist and nurse until Greg himself came on the line. He'd been my physician, and friend, for as long as I'd been in Chicago, and I trusted him. I briefly explained Jessica's situation and he said he'd come over and check on her.

I heard the bell chime and answered the door. Brandt stepped grinning over the threshold and wrapped me in a bear hug. The top of his graying head come up only to my nose.

"I missed you," he said, stepping back to take a look at me. "Life here has been dull and ordinary without you." His voice still had a trace of soft Texas twang after all these years in Chicago.

I laughed and shut the door against the blustery day. "I'm sure you found things to keep yourself occupied in my absence. Come in. Take your coat off. And yes, I missed you, too."

"You look well—tan and healthy."

"Retirement, in small chunks, agrees with me. You taught me well." I led the way back to the kitchen. "How go the wars?"

Inches shorter than me, but wiry and barrel-chested, Brandt Williams is a giant of a man in many ways. A friend in Denver had recommended I look him up when I got to Chicago. I had, and Brandt and I had clicked for some reason.

He'd been my best friend ever since, though I've never been able to figure out why.

Brandt is semiretired. Originally from San Antonio, he comes from an old, monied family that is connected in all the stratospheric social and political circles from Austin to Washington. But he'd been a maverick, and had felt a need to prove himself. Armed with an MBA from Wharton and a pot full of cash from a start-up venture he put together in college, he went out into the world and made a small fortune building companies from scratch. Eventually he went back to his family and asked their forgiveness, then offered to manage the family money. They forgave him, but the vested interests of a small army of accountants and lawyers precluded his attempts to take over their investments.

"You know how it goes. Everyone needs money. The zoo is trying to finish the additions to the kids' zoo. The symphony is trying to raise more money for next season. Northwestern is trying to buy up all of Streeterville and expand their programs. The same old stuff."

His energy amazed me. Relieved of guilt and family obligation, he stayed in Chicago, dabbled with his own money, and volunteered for everything. The family connections put him on the boards and committees of nearly every charitable organization in the city, and he loved every minute of it. But he took even greater delight in his independence and seemed to prefer sitting on my patio with a beer in his hand or slumming with me in neighborhood bars to suiting up in a tux and charming the city's elite.

"Well, it sounds as if you've managed to keep busy."

"Elizabeth's off skiing in Vail and the house is finally quiet. I couldn't get anything done with that woman around. She's a dervish."

Brandt's house was only a few blocks away on Astor, and he usually lived there alone, except for an old Maine 'coon cat and walls laden with books. Though alone, he rarely seemed lonely. Unlike me, he'd been married once, at a young age, but his wife had died, something he didn't talk about. Now he played the field, and was hardly ever without female companionship unless he chose to be. And amazingly, none of his current steadies minded that he dated other women. He had that kind of effect on them all—kind, generous to a fault, full of life, and fascinatingly knowledgeable about everything. He loved them all, and they all somehow understood, and accepted, that he would never marry again.

"Wednesday's bridge sessions have been terrible since you've been gone," he grumbled, helping himself to a beer. "Dean is awful—he doesn't know the difference between Blackwood and Gerber."

I laughed. "Neither do I. You're just used to playing with me. You know my faults better than you know Dean's."

"Maybe." He handed me a beer. "So how was the vacation? It must have been good—I expected you home a week ago."

"It was great, but I cut the vacation part short. I got off the boat in Eleuthera. I ran into an old friend who needed help."

"You just can't leave the white horse at home, can you? Anyone I know?"

"Jessica Pearson. Or Jessica Johnston, I should say."

"You mean *the* Jessica?"

I nodded. "She's upstairs."

"Sly dog."

"No, it's not like that." I took a long pull on my beer, then launched into the story.

He had a grim look on his face when I finished. "Scum."

"Yeah, that says it all. I'm worried, though. It's been more than a week, and there hasn't been any change to speak of. She's lost in there somewhere, and I can't reach her."

"She'll come around. From everything you told me about that woman, she's strong enough to make it."

"I don't know. I just don't know."

"Can I help?"

"I'm sure you can. You have a gift for helping. But not just yet. Better to let her get adjusted, find her way around. When I think she's ready for people, you'll be the first person I call."

We were silent for a moment, then we fell into the easy conversation that was so common between us, a kind of shorthand that those who didn't know us found peculiar. We tended to finish each other's sentences sometimes, and speak volumes without actually talking at other times. He moaned about how miserable and cold and boring it had been since I'd left. And I laughingly told him how warm and wonderful it had been in the islands. Finally, he excused himself to get ready for a dinner date.

I went back upstairs and looked in on Jess. She was awake, reading a magazine by the light on the nightstand. She actually seemed to be engrossed in it. I thought it must be a good sign.

"Who was downstairs?" She said it hesitantly, a little fearfully.

"My friend Brandt. You'll like him. How about some dinner?"

"I'm not hungry."

"You have to eat something."

"Then I'll have whatever you're having."

"Fair enough. I'll have something put together in half an hour. Can I get you something in the meantime?"

"No, thanks."

I cooked a light dinner of grilled chicken breasts, rice, and salad, thinking she could at least handle some of it. She hardly ate a thing.

For days, she stayed in her room. I'd bring up trays of food and an occasional magazine she asked for. And then I'd collect the barely touched trays. I was patient, understanding, and did my best to make her comfortable. I cajoled her into a bath every day, and changed the sweat-soaked sheets every other day. On the fifth day, I did not take up a breakfast tray. Instead, I insisted she get out of bed and into the shower. I selected a simple dress from the closet, some underwear and pantyhose, and a pair of flat shoes to match the dress. I hung them up in the bathroom while she was in the shower, and told her that she could come out when she was dressed.

She did as she was told, but not without looks of shock and small protestations. I smiled to myself. It was progress. It was the first time she'd shown even a little spunk since I'd found her on the island. I sat on her bed and waited a long time. The water stopped running, and still I waited. She finally poked a wet head out of the bathroom, then stepped through the door, a bit bedraggled but dressed.

"I look like hell."

My smile widened. Progress, indeed. "You look fine."

"What now?"

"Breakfast will be served in the kitchen in fifteen minutes. I expect you to be there. I don't care if you're not hungry. You'll sit, sip some coffee, and be sociable for as long as you can stand to be out of this room."

"Okay."

I went down to fix French toast and bacon. I didn't think she was going to come down, but I heard tentative footsteps twenty minutes later. She sat demurely at the table and asked if she could have a cup of coffee. I poured her one.

"I need makeup."

Another good sign. "Make a list. I'd be happy to get whatever you need."

"The bacon smells good."

"Would you like some?"

"Um, yes, please. And maybe just one piece of French toast."

She did a pretty good job. I was pleased. And after breakfast, she wandered around the first floor, looking at the books in the den, admiring the prints on the wall in the living room. I caught up with her in the living room after washing the dishes.

"This is weird," she murmured.

"What is?"

"I know you. I've known you a long time. But walking around this house is like getting to know you for the first time."

"I haven't changed much."

"I know. It's just weird, that's all."

It got better. She started eating more, and spent more time downstairs, reading books, magazines, and the paper—every day the paper, from front page to back. She had an unslakable thirst for news of what was happening in the world, even though she wasn't ready to jump back in. For the most part, I left her alone to feel her way back, to find her self-respect. I spent my time in the den, organizing notes and photos of the sailing trip and knocking out a couple of travel articles.

In another week, I invited Brandt over for dinner. Jess was nervous, as though anticipating a first date. She spent an hour primping to be sure she looked all right, and when she was done, she'd overdone it. I told her she looked wonderful. When Brandt arrived, I thought she would crack. She looked ready to bolt at any moment, and the first fifteen minutes with all of us in the living room were difficult. But Brandt soon had her at ease, as I knew he would, and even had her laughing at one of his outrageous stories. I hadn't heard her laugh since Denver. As she'd put it a few days before, it was weird.

Dinner was fabulous. I cooked, of course. And the evening was successful. Toward the end, Brandt invited Jess to go to the Art Institute with him the next day. She accepted without hesitation, and then realized that she'd committed herself to something she might not be ready for. Brandt gave her an out, but she gamely said it was time that she saw Chicago.

Brandt was the perfect therapy for her, and gave her a break from me, from the constant attention I'd given her. Her first day in public was tough, but Brandt had guided her through it with encouragement and caring. That and a pair of sunglasses did the trick. But she insisted on staying in the house for a few days afterward, and I was afraid it had been too much for her. She spent most of that time in her room, and I wondered when she would return to the land of the living. She seemed to have lost all the ground she'd gained, and she slipped into a kind of trance.

It lasted only a day or so, then she began to come out of her lethargy. I noticed it in small degrees. She again began to take more notice of her surroundings. Her eyes lost their dullness, but she became more remote and thoughtful. We did not talk much. Her night ramblings had stopped long before. She now ate ravenously, and soft curves began to cover the bony protrusions. And when she was ready to try city life again, she let me know. I took her out for long walks through Lincoln Park, to the zoo, to the museums, to quiet out-of-the-way neighborhood restaurants where she felt at ease, and more long walks up and down the beach, bundled up against the cold.

And one night, after a particularly long and tiring day, after we had cooked dinner and eaten and retired to our rooms, I heard footsteps and felt her ease into my bed. With small tuggings and pullings and repositionings of arms and legs, she snuggled in close to me and sighed contentedly. I held her with one hand in the small hollow of her back, feeling one of the little dimples on either side of her spine where the curve of buttocks meld into the smooth back. My mind raced between passion and concern as I lightly and tenderly stroked her long flank. Her breath caught, then she exhaled slowly, and I knew what her night thoughts had been. I sniffed the piney scent of her hair and smelled the sharp-sweet odor of sweat and woman. Her breathing quickened and her body grew heated, and suddenly she stiffened and went rigid. I sensed that fragmentary memories had come back to her, mocking her, debasing and vulgarizing the act on which she had embarked. I let her fall away from me and thought for a moment in silence, then decided to take a chance.

"Poor thing. The lady corrupted, defiled, forever soiled and tainted."

Immediately, the sobs began. "But I wanted you. Y-you've been so kind and p-patient. And I—I love you."

"Very dramatic and touching, Jessica dear. Purity stained, reputation tarnished, hopelessly doomed for innocence lost."

"Damn you, you bastard."

"What do you take me for? A high-schooler leching and leering at anything and everything in a skirt? I like my sexual encounters spiced with kindness and gentleness, a sharing of laughter and tears. Every so often I get lonely and succumb to the weakness of the flesh and take whatever happens my way, but it leaves a bad taste. I keep thinking of the fiery-eyed, iron-willed, vibrant Jessica I knew long ago, and set next to her, your dramatics just don't stack up. No, I think you're a clean, sweet, beautiful, and somewhat silly woman who has forgotten her own worth." I stopped and held my breath, knowing that this moment would decide things between us. She was silent for a long time, unmoving.

"I'm sorry, dear. I was upset because I forgot to turn down the furnace before we left," she finally said in a peculiarly plaintive, subdued, wifely voice. I frowned, momentarily confused, then I burst into laughter, and after a moment she joined in and we laughed until tears rolled. Laughter subsided, but a giggle would set it off until we were too weak to laugh anymore.

After holding each other for a time, we began again. She melted, sighing into my arms, and I gentled her along, telling her of her sweetness, caressing her with kindness and love as much as with hands. I kissed her tenderly—eyes, nose, lips, throat, breasts—stopping to breathe gently, warmly on first one nipple, then the other. My lips and tongue pursed and licked each one to erection, and she gasped and arched her back to thrust a breast farther into my mouth. I lightly pressed a palm against her mons and rubbed in a circular motion while kissing my way up her taut throat to a delicate earlobe. She panted now, and I rolled to cover her warm, moist flesh with my own, and slowly, slowly entered her, a delectable fraction of an inch at a time. And soon, in a single gasping moment, she caught and flamed, a tremor ran the length of her, and she gave a shuddery exhalation that spoke of tumbling releases. In the pleasant afterglow, she spoke with a soft and tender voice husky with emotion, "Emerson, Emerson . . ."

The days that followed were filled with laughter and caring, and the nights were filled with exploration of bodies and souls. It had started out as therapy. She had recognized and acted on a need to prove that she was still a desirable woman, not a degraded piece of chattel. She needed to know that she could still feel and respond, to know that she could be as she once was, be accepted, wanted, loved, cared for. And I had desired her. But I had felt a vested interest, and had expected no less as a reward for my efforts to nurture her back to health. It had turned into more than that. To see her blossom reminded me all the more of the woman she had been and the woman she was becoming. I was at first alarmed to discover what I felt for her, then at ease because it was good, then happy because she loved me as much as I loved her.

Love. The word tripped and rolled wondrously over my tongue, tinkled merrily in my mind, expanded rapidly in my heart, voraciously consuming my being. I became misty-eyed at the sight of her, began making up names for unconceived children, luxuriated next to her on a fantasy porch swing fifty years hence. I was in love, and loved being in love. And I wondered how I could have let her slip through my fingers those many years before. I had been as blind in a different sense then as I was now.

When a month had passed, I awoke one morning to find her dressed, packed, with a grim and purposeful look on her face. I followed her around as she made sure she had everything, bleary-eyed, stunned, numbed, unable to say anything but a repetitive "Why?" She finally shouldered her bag and stuck out her hand to shake mine.

"We'd better say good-bye here."

"Damn it, why?"

"Emerson, I love you, and I will always be grateful to you, but let's not make it harder than it has to be." Her mouth trembled.

"Then tell me why," I repeated. My eyes burned, and I swiped at them with the back of my hand.

"Vince nearly destroyed me, and with kindness and love you put me back together. But everything I know and feel now is related to you. I am fighting for my emotional life. I have to try to learn to walk without you. I have to see if I can feel with someone else the things you have made me feel. If I don't, I will be a whole person only as related to you. Nothing I think or do will have any meaning unless I'm with you, and I can't live with that. But if you want me to be dependent on you, if you want the total responsibility of another person for the rest of your life, then tell me, and I'll stay." She looked searchingly at me, and her lower lip quivered.

"Where will you go?"

"I'm going to stay with Martha for a while. When I feel ready, I'll go home to New York and pick up the pieces of my life. *My* life. Do you understand? I have to go. I have to do this by myself." She turned away so I wouldn't see the tears, leaving me no way to respond.

*   *   *

And now, nearly two years later, she had come running back, exhausted, excited, but with what seemed to be an underlying feeling of calm and serenity. I couldn't tell whether she had come back to ask me to help her pick up the pieces a second time. I didn't know if I would be able to. I paid the bill for my drinks and the barely touched steak, then headed the long way home. I still had some thinking to do. Jessie's sudden reappearance had opened some emotional cupboards that I had thought were bare. Now I had to take an inventory. So I walked along the lake shore, caught between a wall of brightly lit city buildings and a vast expanse of darkness. The cold night air felt good, and for a time I stood with my back to the lights, losing myself in that velvet infinity. The night gave me no answers. Feeling the chill seep through my clothes, I finally turned and hurried home.

Jessie seemed to be sleeping well, so I went to the kitchen to put coffee on. She had arrived with a large suitcase and a small overnight case. I brought them into the living room. The overnight case contained a minimum of clothing and a few toilet articles. I replaced everything neatly, then opened the larger case. A manila envelope lay on top, and underneath it in tidily stacked and banded bundles was an extremely large amount of United States currency, legal tender for all debts, public and private. It took the breath out of me for a moment. I took a quick accounting and came up with an approximate sum of a quarter of a million dollars. It boggled the mind. Where the hell had she gotten that kind of money and why was she carrying it around in cash? I was both frightened and curious. When I recovered from the initial shock, I turned my attention to the contents of the envelope. It contained prospectuses, receipts of stock transactions, and various letters and notes from stockbrokers, none of them addressed to Jessica. I looked it over carefully, then sat back and thought.

Vince Johnston had not left Jessica penniless. That much

I knew. There had been one trust fund that he had not been able to get into, and there were a few scattered investments that she had used to get a fresh start. But carrying around that amount of cash in a suitcase was ludicrous. I could think of nothing but sinister reasons for doing so. It could only be ill-gotten booty of some kind, and that had me worried as hell. I could make no sense out of the contents of the envelope, either. My imagination ran rampant with wild schemes that might explain how and why she had stuffed a suitcase with portraits of past presidents and had suddenly reappeared on my doorstep. My own sense of larceny made me mistrust her motives for coming to see me. I had, on propitious occasions, operated outside the boundaries of the law and snatched loot from looters; it was dangerous ground. The fact that she was here meant that she had put me back on dangerous ground and made me realize that I would have to help her if she was in trouble. I would have anyway, I knew; despite my fears, I was still deeply in love with her.

It had been late when Jessie had arrived, and the windows were turning gray when I finally decided to turn in. I was drained in every respect, and my limbs groaned accusingly when I stood up and stretched. Years ago I had proudly and fatuously patted myself on the back. I had rescued a priceless treasure from destruction. Now I wasn't sure I'd done her any favor. I brooded about that as I brushed my teeth and splashed my face. It would have to wait until morning. I slid into bed and fell instantly asleep.

It was almost afternoon when I awoke. Jess was still sleeping, looking younger, her face softened with tensions gone. I tiptoed to the bathroom and took a shower to wash the sleep-grit out of my eyes and rinse away some of the body fatigue. I put on coffee to brew while I scraped the stubble off my face, and by the time I dressed, the smell of the coffee woke Jess. When she saw me looking at her, she smiled, and my heartbeat went into double time.

"My God, you're beautiful," I murmured. Her smile grew radiant. The years had given her a new loveliness, a maturity that suited her well. She clambered out of bed and gave me a quick, light kiss as she passed me on her way to the bathroom.

"How do you want your eggs?" I asked through the bathroom door when the water stopped running.

"Soft-scrambled."

I went to the kitchen and grabbed six extra-large eggs that seem, these days, to be no larger than robins' eggs, cracked them into a bowl, minced some mild onion, grated some sharp cheddar, added salt and pepper, folded it all together, and, after applying heat, had breakfast ready. Jessica emerged from the bathroom in one of my robes, shiny and squeaky-clean, and she slid into my arms to hold me for a moment, face pressed into my neck. We ate in silence. I didn't want to press her, but I wished to hell she'd say something. She had a faraway look on her face. I was full of questions but knew she must tell her story in her own time. I wanted desperately to believe she had come back to me and was fearful that she hadn't, that she merely wanted my help. Finally, she spoke.

"How long have we known each other? Ten years?" Her voice was soft. "It's funny, when we first knew each other, I wanted you to fall in love with me. And I thought, that's foolish; why would I want one of my best friends to fall in love with me? Friendship and love seemed, well, mutually exclusive concepts. And then when you brought me back from Eleuthera, when you wanted me to fall in love with you, I didn't dare, even though I wanted to. Life's unfair, isn't it?" She paused, and I smiled faintly. "Oh, I do love you, Emerson," she whispered.

Did I really hear it? There was a lump in my throat and a familiar burning in my eyes, the sting of salty wetness that came from a schoolboyish embarrassment of being too sentimental.

"Well? Say something."

I swallowed hard. "More coffee?" It came out a hoarse croak, and I could feel my ears redden and my face flush.

She laughed, and I grinned with her, feeling a lessening of the pressure in my chest. It would somehow work out, I knew. I saw strength and confidence in her now that I had overlooked, and my fears diminished. We took our coffee to the end of the living room where the midday sun streamed through the big bay window, warming ourselves in the rays, quietly watching cigarette smoke drift up in the shafts of light. I opened one of the smaller windows on either side of the bay, and street sounds came floating in with a touch of the winter chill outside.

"Why?" I asked softly. I didn't know where to begin. She looked up at me, silhouetted against the half-drawn drapes, back to the window.

"The money?"

I nodded.

"It's not a dowry or a bribe, in case you're worried. I had some things to accomplish when I left you. I hope you understood that. I had to find out if I was the same Jessica I'd been before I married Vince. Part of that was seeing if I could feel things with other people that I felt with you. Part of it was seeing if I could stand on my own two feet, could make my way again in the world. I did what I set out to do. I met a man, and it was good while it lasted. I only recently got out of that—it had started to get a little messy. And I proved to myself that I have what it takes to be a whole person. Now I want to stop running and settle down and relax. So, here I am. I know it sounds strange, and I didn't really expect anything when I arrived here. For all I knew, you could have slammed the door in my face. But you didn't, and maybe that's a start."

She paused as I waved a peremptory hand. Then I stopped as I realized that she was right. For all she knew, I *could* have slammed the door in her face. "I tried," I said after a moment, "but I don't think I ever stopped loving you."

"I'm not asking you to promise anything, nor will I promise you anything. I'm here because I want to be, but if you would rather not have me, I'll leave. I didn't come looking for help; I came looking for you."

"Right now, I'd rather have you here more than anything I can think of." I felt comfortable. This was a woman I could easily spend my life with, I realized, someone who could accept me and my crazy existence. We sat in silence. I listened to the traffic and caught what sounded like the beginnings of an argument from an open window in the hotel across the street.

"I'm a little concerned," I said abruptly, remembering what our conversation had been about, "that you might be in some kind of trouble."

"Oh, that." She laughed. "I didn't steal it. I'm not sure whose money it was, but it's legally mine now." Her face flushed with excitement. "I know it was foolish to carry all that cash, but I just had to show you. There's more, in fact, but I reinvested it so it would be safe. This is something different, something special."

"What the hell are you talking about? You're crazy." I was still mystified.

Her eyes gleamed, and she smiled at my impatience. "It's a long story," she said, then paused, thinking of a way to tell it. Before she could begin, there was a sharp, echoing crack outside the window that startled both of us.

"What the hell . . ." I muttered, and stood up to see out the window.

It seemed to be one of those things that happen all too often but always to someone else. And it happened so quickly that it took on an unreal, dreamlike quality. A man came running out of the hotel across the street as though the devil were at his heels. Following him was a nut with a gun, and the gun barked again. The running man was heading toward us in a jagged, erratic pattern. In police stance, the man with the gun stopped and grasped the pistol in a two-handed grip. With horrified fascination, I watched as he carefully sighted and squeezed the trigger a third time. It almost appeared as though he were aiming at us, and when the third shot came, the plate-glass window fell in sheets to the floor in front of me with a shattering and tinkling that made me jump. I dimly heard screams from people on the street and the sound of sirens not too far off. The man with the gun looked in our direction with a peculiar expression, then broke and ran as two police cars turned the corner and converged on the hotel. The cops from the first car gave chase, but the man had disappeared around the corner and down the alley. I was riveted by the scene. I could not turn away to look at Jessica, to see if she had been hurt. I knew I must, but it took all my effort. I did not want to see . . .

She had slumped to the floor, and sat with her back propped against the window seat. She looked up at me ruefully, apologetically, then coughed, and blood ran out of the corner of her mouth and down her chin. "No," I whispered. "Don't . . ." I kneeled in front of her. The last slug had come angling, tumbling in, had taken out the window, and then had hit Jess, entering just behind and under her left arm, undoubtedly tearing the hell out of her chest. She frowned at me, as though annoyed that she was being a nuisance. Then she coughed again, slowly drowning in the blood that filled her lungs. She looked at me and her eyes saw me, then glassed and saw through me and somewhere way beyond.

I howled. I howled in pain and rage. Something snapped in my mind, and it all broke loose and went to hell. I did not hear the cops come running across the street, clambering over the empty window frame. I did not hear them shouting.

I did not hear the sirens as the ambulance pulled up. I was only vaguely aware that it took three strong men to pull me away from her body and hold me while one of the white-coated ones fiddled with my sleeve. I did not hear them ask me questions. I could not see them take her away through the wetness that filled my eyes and coursed down my cheeks. I howled and felt pain. That slug had lodged itself as surely in my chest as it had in hers, but I was not dead, for I felt pain. Oh, Lord, it hurt!

The ambulance took her away, settled and shrunken in my robe, with no lights flashing, no siren wailing. The cops left, having given up asking questions. I was alone, feeling the effects of the shot one of the paramedics had given me, craving the oblivion it would provide. I wandered into the bedroom—and saw the suitcase that sat silently by my bed.

II

IT WAS COLD. The sky had turned slate gray, and a light sprinkling of feathery snowflakes dusted the street, swirling in eddies as cars passed. But the cold winter wind swooping through the broken bay window could not match the chill in my heart. The bleak emptiness in my chest numbed me more thoroughly than any weather Chicago could offer. The sedative, too, was taking effect, making thought almost as difficult as feeling. It had lessened the shock, but had made it harder to accept the fact that Jessica was gone. She was as cold as I was now, lying on a slab in the morgue, waiting to be placed in frozen earth somewhere, never to feel warmth again.

The living room grew dark suddenly. I turned to watch the sheet of plywood being put in place over the frame of the bay window. I had called a window repair service, and the two workmen had arrived within a half hour. They would be back in the morning to replace the glass now that they had the proper measurements.

"What happened here?" one of them asked conversationally.

"A woman was shot," I replied dully. The man paused, eyeing me reflectively, slowly chomping a dead cigar butt. "Some idiot over at the hotel decided to play cowboys and Indians," I went on, suddenly feeling strangely guilty under his gaze. "He came running out shooting at another man in the street, and one of the shots went wild." I remembered too vividly how the man had stopped and carefully set up, seeming to aim right through his intended victim directly at Jessica.

"Guess you can't be too careful these days, huh?" The man turned back to his task. "She okay?"

I looked up sharply. "She's dead."

He was silent for a moment. Then, just as casually, "They catch the guy?"

"I don't know. I don't think so."

"She a friend of yours?" he asked as he tightened a nut with a wrench.

"A close friend." This time I couldn't keep an edge of annoyance out of my voice.

He paused for a moment, then slowly took the cigar out of his mouth. "Sorry. Stupid question."

"That's okay." I shrugged. His gaze made me uncomfortable. "Look, you guys want a beer or something?"

"Nah. Thanks, anyway. We're just about through here, and we have a couple more jobs to go to."

They finished the job in silence, for which I was thankful, although I didn't know which was worse, enduring inane questions or the empty loneliness of silence. I didn't want to be alone, but I couldn't stand intrusions into my private grief.

When the workmen left, I turned my attention to the suitcase. Jessie's legacy now held more questions than money, but the money, at least, could not be left lying around. Anything to keep busy, I thought.

I didn't want the money in the house, so I lugged the suitcase out to the oversize garage where I still kept the motor home. One of the modifications I'd made was the installation of a strongbox hidden beneath the platform bed in the stateroom—one of three specially constructed hidey-holes in the bus. The bus smelled musty with disuse, and the interior lights burned dimly.

There was a small nylon duffel in one of the closets that

contained some odds and ends. I emptied it out and transferred the money to it bundle by bundle. Then I pulled the
mattress off the bed and slid back the panel underneath,
revealing the reserve water tank, only half of which held
water. I popped the hidden catches on the strongbox and
stuffed the duffel into the small space, squelching an impulse
to find a flower to drop into the hidey-hole. After putting
everything back in place, I hurried back to the house, feeling
furtive and guilty.

I had just gotten back inside when the doorbell rang. It
startled me, and I checked the peephole to see a man in a
rumpled gray topcoat blowing on his hands and stamping his
feet in the cold. I opened the door a crack.

"Emerson Ward?" he asked. I nodded. "I'm Lieutenant
Lanahan, police department. I'm sorry to bother you, but I
have to ask you some questions before I can finish the initial
report on that shooting this afternoon."

"Sure, come on in." I shrugged, swinging the door open.
He stepped inside and looked around appraisingly. He was
a burly man with a round, friendly face ruddy from the cold.
"Would you like some coffee?" I asked as he shook off his
coat. "It's already made," I added.

"Sure." He rubbed his hands, then fished in his coat pocket
and pulled out a stenographer's notebook.

"Have a seat," I said on my way to the kitchen. I poured
coffee into two mugs and put them on a tray with cream and
sugar, then set the tray on the table in front of him. I went
to the liquor cabinet and brought back a bottle of Tullamore
Dew. His eyes lit up and he hesitated, but finally took the
bottle.

"Thanks, I think I will." He splashed a dollop of the Irish
whiskey into his mug. "It's just too damn cold out not to.
Ah, that's good," he said, taking a sip. I fixed my own, and
took a chair across the coffee table from him.

"Look, I apologize for intruding," he continued. "I understand you were pretty upset earlier, but I'd like to know what happened from your point of view."

I briefly described how we had been sitting, how the men had come running out of the hotel, how the third, and fatal shot had shattered the window, and how my attention had been glued to the scene because somehow I had known that Jess was hurt, and I hadn't wanted to see it. He nodded and scribbled in his notebook, occasionally stopping to tap the end of his pencil against his lower lip as he watched me intently.

"Could you describe the man with the gun?"

"I don't know—medium height, medium build." I was peeved at the question. "Surely you have a description from all the eyewitnesses on the street."

"Yes, we do," he said quietly. "Just verifying what we have."

"I'm sorry." I paused, then described the man as accurately as I could, remembering the expression on his face, the clothes he wore, the way he stood, and the way he had run at the last possible moment. He had been a powerful man, and he had seemed comfortable with a gun in his hands, I realized as I recalled the scene.

"What we don't know," he said, almost apologetically after a pause, "is the name of the victim."

"Jessica Pearson Johnston."

"No relation?"

I shook my head.

"She was someone special, however?"

I nodded, then told him a little about how we had met and how we had gotten together again after so many years, knowing he probably would have asked anyway.

"I'm sorry. It's a lousy way to die." He looked angry, and was silent for a moment.

"Lieutenant, what the hell happened out there anyway?"

He sighed. "As far as we can tell, it appears to have been

an argument over a woman. The suspect caught his girlfriend or wife—a hooker, more likely—in the room of one of the hotel's guests. The desk clerk has identified the guest as a William Hodges from Green Bay, Wisconsin, in town for the hardware convention; we haven't found him yet. The man apparently chased this Hodges fellow downstairs and through the lobby, waving a gun, then started taking potshots at him when they reached the street. We don't know any more than that at present."

"Wonderful," I said sarcastically. "What are the chances you'll catch this guy?"

"With the description we have, about fifty-fifty." He saw my angry stare. "All right. Look, I don't know if we will find him. I know you're angry, and I understand your frustration, but we will look for him. And we do have a chance. We didn't find the gun anywhere near here, and we know the victim—Mrs. Johnston—was killed by a thirty-two-caliber slug. Maybe he kept the weapon, in which case when we find him we'll be able to nail him." He paused, and I got up from my chair and paced the floor, trying to get my anger under control.

He had something to go on, but he would give the matter of Jessica's death the same amount of attention as the nine hundred eighty-seven other files he undoubtedly had on his desk. It had simply been a tragic accident, and if they caught the man responsible, fine. The matter held greater importance for me. I would have to find him myself, I sensed, if I wanted to avenge Jessica's death. Emerson Ward, Dragonslayer. Any excuse to hop into the saddle of the faithful old white steed, bang the beer-can armor, wave the broomstick lance with the fluttering pennant that cries "Virtue," shout huzzahs, and leap into the fray to protect wanton waifs and distressed damsels from the cold, harsh realities of the world, from wicked men who would corrupt and defile them, and, in the name of all that is good and true, make them whole and

fulfilled and happy with that therapeutic marvel, a dose of
Emerson Ward's old-timey romanticism. I had used clever
sayings and sly designs to bundle the lady sweetly into my
bed, saving her from the clutches of the brutal Vince Johnston
and a marriage turned sadistically sour, but the tin armor
had not been enough to stop a stray bullet from killing her.
Perhaps this righteous indignation I suddenly felt was an
excuse to rationalize my own sybaritic existence, a means of
polishing spots of a character tarnished by self-indulgence.
I didn't know. I knew only that I had to find the man who
had taken Jess away before I'd had a chance to find out how
much I could truly love her.

"Do you know of any relatives?" Lanahan interrupted my
thoughts. "We'd like to notify her next of kin."

"Her father was all she had, I think. Let me call him,
please. It would be more . . . personal."

He nodded. "By the way, do you have her personal effects?"

"Sure," I said, frowning. "I'll get them." I couldn't imagine
why he wanted them, but I went to the bedroom and brought
back her purse and the overnight bag. He briefly rummaged
through them, taking note of the contents.

"Fine. I know you'll make sure her father gets these." He
rose and put on his coat. "I'll have your statement typed up,"
he said on his way to the door. "I'll call you when it's ready
so you can come down to the station to sign it. I'd also
appreciate it if you could take a look through our mugbooks
as soon as possible. It doesn't appear our man is the sort to
have a record, but one can never tell."

"I'll do that," I assured him.

"Thanks for your help. Call me if you think of anything
else." He handed me a card, then bundled up his coat and
hurried down the walk to the unmarked sedan parked at the
curb.

Now came the distasteful task of calling Jessica's father.

Better to do it while I was still anesthetized by the sedative, I thought; maybe it wouldn't be as difficult. I went into the den to get my address book. It would be about four o'clock in New York, so I would try John Pearson at his office first. He was the only family Jessica had had. Her mother had died when she was a baby. Since I had last seen John, I had spoken to him only occasionally over the phone. I dialed the number, and it rang twice before a secretary answered. He was in, she said.

"John," I said when he got on the line, "this is Emerson Ward. I'm not sure if you remember me; I'm a friend of Jessica."

"Of course, of course. How are you, Emerson?"

"I'm afraid I have bad news. I don't know how to tell you." I paused, steeling myself with a deep breath. "Jessica's dead, John."

There was a profound silence. "Oh, Jesus," he finally whispered. "When?"

"This afternoon," I choked out. "A few hours ago."

Again there was silence on the line. "How?"

"She was shot—accidentally." I didn't know what else to say.

"What happened? No, no, never mind. I'll get the details later. You're still in Chicago?" His voice was controlled, but strained.

"Yes, sir."

"Jessica—she's there, I take it. All right, I probably won't be able to catch a flight tonight, so I'll get on one first thing in the morning." He gave me the airline.

"I'll check the arrival time and pick you up." I paused. "Do you want me to start making arrangements?"

"No, that's all right," he said quietly. "We'll do it in the morning. I better make some phone calls."

"John, I'm really sorry."

"I know. I'll see you tomorrow."

I gently cradled the phone. I sat for a long time, thinking of nothing, unaware of the darkness that settled in. I had floated too long unattached, an amoeba in a self-contained world surrounded by distilled water in which nothing else seemed to live. Occasionally, I opened the gates of my self-imposed solitude and let friends in to change and brighten my existence with chatter, a once-in-a-while bridge game, a dinner or two. But something had been lacking in my life for a long time. Chicago was a nice city; I had nice friends. But life seemed bland. I sat, full of self-pity. Jessica could have been the attachment I had avoided for so long, the ground wire I had sought. I had not been fully plugged into life around me, and she might have been the outlet linking me to everything I was missing, providing me with more than vicarious thrills. Three times she had slipped through my fingers, and now there would be no more chances for us.

I finally got up to turn on a light, and went to the kitchen to heat up some soup. But I wasn't hungry. I left the half-finished mug on a counter and wandered from room to room, feeling trapped and haunted by my own inadequacies and the ghost of the woman who was shot. I needed a cause, it seemed, to feel alive, to feel worthwhile. Without one, time seemed wasted, life was little more than treading water. Well, I'd found one at the expense of a life, and perhaps at the expense of a relationship in which I would have had no need of causes. All this aimless self-recrimination was making things worse; I was beginning to feel claustrophobic. A walk might do some good, I thought, so I bundled up, turned out the lights, locked the door, and headed toward the lake.

It was a bitterly cold February night. The wind had died, and the clouds that had earlier dusted the city with snow had scudded out across the lake, leaving the sky clear and starlit. My steamy breath hung in billows in front of me, and as I walked it condensed and froze in little icicles on my mustache. The air was brisk and clean, and with no wind to penetrate the layers of clothing I had on the cold touched only the exposed parts of my face, nipping my nose and ears. The ice along the lakeshore had been broken up by winter storms, but large icefloes still bobbled in the waves, moving eerily like ghosts on the inky background of the water. I walked almost a mile up to Diversey, then turned and headed home through the park, past the botanical gardens and the zoo that lay in dark and silent hibernation waiting for spring. Finally, I was back on brightly lit city streets, just a few blocks from home. I had solved none of the world's problems, or any of my own, but the walk had made me feel better, and I went up my steps a little less morose.

I sensed something was wrong as soon as I opened the door. I took a few steps into the living room and waited, listening intently, then moved to turn on a light. There was a soft footstep behind me, and a massive forearm snaked around my throat before I could reach the switch. My hands went to the intruder's arm, scrabbling and clawing to pull it away. I bent forward to pull him off balance, and together we stumbled into an end table, sending a lamp crashing to the floor. I kicked backward, trying to rip the flesh off the man's shins. He merely grunted and tightened his grip on my throat. I tried to force him backward into a wall, but could get no leverage. The man had to be inches taller than my six-foot-four, and probably outweighed me by thirty or forty pounds. His sheer size and power, and the fact that I was being choked to death, sent a surge of adrenaline through my system. I half carried him across the living room trying to loosen his grip, but my head was spinning, and my lungs were screaming for air. My vision went black, and I went slack in his grip. He suddenly let go, and I collapsed on the floor, taking huge gulps of air with great wheezing sounds. I shook my head to clear my vision, and struggled to my knees, then something thokked against the side of my head above the ear. My muscles turned to jelly, and I went down, feeling nothing.

When the buzzing in my head finally lessened, I could hear again, and dim shapes materialized in front of my eyes, but I couldn't move. I felt as though under water; everything was hazy and remote and moved in slow motion. And I was disembodied. I could feel nothing. I heard sounds of the man moving around the house, sounds of doors opening and closing, drawers being pulled open and pushed shut.

Eventually, I found I could turn my head slightly, and I could see clearly. The living room was still dark except for the light that filtered in from the hallway and from the street. The man returned to the living room, glanced at me, and began poking around, searching systematically in the half-light. He was as big as I'd thought. My mouth didn't work, either, and I watched helplessly as he searched, unable to protest. A shaft of light from a street-lamp cut across his face. It was large and round, with features that were too small for it. He was not unhandsome, but the small eyes and mouth gave him a mean little-boy look.

Suddenly, he was standing over me, watching my squirming efforts to make everything work again. He reached down with a massive paw and grabbed a handful of coat fabric beneath my chin. With one hand he lifted me effortlessly, leaving me openmouthed and bewildered, feeling a mix of awe and terror. Then he hit me with an open-handed blow across the face that rang my ears.

"Where's the money?" he asked when my eyes uncrossed.

"Don' hab any," I said thickly. Why didn't he just take the television or something and be done with it? He backhanded me across the other side of the face, and the ringing in my ears became a dull roar.

"Where's the money?" He spoke calmly, almost politely. He had a funny little smile, and his small eyes flicked rapidly back and forth, searching my face for some hint.

"Who are you?" I asked stupidly. He hit me again in reply, and I tasted blood.

This would not do. I stiffened my fingers and jabbed him in the face, poking him in the eye. He grunted and dropped me, his hands going to his face. I managed to hook one foot behind his ankle, then lashed out with my other foot as hard as I could, kicking him in the knee. He roared in pain and fell backward. I tried to scramble away, but he grabbed me, lifting me to my feet while he hit me again and again across the face. Things were turning fuzzy. My knees quivered, feeling deserted me, and I toppled to the floor. Through the roar in my ears, I dimly heard pounding and thought I heard someone calling my name. Then blackness washed over me and the world receded into nothingness.

Someone *was* calling my name. The voice was faint and faraway at first, but gradually came closer and became more distinct. I opened my eyes and saw Brandt's concerned face peering down into mine. The lights were on, and I squinted against the brightness. The side of my head was tender, and my whole head ached. I gingerly reached up to touch my neck and felt an icepack. I tried to speak; nothing came out. I wet my lips and tried again.

"How did you get in?" I asked Brandt.

"I came around the back. Whoever did this slipped out the back, but left the door wide open."

I nodded. I wasn't thinking clearly.

"I heard about the shooting on the six o'clock news," he continued. "I tried calling a few times, then figured you must have taken the phone off the hook, so I came over. What the hell went on here?"

I looked around. The place was a shambles. My eyes watered, and I bit my lower lip. "It just hasn't been my day," I said, thinking of Jess. I tried to sit up, but everything seemed to hurt at once.

"Take it easy," Brandt said, helping me up. "I called Greg;

he's on his way over. I thought he better take a look at you."

Greg had tended to my hurts before, and had never questioned where I'd gotten them.

"Did you surprise a burglar or something?" Brandt asked.

"Is anything gone?"

"I don't think so," he said, looking around.

"It was no ordinary burglar. A burglar would have run when he heard me at the door. Oh, Jesus." I groaned. What had Jessica gotten me into? I suddenly realized, stupidly, what he'd been after.

"What is it?" Brandt looked at me curiously.

"There's a duffel in the hidey-hole in the bus. Bring it back in and I'll tell you about it."

He hesitated, then nodded and left. I slowly got up and poured two stiff Scotches on ice, then sat on the couch. Brandt returned and traded the duffel for one of the drinks, then sat down opposite me.

"That's a lot of money in there."

"Jessica Pearson showed up last night with that money in a suitcase." Brandt waited for the rest of it, and I gave him the story of what had happened during the past eighteen hours. "So, somebody knows she had the money," I finished, "and followed her here. But I don't know where it came from or who wanted it."

"I would say you've got yourself a problem." He stopped to think.

The doorbell rang, and Brandt answered it.

"Emerson, you don't look too good," Greg Edwards said.

"I don't feel all that well, either."

"Okay, let's have a look-see what the damage is." He sat next to me and opened his black bag. He gently probed the lump on my head, saying, "Hmm, got hit here twice, I see." Then he shone a light in my eyes, looking into one, then the other. He poked and prodded, then had me cross my legs, and hit my knee with a little rubber hammer. I uncrossed them, recrossed them, and he hit the other knee to test my reflexes. After some more poking and "hmming" he closed his bag and sat back with his fingers laced behind his head.

"If you'd been hit any harder in the head, you'd have a nasty little concussion right now. As it is, you have a teensy-weensy one, I'd say—enough to give you a headache for a day or so. I'll leave you a couple of codeine tablets. Being knocked silly like that could cause temporary paralysis if you were hit just right. Your face will be swollen and puffy for a few days, but there won't be any lasting bruises. You were lucky, my friend; I'd say someone knew what he was doing. He was careful to hurt you but not do any permanent damage."

He paused. "All right, I won't ask," he said, shrugging. He stood and picked up his bag. "Next time, be more careful who you pick to dance with."

"Thanks, Greg. Put this on my tab." I knew he wouldn't even bother to send me a bill. "Have a drink before you go?"

"No thanks. I've got to run. Sally's expecting me back; it's my turn to put the kids to bed." We said our goodbyes, and Brandt showed him to the door.

"How do you feel?" Brandt asked when he came back.

"Lousy. I still feel numb. Jessica was the one," I said softly. "She was the one I think I could have settled down with. I could have given up all this quixotic nonsense about having a cause; she would have been my purpose in life. I think I could have lived with that one. But now I'll never know. Maybe that's what hurts most—not knowing."

"What are you going to do now?"

"I'm not sure. I called her father in New York. He'll be here first thing in the morning. I'd like you to be here. You might be able to help us determine what to do with the money."

"Sure. What time?"

"Make it about eight-thirty or nine. I'm picking him up at

the airport, and we should be back by then." I was silent for a moment, then Brandt spoke.

"Emerson, don't you think you should report this?"

I thought a minute. "No. On top of the shooting, this may seem a bit much to be coincidental. The police might think I was hiding something, and I don't need the hassle."

"I guess I see your point. Well, I'll be going if you're sure you'll be all right."

"Yeah, fine. Thanks."

After he left, I called the airline to find out when John Pearson's flight was getting in. Then I wandered around the house, trying to put things back in order. I washed down one of the pain pills with another belt of Scotch, and finally, exhausted, I climbed into the empty double bed and fell into a deep sleep.

III

DURING THE NIGHT, moisture rolled up off the Gulf of Mexico creating a cloud cover over the city, and a mass of warm air swept in from the Southwest putting a cap on top of that. The combination produced almost four inches of snow and freezing rain, and now in the early morning hours I watched the snow taper off into a fine drizzle. I had awakened early and had gone for a short walk. Though the temperature had risen almost twenty degrees, it was cold and raw. The dampness chilled bones more thoroughly than even the bitter cold of the day before.

The emptiness of the bed had wakened me. My body achingly recalled all the contours of her, all the curves and valleys, and the secret places that could be touched just so. I could feel her snuggled tightly into my back, her breath warm between my shoulder blades, my buttocks pressed warmly into her lower belly at the juncture of the thighs, her legs snaking down the length of mine, her toes grasping my Achilles tendon so that every inch of her touched some part of me. Now the silky flesh was cold, and the warm blood that had pulsed beneath it was stilled forever. She had come back to save me from myself, from my own little world that had somehow become tawdry and banal, just as I had once saved her. She would have meant an end to a life I had curiously outgrown and become increasingly cynical about, an end to a life of rambling as loose-jointed as my gangly frame. But she had deserted me, leaving me shackled to my self-created image of white-plumed knight on a white horse, symbol of gallantry, bumbling from one windmill to the next in search of value and sense of purpose, half-crippled by emotional immaturity and puritanical hang-ups that went deeper than I wanted to believe.

I felt a great selfishness as I sipped coffee in the cold gray morning light, and I wondered what I really felt underneath. It is as if we twitch emotional cords in a room of the house and wait to see who will come running to answer the bell. I was afraid that under the pain was a selfish anger that she had not repaid the favor I'd done her, or perhaps some sort of relief that I would not be forced to play the charade of a togetherness that was alien to my staid and fussy single ways. But no matter which cord I pulled, the answer came back the same: I had lost my girl, the one I had been destined for, and the loss seemed larger than life, larger than my sad and superficial existence.

I pushed away the coffee and the sense of loss that was almost too much to bear, and got up. I went to the garage to start the red Alfa coupe that sat squatting buglike next to the bulk of the motor home. It didn't like cold mornings any more than I did, and growled throatily at the imposition of being asked to go out on a day like this. The streets were slushy and slick, and I drove tentatively, wary of the nonchalance of other drivers, especially Chicago cabbies forging blithely through the snow, unmindful of its icy treachery. The expressway was clearer, and I let the little car have its head, making good time to the airport, lulled by the steady hum of the engine and the slap of the wipers smearing the sad rain against the windshield.

I waited at the gate as the plane rolled up to the terminal, nosing into position. A muffled bell clanged as the jetbridge was moved and snugged into place against the fuselage, and a moment later John Pearson emerged at the rear of the first group of passengers to disembark. He was tall and lean with

gray, thinning hair and pale, pale blue eyes. The high cheekbones, thin nose, and square jaw gave him the same look of
elegance that Jessica had had. He paused, searching the gate
area, then his eyes met mine and he strode forward to meet
me. I held out my hand and he took it. His hands were long
and slender, but his grip was firm. He paused again, his eyes
searching my face, then he pulled me to him and embraced
me. Perhaps he read in my eyes how much she'd meant to
me. Without a word, and with no self-consciousness, I hugged
him back, knowing that we shared not only a common sorrow,
but the memory of someone very special as well. When he
pulled away, tears silently streamed down his face, and
he tried to smile and wipe and them away. I did not think
he was a man who shed many tears. I fought back my own
and patted him on the shoulder.

"Come on, I've got the car waiting outside."

He buttoned up the gray herringbone overcoat, tucking in
the navy scarf, picked up the small suitcase he'd carried off
the plane, and followed me out of the terminal.

The car warmed up quickly, and I turned off the heater
fan and loosened my coat. We threaded our way through the
construction that seemed a way of life at O'Hare. For nearly
ten years, they'd been building one thing or another at the
airport. The half-melted snow made everything look grimier,
covering the ground in a wet gray a shade darker than the
sky. John looked back and forth with a dazed expression,
hypnotized by all the activity, the traffic merging and flowing,
construction equipment lumbering along in the median, air-
planes moving to and fro on ramps and runways on either
side. Finally, we were on clear road back to the expressway,
and he gave his head a little shake, then turned to look at
me.

"I guess I still can't comprehend the fact that she's gone.
Why?"

"I don't know. I just don't know." I could not yet fully

comprehend it either. I kept hoping her death was some kind of cruel joke, that it had been ketchup instead of blood, that it had all been staged to give me a fright, that she would come running back into my life, warm and safe and happy, apologizing for the scare they had given me.

"How did . . . how did she die?"

"There was a quarrel outside the hotel across the street. We were sitting in the front window having coffee. One of the men had a gun and started shooting, and one of the shots just went wild, I guess. It happened so fast I'm not even sure of what I saw anymore. For a time, it seemed as if we were removed from what was happening out in the street. We were not part of it. But when that bullet came through the window, we suddenly became bystanders who got caught in the line of fire. I didn't think such things were possible. I thought we were safe within the walls, the privacy, of my house."

"Jess, an innocent victim? I don't know."

I glanced at him, puzzled. His face was full of sorrow, but his voice was cool and detached.

"We live in a sick and savage world," he continued after a pause. "Every day the newspapers tell us such stories, and every night the television tells us more. Each day more and more people are dying in a variety of bloody ways. There are too many of us in too small a space, and the edges of our society are beginning to curl back in on us. It's almost to the point now where this kind of thing is no longer an outrage but a common occurrence. We just never expect it to happen to one of our own. We go on pretending that the four walls of our houses or the manufactured boundaries of our own lives will shut the rest out. We continue merrily on our narrow paths, wearing blinders, hoping that nothing unpleasant will intersect us. But all the time we are aware of what surrounds us. Can any of us call ourselves innocent victims or innocent bystanders? Victims, yes. Innocent, no. We have let the killing go on too long to consider ourselves innocent any-more."

"Could I have saved her? Should I have somehow foreseen that idiot staging a shoot-out in the middle of the street? Who could have warned me? My horoscope?"

"I'm sorry, Emerson. No, we can't take on any more guilt than we already feel. I didn't mean to say that because we're no longer innocent we're to blame. I'm sorry I didn't know her better. She was my child, a part of me. I've known her all her life—more than half my own—and I'm not sure I really knew her at all. I guess what I'm trying to say is that we should expect the savagery to touch our lives in some way and learn to accept the things we can't change."

I was silent for a long moment. "I can't do that."

He looked at me intently, face impassive, for a long time, then turned away. "Why was she here?"

"I'm not sure. She arrived on my doorstep the night before last. I don't know where she came from. New York, I assume. She said she wanted to stay."

"Ah. She mentioned she was divorcing Vince." He lapsed into silence. I couldn't tell if there had been disapproval in his voice. I didn't think so.

The rain had stopped and the cloud cover had lifted some. The skyline spread out in front of us, but the tops of the city's three megaliths—the Hancock, the Sears Tower, and the Standard Oil building—disappeared into the fog. We finished the drive in silence. I sensed we both had more to say, but, for the moment, no way to say it.

Brandt had let himself in and had both coffee and a pitcher of Bloody Marys waiting for us. I gratefully poured a Bloody Mary into a king-size glass and drank half of it before I remembered to introduce Brandt to John. Brandt expressed his condolences while I took John's coat and hung it up in the hall closet.

"Do you want to freshen up?" I asked when I came back.

"I'm putting you in the spare bedroom just down the hall."

"No, thanks. I'm fine. But I think I will have a drink. Somehow, it doesn't seem too early."

I filled a glass for him, then poured refills for Brandt and myself. John pulled out a chair at the kitchen table across from Brandt, and I hitched up a hip to perch on the edge of the counter.

"I guess I'll call Lieutenant Lanahan down at the police station in a few minutes and let him know you're here," I said.

"That would be fine." There was an awkward silence.

On a hunch I decided to be honest with him. From what little I knew of him, he deserved that much at least, and I had come up with no other way of determining the source of Jessie's legacy.

"John, Jessica did not arrive here empty-handed, but I don't know why she brought what she did. I asked Brandt over here because he knows more about these things than I do."

"What are you talking about?"

"Wait here. I'll show you."

A few minutes later I returned with the duffel bag. We all stared at the contents, spellbound.

John cleared his throat. "How much is there?"

"Two hundred fifty thousand exactly," I replied.

"Jesus." John shook his head and looked at the money again, then sighed and turned to look at me, rueful and dismayed.

"No clothes? I thought she said she planned on staying?"

"She could certainly buy enough clothes with that kind of money," Brandt said.

"I guess so."

We moved our drinks to the living room. I noticed that the bay window had been fixed. Brandt told me he'd gotten there early, and that the workmen had arrived and replaced it during the hour I'd been gone. I was grateful; it was one less thing to worry about.

I got the envelope with the stock receipts and gave it to John. "See what you make of these. They were in the suitcase with the money. She was about to tell me when . . . when she was killed." I told him briefly about our conversation just before the shooting.

He shuffled through the papers, pausing occasionally to look at one more carefully. "I don't know. It could take awhile to sort this out." He stopped and looked up. "First, let me call my lawyer and see what he knows. I told him last night to start work on Jessica's estate, that I'd be calling him this morning. May I use the phone?"

"Sure, help yourself."

The conversation was strangely one-sided. "Peter? John Pearson. How do things stand?" Long pause. "That *can't* be." Shorter pause. "She *what?*" Another long pause. "I don't see how that's possible, but . . ." Short pause. "Okay, but she was living on something. Check around and see what you can find. I'll look into it as soon as I get back.

"I don't believe it," he said as he cradled the phone and turned to face us. "Jessica was flat broke. She had nothing."

"I wouldn't go that far," Brandt said. "That's quite a bit of cash she was carrying."

"No, no, what I mean is, all her accounts were closed out. She signed everything over to Vince Johnston almost two years ago. I just can't believe it." He shook his head incredulously.

"I thought you knew," I said softly.

"Knew what?" He looked at me sharply.

"When I ran into Jessica down in the Bahamas awhile back," I said after a pause, "she was pretty down on her luck. Vince had . . . well, given her a rough time, and had forced her to sign everything over to him. I don't think she had much choice. It was either lose everything and keep what little sanity she had left, or hang on to the money and be pushed over the edge. I spent some time with her, tried to help her pick up the pieces of her life. I guess she had pretty much done that by herself when she came back. I've never seen her happier. She seemed . . . at peace with herself."

He stared into his drink. When he looked up, his eyes were glassy and shiny with tears. "Damn it to hell, Emerson. Why didn't you marry that girl years ago?" His vehemence startled us both.

"I never liked Vince Johnston," he said, calm now. "Oh, hell, why didn't she tell me?" I could feel his anguish.

"I guess because she knew you'd do something about it. She was finished with Vince. There was no doubt about that. But she had some pride left. She had to get back on her own two feet. 'I have to prove to myself I have what it takes to be a whole person' is what she told me. There's another thing. You would have gone after Vince, just as I wanted to for a time. She couldn't have taken the thought of it being known. Vince humiliated her in a very . . . personal way. I don't think she could take being humiliated in public if it ever got out. So, she probably just looked for a quiet divorce, hoping to erase that part of her life."

"We weren't close for a long time," he said quietly. "I didn't approve of her marriage, but it was her life, so I kept my nose out of it and stayed away. She knew how I felt. It saddened me, though. After her mother died, we had been just about as close as a father and daughter can be. She came and spent a month with me—I suppose right after the time she was with you—and said she was leaving Vince, but she wouldn't elaborate. She was changed, distant. I think I see why, now. She got an apartment and moved out, and it was only recently that we were able to talk again. She did seem happier, more content. She never mentioned that time in the Bahamas, or the time she spent with you, but she did say a couple of times how much she cared for you, Emerson."

"Thanks. I think I know how much." I swallowed hard, trying to dislodge the lump in my throat. "Right now, however, we seem to be faced with something of a dilemma. Your lawyer says Jessica was broke, but she showed up here with a quarter of a million dollars. And she said there was more where that came from. We don't know where it came from or what to do with it, and someone knows she had it and brought it here, or at least thinks she brought it here."

"What?" John looked surprised.

"Someone broke in last night," Brandt explained. "I came by and found Emerson unconscious. Apparently, he surprised whoever it was."

"No wonder you don't look too well," John said to me. "I didn't want to say anything. How do you know the burglar, or whatever, was after the money?"

I explained to him what had happened, why I thought the man had been after the money and not the standard burglar's fare.

"In any event," I said, "something should be done with it for safekeeping at least. I would prefer not to have that amount of money lying around, especially if someone is looking for it. I don't know if you're the executor of Jessie's estate or not, John, but I think you probably should determine what happens to the money."

"I never really expected this eventuality, but I'm the sole beneficiary. When her mother died, she left everything to Jessica in trust until Jess was older—a pretty sizable estate, too. Her mother had a fair amount of family money. Anyway, I've always been Jessica's beneficiary. I thank God she never named Vince Johnston in her will."

"If she had," I mused, "he might have just outright killed her."

"You don't think . . ." John's thought went unfinished. It

didn't much matter—Jessica was dead. "The problem is," John continued after a moment's silence, "we don't actually know if this is part of Jessica's estate. And even if it is, until we find out how she got it, I don't know what to do with it from a tax standpoint. It may be subject to capital gains or income taxes before estate taxes. Jesus, what a mess." He sighed.

"It may not be subject to any taxes, depending on its source," Brandt said softly. John looked at him curiously. "Anyway, for the time being you could put it in a trust until you determine where it came from."

They began discussing various options and the relative merits of different financial instruments. I went to the kitchen to mix another Bloody Mary pitcher. I wasn't bored, but I no longer cared about the intricacies of money management that they were now discussing, which is precisely why I had asked Brandt to come over. And I didn't really care what happened to the money as long as it was safely removed from my premises. I was assuming, of course, that John Pearson held the strongest claim to it. Whoever had rapped me on the skull might not agree.

When I came back, Brandt was on the phone to his lawyer. I poured another round of drinks while he finished his conversation.

"Okay, we're all set," he said. "I made an appointment at the bank for ten-thirty." He looked at his watch. "That gives us about half an hour. From there we can swing by Arthur Ryan's office. I asked him to call your man in New York, John, and have the necessary documents thermofaxed here to Chicago. He'll have copies of Jessica's birth certificate, will, and so on waiting for us."

"Fine," he said, nodding.

"What are you going to do? Deposit the cash in your friendly neighborhood savings and loan?"

"No, John and I have talked over the options, and he's

going to take a cashier's check back to New York with him."

"Okay. Look, why don't you take my car. That's easier than lugging the money over to your house."

"Good idea."

"John, I've got to go to the store for supplies anyway—it's just a short walk. I'll do that and call Lanahan, then meet you and Brandt down at the Chicago Avenue police station in, say, an hour and a half, two hours."

"I'll ring you from Ryan's office when we're done there," Brandt suggested.

"Okay." I gave them the money and let them out the back door. I didn't want any part of Jessica's legacy, the weight she'd barely been able to drag across the doorstep just two nights before.

Brandt and John were waiting for me at the curb when I arrived at the police station a little after one o'clock. The bank had taken longer than they'd expected to count all the money. Brandt had called on one of the bank's veeps, an old crony, and he, in turn, had pulled five girls out of the tellers' cages to sit in the hushed conference room and count each of the banded stacks twice. Even so, it had taken time. I told Brandt he was under no obligation to come with us to see Lanahan. He said it was no imposition. I told John I didn't really know what to expect from Lanahan. He said it wasn't important. We went inside and were directed to a small, glassed-in office on the second floor.

Lanahan rose to meet us before we were through the door, and I introduced everyone. He told John how sorry he was, then asked us to sit down. There weren't enough chairs or enough space, so I stood. They are very kind to kinfolk nowadays; they show a picture of the departed instead of the body. Lanahan handed a five-by-seven glossy to John. I didn't want to look. John made a small snuffling sound and nodded silently. He handed the photo back to Lanahan. From a folder he pulled a sheaf of papers and handed them to me. It was my statement, neatly typed. I read it while he asked John questions, then answered questions. "I assure you, we're doing everything we can to find the man responsible," I heard him saying. I took out a pen and signed the statement when I had finished reading.

". . . we can release the body now that we've seen the proper papers," Lanahan was saying as I handed the statement back to him.

"Oh," I said tentatively. They turned to look at me. "Where are we going to release the body to?"

"Brandt took care of it while we were in Art Ryan's office," John said gently. "All the arrangements have been made."

One more thing I'd forgotten, but one less thing I had to worry about now. That was fine. I felt despondent, listless, and I wasn't sure I could cope with anything more. I was suddenly very grateful for Brandt's presence; he seemed capable of managing things for me. I wondered if John felt as I did or whether he was holding up better.

"I'll send these documents down to the morgue," Lanahan said. "They'll be picked up with your daughter's body, Mr. Pearson. You'll be able to get them later."

"Thank you, Lieutenant. I appreciate all your help." He stood and shook hands with him, and we all left.

Brandt took us to lunch at a little place on Dearborn Street that serves an excellent fish chowder and a better than average lunch menu. I don't remember what I had. My head ached, my face hurt, there was a sour knot in the pit of my stomach and a hollow spot in my heart. The damp and cold had gotten to my knees. Too much strain during the days of college football had left them susceptible to arthritis, which stiffened and inflamed them. I felt small and mean and as leaden as the sky. Brandt and John's few attempts to include me in conversation had met with ominous growls. I was not good company.

We went back to the house where I filled the largest old-fashioned glass I could find with Glenfiddich. And later that afternoon, we got the call from the mortician. Your order is ready. We don't deliver—cash and carry pick-up only. When do you want to come get it? We told him we would pick it up now, thank you, and so we bundled back up, got in the car, and drove in somber silence to the funeral home to collect the remains of my girl.

She had been cremated. It was her wish, John said. The bronze urn was more ornate and shinier than I expected. The mortician was brighter and more cheerful than I expected. They packed the urn carefully in a cardboard box that measured about a foot square and a foot high, padding it with paper, and tied it up with string. While that was being done, Brandt pulled the funeral director aside and haggled over the price, then went into his office to pay. I guess he used some of Jessica's money. When he came out, John hefted the small box, and we stepped out into the raw wind blowing off the lake.

"I think I'll put her next to her mother," John said as we walked to the car. "She's in a pretty little cemetery up in Westchester County, up in the . . ."

I didn't hear the rest of what he said. I had caught a fleeting glimpse of the face of the man in the car pulling away from the opposite curb, and I strained to get another look as the car went by.

"Get in the car," I yelled, scrambling around the hood, slipping on the icy street in my haste to get behind the wheel. They jumped at the sound of my voice, and scurried for the passenger door when they saw how frantic I was. I turned the engine over, slammed it in gear, and popped the clutch, sliding into a U-turn before Brandt even had the door shut.

"What in God's name are you doing?" Brandt shouted over the whine of the engine as I accelerated up Lincoln Avenue.

In the mirror I saw John sitting wide-eyed in the rear seat, clutching the cardboard box on his lap.

"I think that's the man who shot Jessica," I said grimly, winding the car up through the gears.

"What man?"

"The one in that car up ahead."

"Are you sure?"

"I don't know. I think so. Just keep your eyes on that baby-blue sedan."

"Don't look so exasperated, Emerson. We didn't see him. I'll watch the car. Why would he have been following us anyway?"

"How should I know?"

He'd had a two-block head start, but had obviously seen me swing into his lane in pursuit because he'd spurted ahead before I could get any speed up. He had to slow momentarily until the light changed at an intersection, and we barreled right behind him, beginning to gain a little now. Then he tapped his brakes and threw his car onto a side street, narrowly missing a parked car as his rear end broke loose for an instant. I double-clutched the Alfa, swung wide, and accelerated into the corner, hoping to gain on him. He led me on a confusing chase, roaring down narrow, one-way streets, parked cars whizzing by on either side, turning north then east then north again. Finally, he swung east, and I had to wait at the corner for traffic. I nosed out and swung in about six cars behind him. The street was congested and I pounded the steering wheel in frustration at the start-stop traffic. But he was no better off than I, and we crept along block after block. He made no move to turn, and I suddenly saw why. We were almost at the lake. The traffic cleared some as one lane turned into two, and he squirted through the intersection at Sheridan Road. I put my foot down, but the light changed before I got to the intersection and I had to slam on the brakes to avoid sliding into the cross-traffic.

We watched as the blue sedan turned onto the Lake Shore Drive ramp heading south.

"Damn," I swore softly.

When the light turned green, I turned right on Sheridan and headed slowly home.

I fixed supper for us that evening. I turned on all the lights, lit the candles, and put happy music on the big stereo. Then I uncorked two bottles of good red wine. Nothing more had been said about the man in the blue sedan after it had been determined that none of us had thought to get the license number. We didn't want to think of such things now. We wanted to laugh a little and share good memories, happy memories, of the woman who had died. It was a wake, and though we were a small group, we sent her off in style, with boisterous stories and a cheerfulness we did not really feel.

I drove John to the airport the next morning. He was thoughtful and quiet the whole way there. When we pulled up outside the terminal, I climbed out and got his suitcase and the cardboard box from the back seat. I handed them to him, and he set them on the curb and turned back to face me.

"Remember that little speech I gave when I first arrived? I'm sorry I said it because now I can't accept what's happened, either." He slipped an envelope out of his breast pocket and gave it to me. "I don't care what you call it— a retainer, expenses—but I want you to have it. And I want you to find the man who killed my daughter." He looked intently at me, then turned and was gone, lost in the throng of passengers.

I got back in the car, looked in the envelope, and counted out twenty five-hundred dollar bills. I didn't need ten thousand dollar's worth of motivation to look for the killer. But John probably didn't need it, and Jessica certainly had no

use for it now. I would keep track of my expenses, I decided,
and return what I didn't use. Or donate it to some worthy
cause. I put the envelope in my coat pocket and kicked the
little car in gear. As I drove home I realized I had no idea
of how to find the man who had killed Jess. But maybe he
would find me.

IV

WILLIAM HODGES from Green Bay, Wisconsin, was a distasteful, insignificant little man who tried to make an impression on the world by wearing maroon trousers, a checked shirt, paisley tie, and plaid jacket. We stood in his hundred-dollar-a-night hotel room, he suspicious of me, and me intensely disliking him. He was in the process of packing.

"Look, mister," he said, throwing a shirt into his suitcase, "I told the cops everything I know, so go ask them, okay?" His voice was as loud as his outfit.

"I just want to know what happened in your own words."

"Hey, I don't know from hardware, 'cause hardware's all I know."

"Damn you, that was my woman who was killed," I roared.

He jumped with a little squealing grunt of fright, like a stuck piglet, and backed away slowly, hands held out in front of him as if to ward off my anger. I wanted to pound the top of his shiny bald head with my fist until it turned to mush.

"Okay, okay, mister. Don't get your feathers ruffled. I guess I can spare a few minutes, all right?" He relaxed a little when I made no menacing moves. "I'm from out of town, right? So I'm here to have a good time. I come back from the show a little early that day because my feet are killing me and I'm dying for a drink. I mean, I'd already been here two days, and you can end up walking for miles through that show. Anyway, I meet this girl in the bar, and she starts coming on to me. So I suggest we come up here and kick off our

59

shoes and have another drink—you know, real subtle like. Well, she's real cool, like she's not sure, but she finally says okay, why not. So we come up here, and I'm thinking I hit the jackpot—we're going to get it on, have a few laughs, and like that."

His eyes shone and little beads of perspiration popped up on his forehead as he thought of how he had been planning to grab a little ass, squeeze a little tit, and then poke his meat into the warm, scented snatch of Cathy Callgirl. If she played her cards right, she could hold him off long enough and get enough liquor into him so that after his little squirt of release he would tumble off her with loud snores, and she could quietly slip away with his wallet. The thought would never occur to him, I realized, as I noticed the pale indentation around his left ring finger. Until he awoke to find his money gone, he would think the jollies were free, that the girl had been unable to resist being excited by his grunting, sweating effort.

"Anyway," he said, giving his head a shake, "when I open the door, there's this guy in the room. A guy in my effing room. Can you believe that? He's standing by the window there, and I ask him what the hell he's doing in my room. All of a sudden he starts yelling something about me stealing his woman, and waves this gun around. Now, I says to myself, 'Billy-boy,' I says, 'Billy-boy, you have really got yourself a problem this time.' I figure the easiest way to solve the problem is to just turn around and get the hell out of there. But would you believe it? That son of a bitch starts running after me. I beat it for the stairs and took them three at a time, and when I got downstairs I just kept heading right on out into the street. That's when the crazy bastard starts taking shots at me. I guess you know the rest."

"Where was he standing?"

"Right over here." He moved toward the window and

pointed to the floor. I walked across the room and stood on the spot.

His room was on the third floor of the Ambassador East, a first-rate European-style hotel with excellent service, the still-famous Pump Room, and prices that are too high. His company had probably had a good enough year that for the first time it could afford to send him to the big city for a convention. And now here he was, trying to live out a fantasy, attempting to create his own legend with which to regale the boys back home: "Fellas, I gotta tell ya she was the most gorgeous chick in the place—in the whole city of Chicago— and she was just dyin' for what I got in my pants. She was all over me. We musta shook the building half the night."

Brandt says that I tend to judge too hastily, that my own self-righteous morality is just that, my own. Perhaps he's right—I have bedded my share of women with the intent of assuaging and adding a notch to my male ego, but those encounters almost always left me feeling something was lacking. Brandt says that is because I try to reshape the scenes in which I find myself to my image of what they should be like. I try to rewrite my lines, looking for emotions and reactions that are larger than life, believing my life has more depth, more meaning, than the role given to me. And maybe I just believe Hemingway was right when he said you had to be friends with a woman first.

"What was he doing?" I asked.

"Yelling his damn head off." He moved back to the bed and started packing again.

"No, no, when you first walked in?"

"Just standing there, looking out the window."

I looked out. Directly below, three stories down, was the canopied walk. A doorman hailed a cab for unseen passengers. Across the street and down to the left was my house.

"Where did the girl go?"

"I don't know, and I don't care. I just left her here, and

she sure as hell wasn't here when I got back." He snapped the suitcase shut and headed for the door. "I'm checking out. You can keep this crazy fucking town. I'm going home." He paused at the door, put down the suitcase, and patted his pockets. He reached deep into his coat, pulled out a gold wedding band, slipped it on, and left. I turned to take one last look out the window, then walked out the door, pulling it shut behind me.

Outside, I turned my collar up against the cold and walked north to join some friends for a late brunch in a little bar overlooking the park. The storm front had passed through. It was a sunny Saturday. Winter would be over soon. I wondered how many millions of souls had been claimed in the world since Thursday, since the day the soul of my Jess had been claimed by a fruitcake with a gun. It made no sense. Maybe he was a jealous pimp. And maybe he had simply been a victim of cabin fever, the strange loss of sanity that comes with too many weeks of cold, winter weather. John was back in New York by now, confining her ashes to their resting place. But her soul was out there someplace, mingling with the ether of the azure winter sky.

I hadn't wanted to go to brunch, but I had promised earlier in the week. They were people I didn't know well, but it was better than I anticipated. And I was glad to have something to take my mind off myself. They were bright and entertaining people who drank merrily and told tall tales and bawdy jokes. We shared some common interests, and they made me feel comfortable. I drank along with them and joined in with some tales of my own. And finally, late in the afternoon, the party broke up. I found I'd drunk too much, and decided to walk home and let the cold air clear my head. Everything seemed just a little too bright and a tad fuzzy around the edges.

The shadows lengthened quickly as I made my way through the park. The sky was already a deep, dusty blue out over the lake and turning pink in the west. The air felt good, and smelled of oak and pine burning in fireplaces. I paused at the edge of the lagoon and watched a solitary oarsman bundled up in a sweatsuit row his shell up the glassy length of water. I glanced up as another man walked to the water's edge about a hundred yards away, then I turned and strolled off toward the baseball diamonds. A few minutes later on impulse, I glanced back over my shoulder and saw the same man walking in the same direction still some distance away. To see if I was being followed, I worked my way over to the pedestrian bridge crossing Lake Shore Drive to the beach.

On the other side, I furtively looked back to see him approaching the bridge. I couldn't see who it was; his face was half hidden by a scarf, and he was too far away. He would not have to stay close to keep me in sight for a while, so I sauntered casually down the beach. I could feel his presence behind me, and now I was perturbed and curious. Why was I being followed? It was getting dark, and I knew he would probably quicken his pace to keep me in sight. I stepped up my own pace, and when I got to North Avenue, I ducked into the pedestrian subway and broke into a run. I sprinted down the length of the tunnel, hoping he hadn't seen where I'd gone. I wanted him momentarily confused. I reached the end and turned the corner, leaning against the wall at the bottom of the steps leading to the street, trying to catch my breath. I waited, then heard faint, tentative footsteps echoing down the tunnel. Then I heard running footsteps as he made up his mind that I must have come this way.

I tensed, and when he rounded the corner, I took a step away from the wall, grabbed his coat, and used his momentum to spin him around and slam him against the wall. His breath left him with a whoosh, and before he could get it back, I shoved a forearm across his throat. He was making strangled, gagging sounds, and his eyes started bulging out of their sockets.

"Why are you following me?" I demanded.

The scarf had slipped down below his chin, and when the streetlights suddenly winked on overhead, I recognized the man who shot Jessica. In momentary shock, I relaxed my grip, and he swung both arms up and clapped me over the ears. It sounded like an artillery shell going off in my head, and I staggered backward, thinking he'd ruptured my eardrums. He scrambled up the stairs. I went up after him, taking the stairs two at a time. I finally caught up with him a hundred yards into the park and brought him down with a flying tackle that sent us both sprawling in what was left of the wet snow. I slithered on top of him and sat on his chest, then punched him with a short, straight left, square in the face.

"What the hell did you kill her for?" I was consumed by a furious, frustrated rage that left me blinded with tears. "Why did you kill her?" I screamed, punctuating each word with another left to the face. Blood spurted from his broken nose. He wriggled and squirmed like a demon, and finally bucked me off.

He rolled into a crouch and charged at me before I could regain my feet, butting me in the stomach. My head snapped back and cracked against the back of a bench, and the world went momentarily black. I fell on the ground, stunned, and when I could see again, the man was gone. There was nothing left to do but gingerly test everything to make sure it worked and walk slowly home, rueful and frustrated.

The anger slowly subsided, but was not yet gone when I got home. I switched on the lights and poured myself a Scotch. I wrapped a couple of extra ice cubes in paper towels and pressed them to the back of my head as I took my drink into the living room. I took two big swallows, then set down the drink, took off my coat, and fell into a chair. I was just about to pick up the phone to call Brandt when it rang. I hesitated, then picked it up.

"Where's the money?" It was the voice of the man who had burgled me.

"Who are you?"

"Never mind. Just tell me where the money is and you won't get hurt."

"For chrissake, I don't have it! It's probably in a bank in New York by now. What the hell do you want from me? And who *are* you?"

The line went dead. I held the receiver away and looked at it, then slammed it down in anger. Things were getting stranger by the minute, and I didn't like one bit of it. What in God's name had Jessie gotten me into? I picked up my drink, and the phone rang again. It startled me, and I slopped half the drink in my lap. This time it was Brandt inviting me over for dinner.

"Christ, yes. Anything to get out of this house."

"What's wrong? You sound shaky."

I related what had happened, and he let out a low whistle.

"Sounds sinister and very strange. I'd like to know more. Come on over."

"Ten minutes."

Brandt fixed drinks, we talked, and I gradually calmed down. About twenty minutes after I got there, people started arriving—for dinner, Brandt said. I protested quietly, asking him what the hell he thought I needed a party for. He shushed me and smiled broadly. And I realized that these were the close friends, the tightly knit group of regulars that make up my small world. Brandt had told them about Jessica, and had gathered them to help me mourn my dead and then cheer me back to the land of the living. They arrived and embraced me warmly and patted me lovingly. There were Jane and Lou Foster from the suburbs, and Georgia and Morgan Grant from uptown. There was Pam McAllister and Judy Snow and the McFadden twins, Justin and Stanley. There were Greg and

Sally Edwards, and Rob and Lonnie White, Susie Toffic, and Paul Rivelli from the bridge group, and others from the circle that formed my sense of belonging, a sense of place in some form of society. I moved through them, accepting their warmth, touching, shaking hands, kissing, thanking them. At one time or another, they had all kept me from being too much the loner, linking me with the rest of the world. They all brought something, bottles or food, and Brandt set up a buffet and cranked up some happy music as I had done the night before. And finally, when too much more merriment would have been in bad taste, they began slowly departing with long good-byes and promises to get together more often.

It was nearly midnight when I dragged myself, exhausted, back to the house. As I approached the front walk, two men got out of a dark sedan, putting me instantly on my guard. The Mutt-and-Jeff pair converged on me as I strode up the walk. Halfway to the door, I spun around to face them, tensed with anticipation. They stopped at a distance far enough not to be threatening.

"Emerson Ward?" Jeff said. He reached into an inside pocket, pulled out a little wallet, and flipped it open, then shut. "Police officers."

"What do you want?"

"We'd like you to come with us to answer some questions," Jeff said. Mutt eyed me warily, ready to cut me off if I made a break for it.

"What about?"

"That's for Lieutenant Lanahan to decide."

I sighed and relaxed a bit, shifting my stance. "Look fellas, I'm tired, and I've had a long day. If you don't mind, I'd like to go to bed. Tell Lanahan I'll call him first thing in the morning."

"No, sir, I'm afraid that won't do. He wants to see you now."

"Can't it wait?"

"Mr. Ward, we have a warrant here for your arrest that we'd rather not use. We'd appreciate it if you just came along with us to answer some questions."

"A warrant? On what charge?"

"Suspicion of murder. Now, will you come with us, please?"

I was stunned. My mind raced furiously. They appeared legitimate, but the charges were absurd. And why would they rather not use the warrant? It made no sense. If they had wanted to take me, they would have waited until I was almost in the house, or yanked me down a dark alley on the way home.

"May I see your identification again, please?" I took a tentative step forward as he held it out. "Yours, too," I said to Mutt. He handed it over, and I stuck both in my coat pocket, then said, "Okay, gentlemen, come on in. This won't take a moment."

They had no choice but to follow me inside. I called the Chicago Avenue station and asked the desk sergeant for verification of the two badge numbers. It matched the names on the ID.

"Okay," I said and shrugged, handing them back the wallets, "let's go."

The ride was short, and when we got there, they ushered me up to Lanahan's office. He looked worn and tired. Mutt left, but Jeff stood just inside the door. Lanahan looked up from his desk and asked me to sit down.

"Any trouble?" he asked Jeff.

"No, but he checked our badge numbers."

Lanahan smiled wanly and looked appraisingly at me. "Being a little too cautious, perhaps?"

I said nothing. I wasn't ready to tell him about the burglary or about being followed. I wanted to hear what he had to say before I decided to tell him anything.

"Mr. Ward, would you please tell me how you spent your day?"

I told him I had gotten up, taken John Pearson to the airport, then talked to the Hodges fellow in his hotel room.

"Why did you do that?" he interrupted, looking curiously at me.

"Just to hear his story in person, I guess."

He waved his hand. "No matter. Go on."

"Then I went to brunch at a place up near the park."

"With friends?" I nodded. "I can get their names later if I need to. Go on."

"After that, I walked home—I guess I got there a little after five—and then I went to dinner at Brandt Williams's house."

"Get him on the phone," Lanahan said to Jeff, "and check it out." He spun on his heel and was gone. Lanahan turned back to face me. "Do you recognize this man?" He pulled a photograph from his desk drawer.

The face was curiously white in the glare of the photographer's flash, making the features stand out grotesquely. The man's nose was crooked and mashed where I'd broken it, and there was still some dried blood on his upper lip. He lay on cold ground, head tilted strangely to one side, eyes glazed, staring at something unseen, mouth contorted in pain and fright. It was not possible; the short, straight left could not have killed him. My mouth felt dry, and my stomach churned. I looked at the photo longer than I needed to, trying to regain some composure.

"Am I being charged with anything?" I looked Lanahan in the eye.

"Not at the moment. Let's just say we're having a friendly discussion so I can get answers to some questions that are puzzling me."

I nodded. "Then let's say I think this could be the man who fired shots in the street outside my house last Thursday."

"Okay. Have you seen him since that time?"

"I may have. It's hard to say."

He sat back, watching me intently, then shifted his gaze and stared at a corner of the ceiling, musing. He said nothing, and we sat in silence for a long five minutes until Jeff came back in the office. Lanahan swiveled his chair around toward the door.

"Well?"

"It checks out. He gave the names of some of the other people who were there, and they confirmed it, too."

"Okay, thanks," he sighed. "You can take off." He swiveled back to face me, leaned forward to put his elbows on the desk, and sighed again. "Sorry for the inconvenience, but I think you can guess why we had you brought in. That is the man who killed Mrs. Johnston—we found the pistol in his pocket and the ballistics match. You had more motive than anyone we know of for wanting him dead."

"Then why not charge me?"

"Not enough evidence. Coroner says he died between eight and nine. We found his wallet, but no money, so it could have been a mugging."

"Who was he, anyway?"

"New York driver's license says he was Jack Saldi, probably a conventioneer. We're checking it out now."

"How did he die?"

"Broken neck, apparently. Killed him instantly. What's curious is that he didn't use the gun. Whoever it was must have surprised him."

I had not killed him, then. That was some consolation. "He looks pretty banged up, though. Someone must have worked him over before killing him."

"That's what's strange. They're having a tough time with this one down at the coroner's office. They say it looks as though he was beaten a few hours before his death. They say, at least in the preliminary report, that only one mark looks fresher than the rest, a bruise over his left ear. It's got me puzzled as hell. Well, I guess you can go. I'll have a car drive you home."

"Thanks, but I can catch a cab." I rose and turned for the door.

"Ward," he called out as I was leaving. "I haven't yet ruled you out entirely. The person who found the body says he saw someone about your size in the vicinity. Don't stray too far from home, okay?"

I went out to find a cab that would take me home to bed. It was not until I was safely inside, doors locked, coat shed, and drink in hand, that I realized what had happened. It hit me like a blast of arctic wind that numbed me and made me shiver. With a ball of ice in the pit of my stomach, I picked up the phone and dialed.

"Hello?" the sleepy voice said.

"John, this is Emerson. Sorry to wake you." I felt wooden, and my heart had turned to stone. "John, you have to find out where Jessica got that money. Because that is the only lead we have left."

Jack Saldi, whoever he was, would answer no questions now. Jessica's death had been avenged by a mugger in the park.

V

MARTHA CRANSTON CULBERTSON snapped me up like a tree frog flicking at a fly. Jessica had been dead for a little more than a month. I had been barely alive for most of that time, but I knew that I couldn't sulk and drink myself into a stupor forever. So I had accepted an invitation to a party at the yacht club. I was in no mood to be sociable, but anything was better than being alone with myself. The club had only recently opened after its traditional closing for the month of March. There were no boats at mooring yet, but it was warm enough to be outside. I sat in a deck chair in a far corner of the patio out of the lights and away from the madding crowd. And while I'd promised myself I wouldn't drink myself silly, I'd had just enough to feel it.

It came as a great shock when a tall, rather striking, it seemed at the time, woman deliberately violated the imaginary boundaries I had circumscribed around my table and sat in the deck chair next to mine. I refused to acknowledge her presence.

"It must hurt a lot," she said softly.

I didn't answer.

"I've been watching you most of the evening. I think I know what you've been going through. I've been there," she added, hitching her chair closer to mine.

"What do you want," I finally said, a poor excuse for a greeting.

"To comfort you." Her voice was soothing, but it didn't

seem like an answer to my question. "You can cry if you want to," she said then.

They were magic words. I suddenly felt warm wetness fill my eyes and a single tear roll silently down my face. Then I felt her arm around my shoulder, and I let myself be pulled closer to her, laying my head on her breast and letting loose all the hurt. My hair was stroked, and soothing murmurs filled my ear. It was a catharsis I'd needed for some time, and it was painful. I had not let myself mourn for Jessica, at least not with tears. Ridding oneself of poison is often more painful than allowing the poison to do its killing work, and I had been afraid of that cathartic pain, even though I knew how much better I'd feel when the poison was gone.

When the moment passed, I raised my face to look at her with a number of half-formulated questions in mind. She answered them all before I even spoke.

"It doesn't matter," she said simply. "Come on, I'll take you home."

She gave me her hand and I took it, glad to have something tangible to hang onto. She led me around the side of the clubhouse instead of through it, for which I was grateful, and had the doorman hail us a cab. My memory of what followed is like a badly edited film run on an old projector with a bad bulb. There is a white blank in place of the cab ride. There are flickering images of arriving at my door. I managed to get my keys out of my pocket. She used them on the door. I helped with magical incantations.

Inside, she sat me down at the kitchen table. I watched her as she moved around the kitchen, not thinking of anything in particular, not really paying attention to what she was doing. I felt comfortable and enjoyed watching her move. She presented me with a mug of tea and a plate of Saltines with grape jelly. I hadn't known I owned any Saltines. I nibbled one tentatively, then nibbled with relish. I ate all the crackers. I finished the tea. I drank a large glass of water. Then she held out her hand. I took it, and she led me to my bedroom. I helped her undress me and put me under the covers. I rolled onto my left side, delighted at the feel of the cool sheets. The light went out with a click, and I heard the soft rasp of clothes being pulled off. There was movement as she got in the other side of the bed, then all that warm weight pressed against my back and buttocks and legs as she snuggled into me so we lay like spoons. I smiled, then slept.

I woke once during the night with an entire bale of cotton in my mouth. I sat up, and she was waiting for me with a quart jar of ice water and three aspirin. When the water was gone, I lay back on the pillows. She leaned over and kissed me lightly on the forehead. I marveled at how psychic she seemed, then slept again.

The feel of her hands softly caressing my back and shoulders woke me the second time. I woke gradually, slowly letting go of the dream that played against the back of my eyes, luxuriating in the gentle touch of her fingers. I opened my eyes to daylight muted by the drawn drapes, then rolled over into her embrace. My eyes searched her face, not knowing what questions to ask, not knowing what answers to look for. The kiss began gently, with fluttery breath and trembling hearts, then slowly turned to a seeking, grasping, needful exploration. Mouths broke away to seek throats, eyelids, earlobes. Hands ran the lengths of gentle curves, swelling curves, hollows, leaving nothing untouched.

I rolled onto my back, taking her with me. The silence was broken only by our breathing, then her quick panting as I entered her, and then by her single gasp as she slid down the full length of my penis. We lay quietly. I stroked her hair and held her close with the other hand in the small of her back. Her breath was warm and moist against my neck. Then, as if controlled by unconscious instinct, we began to move in synchronous rhythm, slow and languidly at first. Time became rhythm, tempo, and we slowed it, stopped it, sped it up, and controlled it with every movement. She rose to her knees, hands on my chest, elbows locked, eyes closed, lips parted. My hands reached to stroke her face, her shoulders, her breasts, and I gently squeezed the erect nipples. And time began to explode and fragment into a myriad of sensations and tinglings, then spasms and shudders of release, ecstatic and exquisite.

Our movement slowed, then stopped. I searched the face above mine, the square jaw, the broad mouth, the nose that was almost too delicate, too thin, for the wide-set eyes. The eyes opened. They were gray. And for a fleeting moment I saw another face in my mind, and the tears started without warning. She leaned down to gently kiss them away, then lay on me as before with her face pressed into my throat. We stayed like that for a long time. She finally raised her head to give me a last kiss, then rolled off and got out of bed.

I heard the shower running. Finally, I rubbed my eyes with my fists, then swung my legs out of bed to head for the kitchen to make coffee. I had juice made, and the coffee was almost ready when she came out in one of my robes. I poured a glass of juice for her, then one for myself and took it with me to the shower. I turned on the water as hot as I could stand it and adjusted the spray to needle-fine, then scrubbed and rinsed until I was pink. I toweled down, brushed my teeth, decided the hell with a shave, put on a robe, and went to the kitchen for coffee. She was busy investigating my refrigerator and cupboards. I poured coffee and sat at the table watching her as I had the night before.

"I hate to break the silence," I said finally. "First, a humble and heartfelt thank-you. Second, who are you?"

She stopped and turned to look at me with a peculiar expression. "Martha Culbertson," she said simply, then turned back to the counter.

"Martha . . . Marty Culbertson?" I knew the name, and now

the face was somewhat familiar to me, but I didn't know what it should mean to me.

"Do you want eggs?"

"Scrambled." I assumed she meant me and not the refrigerator. "Okay, Marty Culbertson, why?"

She turned back to face me and shrugged. "Because you did me a good turn once a long time ago. Because you were so obviously hurting last night. I don't know. When I recognized you and saw how sad you looked, I thought I'd see what I could do to cheer you up and repay an old favor."

It began to come back to me. The incident *had* been a long time ago, long enough that her face had matured sufficiently for me not to have recognized her. She must have been barely eighteen or so when I'd first run into her, and I was probably just out of school. It had been at a large formal dinner party thrown by someone up in Lake Forest, north of Chicago. I couldn't remember whose party it had been, or the occasion, but I remembered taking a walk around the grounds after dinner and coming on two of the more drunk male guests about to do a number on a young girl. They had had her on the ground, and one had held her arms while the other had been all over her and had ridden her dress up over her hips. She had squirmed like a demon and had been making squeals of protest through the hand over her mouth, but she had had no chance against two of them.

I had taken care of the one on top of her first. He had gotten his pants halfway down over his fat ass when I came up behind him and kicked him square in the balls. He had fainted without a sound. The other one had seen me then, and had tried to scramble to his feet to get away. I had been so outraged that I'd picked him up by the front of his tuxedo and had slapped him half-unconscious. The girl hadn't been hurt, but she had been terrified. I had helped pick her up, had gotten her steadied, then had offered to give her a ride home so she wouldn't have to do a lot of explaining inside.

Her dress had been ruined, and she had readily agreed. She had talked it out on the way home, crying some, and I had comforted her. I had given her my name and had told her to get in touch with me if anyone wanted to know what had happened. She had said her name was Martha—Marty, her friends called her. And about a week later, I had gotten a note from her father, Bertrand Culbertson, thanking me for extricating his daughter from a precarious and compromising situation.

She was now probably in her early thirties, stood naked under my robe in my kitchen, was offering to make me breakfast, and had more than paid back the favor I'd done her. When I looked at her, I could see that she must have watched me search my mental filing drawers to find the one with her name on it.

"I wouldn't have recognized you without the name," I said, though there was something disconcertingly familiar about her that didn't match up with the information in my head. "How did you remember me?"

"The man with the funny name—Emerson W. Ward. You were very nice—kind and thoughtful, I remember. I didn't get the impression that you thought it was my fault in the least. And I remember how outraged you were. I think you called it 'righteous indignation.' You gave me your card. I spent months trying to figure out what the *W* stood for. I guess I had a crush on you. I never did find out."

"Woolsey."

"What?"

"Woolsey," I said, and grinned. She laughed. "I'm not kidding." I liked her laugh.

We ate then, heaps of scrambled eggs with grated sharp cheddar, spicy sausage patties, toasted muffins with gobs of butter, mugs of steaming Sumatra coffee, and glasses of juice. I was famished. When my plate was empty, I made her get up and scramble more eggs and she helped finish off the second round. When everything had been eaten and we settled back in our chairs with the last of the coffee, she asked the question, quietly.

"Who was she?"

It was like a hot knife, twisting and turning in my guts, forcing its way up to my heart. I felt my face screw up with hurt and sadness. I took three or four deep breaths, trying to push the feelings away, trying to calm the sudden anxiety that boiled in my stomach. I didn't see Marty move, but she was suddenly behind my chair, leaning over me, hands on my chest, cheek pressed against mine, comforting me.

"It's okay," she murmured. "Go ahead and let it out. I'm here." It was a honeyed voice that could undoubtedly soothe savage breasts. It calmed me. Her touch relaxed me. She felt the tension melt under her fingers. "Okay now?" she asked. I nodded. She kissed me on the cheek, then knelt down next to my chair and rested her head on my thigh.

"She left?" Marty asked after a long silence.

"Died," I said, not wanting to remember.

"I'm sorry. You must have felt very close to her." She absentmindedly stroked my leg.

"We had both gotten to the point where we thought it might just work, where we decided that the feelings were there, and that all the trying and the effort was worth it." I felt the load lighten perceptibly, the constriction in my chest lessen. Strangely, there was no self-consciousness. To tell Marty about it, to give her an explanation, seemed only natural. Not even Brandt had known how deeply the hurt ran. I had carried it silently, stoically, for weeks, trying not to acknowledge it because I hadn't known how to deal with it.

"You don't have to talk about it."

"No, that's okay," I said. But she was silent, and I didn't know what to say. I had the strange feeling—a feeling of disappointment—that therapy session was over for the day.

She got up and headed for the bedroom, so I started clearing the dishes from the table. I put on another pot of coffee, and while it brewed, I sudsed the dishes. I was scrubbing the frying pan and sipping fresh coffee when she emerged, dressed and made up. The thought suddenly occurred to me that I had not even considered what she might do, that she would, of course, eventually leave. It was Sunday morning, so she hadn't had to run off to work, if, in fact, she worked. I realized that I didn't know a damn thing about this woman except her name, the fact that she appeared to be leaving, and the fact that I didn't want her to leave.

"You're going?" My arms were wet up to the elbows, so I only half turned toward her, letting my hands drip over the sink. There was a strange churning in the pit of my stomach, an anxious anticipation. She looked at me long and hard, then there was a twinkle in her eyes and she smiled.

"You look like a lost puppy. I'm sorry, I had to smile." She came up behind me and put her arms around my waist, her head on my shoulder. "Yes, I'm going. There are some errands I need to take care of. I'll be back in an hour, maybe two."

My stomach had dropped through the floor, but now it was settling back into position. She stood on her tiptoes, and I turned to kiss her lips.

"Read the paper, do the laundry, clean the house—find something to keep busy, and I'll be back before you know it." She gave me one last kiss, laughed gaily at my hangdog expression, and was gone.

I kept busy. She came back. I half expected her not to. She had eased some of the hurt, and I didn't want to be hurt by her in turn. So I only half hoped she would come back. She came back with an overnight bag. I was surprised, speechless at my good fortune. From the moment she set foot inside the door, she chattered cheerily about everything under the sun. She told me about her errands, then she took her bag into the bedroom and talked to me from there, suggesting new curtains, telling me that she was requisitioning one of my dresser drawers, admiring a drawing on the wall. Then she was in the kitchen, without having run out of breath.

Finally, she came back into the living room where I lay on the couch, wearing the robe she'd had on earlier, bearing gifts in the form of a pitcher of Bloody Marys. So we played backgammon, talked, and got slightly stupefied with drink. And later, we made love again, slowly and tenderly, then slept in each other's arms. It was dark when we woke. Together, we showered, rinsing away sleep-sweat, and then we dressed and went out for a late supper.

Martha Cranston Culbertson became my life. I thought of little else, tuning everything and everyone out of my mind. I followed her around like a hound after a bitch in heat. I ignored my friends; I didn't return phone calls. My schedule revolved around Marty's. Waiting for her to come back from an errand or an appointment, I occupied my time by fidgeting. I couldn't amuse myself or keep myself busy or interested in anything. I felt at loose ends, couldn't concentrate, didn't know what to do except wait for her to return to fill the void with her chatter, her warmth, her love.

She knew the right words, knew how to comfort me, soothe me, lighten my heart, turn my moods, and make me smile. She was an expert fly-caster, and I was a trout. The hook was deep and would have to be cut out. She played me, brought me out of my brown moods into flashes of iridescence. She was my being, my essence; it was she who gently tugged on the light line making me wriggle and gasp obediently.

Marty didn't work much. She didn't have to work much. Grandfather Culbertson had started a hotel chain way back when, and had set up trust funds for his grandchildren. With little or no frugality, Martha Cranston Culbertson could live comfortably for the rest of her life. She was, however, involved with public relations for the company and did odd jobs and acted as troubleshooter for her father. Bertrand Culbertson was not as fortunate as she. He had to earn his living, and he did so as president of the hotel chain, drawing a substantial salary. I was not as fortunate as either father or daughter, but did not shed many tears over my situation. I work when I feel like it, or when I'm broke. I neither felt like working, nor was I broke; I wanted to do nothing except be with Marty.

Brandt came over late one afternoon when Marty was out. I was glad to see him. I hadn't seen him, or any other friends to speak of, since the yacht club party three weeks before.

"Ah, you're still alive," he said when I answered his knock.

"Good to see you. Yep, I'm alive and well and living in sin. Drink?"

"Why not."

I had a Glenfiddich on ice and gave him a beer. We chatted inanely about things that had been happening, catching up on local gossip. Then there was an uncomfortable silence.

"Emerson," Brandt finally said, "are you all right? Everything okay with you?"

"Yeah, fine. Why?" His question stirred up sediment from the depths of my subconscious, and I felt anxiety knot my stomach.

"We're all a little concerned about you."

"Who's 'we'?" I suddenly felt defensive and ill at ease. Brandt's my best friend. What the hell am I being defensive for? What am I trying to hide? Who am I fooling? The questions ran in a jumble through my head. There were answers there somewhere, but I didn't want to find them. Instead, there was suspicion and distrust.

"We are your friends. Or had you forgotten you have friends? No one's seen much of you lately, and those who have seen you are shaking their heads and wondering what's the matter with you. For the past three weeks you have been absolutely obsessive. We hate watching you throw your life away.

"It's Jess still, isn't it?" He said it so softly I wasn't sure I heard it. I didn't want to hear it. "You still haven't let go, can't admit that she's gone. And this new one—Martha?—she's supposed to replace Jessica. She's supposed to fix it, take away all the hurt, kiss it and make it better?"

"Stop it," I said, feeling like a petulant child.

He shook his head. "Jesus, Emerson, don't do this to yourself. She's not worth it."

"Go home, Brandt. Go away."

He looked at me long and hard. Then he got up and left. I sat and nursed my Scotch for a long time, full of a pain I didn't understand.

VI

It was Marty who suggested the trip to Nassau. There was no reason not to go. Saldi was dead. Lanahan hadn't questioned me again. And I hadn't heard a word from John Pearson.

"Come on," Marty had said, "come with me. I have about two days' worth of business, then we can spend a week just lying around in the sun."

No sane person would refuse. So we packed bags, were chauffeured to the airport in a Culbertson limousine, got on a big mechanical silver bird, and went. In Nassau we were met by another limo and taken to Paradise Island where we checked into one of Grandpa Culbertson's hotels. Rather, I was checked in. Marty was expected. We stayed in adjacent suites, to maintain appearances or something like that.

Business took a few days longer than Marty expected, so I spent a lot of time by myself, on the beach or by the pool during the day and aimlessly cruising the strip at night when Marty couldn't join me for dinner. I wasn't thrilled with the arrangements, but there didn't seem to be much I could do about it. I brought up the subject twice, letting her know I didn't like spending so little time with her, and I got unsatisfactory answers both times. She said that I had known beforehand that she had business to take care of, which was true. She said that if I didn't like the Bahamas, or the current state of affairs, I could fly back to Chicago, which was true. She said that she couldn't help the late dinners or that some matters were taking so long to work out, which may or may not have been true.

On the morning of the fifth day, Marty invited me to join her for breakfast in her suite. We had not slept together; I hadn't seen her since lunch the day before, so I thought the idea was splendid. I rushed right over. Room service was just finishing laying things out when I arrived. Marty was on the phone, so I helped myself to coffee, then poured a cup for her, too. She hadn't dressed yet. She wore a long silk robe, loosely tied, slit at the sides, that revealed some and hinted at other delights of that luxurious body. I sat patiently sipping my coffee, wanting her very badly. I ached with longing at the sight of her, but I couldn't tell her. Something in her manner put me off. I buttered a croissant instead, added a big dollop of orange marmalade, and bit into it hungrily.

"I need a favor," she began when she joined me at the breakfast cart by the window. I tensed, but she didn't notice. "I have some papers that must be delivered in Miami today, and I just don't have the time to go myself. Would you mind flying up there for me?"

An odd request, but not unreasonable, and not as bad as I had anticipated.

"Sure. Fill me in?"

"There's not much to fill in. All you have to do is fly up there, meet our man at the airport, deliver the papers, and fly back. It's simple. The man who will meet you at the airport is named Robert Smith. I told him I'd meet him between eleven and eleven-thirty this morning. He suggested one of the bars in the terminal, but since he's not expecting you, and since you don't know him, you'll probably have to page him. Okay so far?"

"Sure, it sounds reasonable." There was a hint of something in her voice, her businesslike manner—condescension?— that grated, made me feel like an employee. I tried to ignore it. "What's so important that it requires an escort?"

"It's just the result of some of the meetings we've been having." It was a delightfully vague comment. Her shrug, and that same slightly condescending tone, suggested that she felt it was none of my business and that it would probably go over my head anyway. I felt a touch of resentment. She must have sensed it, or else felt that even a lackey deserved some consideration. "The Miami hotels were next on my list, anyway," she continued. "I should fly up there myself and spend the day, but I want to finish up some things here. They really are important papers, Emerson."

"Oh, I don't doubt it. I was just curious, that's all." There was a moment of silence.

"Let's see, it's now nine-ten," she said, looking at her gold Cartier watch. It was the only piece of jewelry she wore unless she was dressed to go somewhere for dinner. "I hate to kick you out, but you'd better start for the airport. Do you have any money? I can get some for you out of petty cash at the front desk. Or I can reimburse you when you get back. Okay?"

I dug in a pocket and came up with some bills, colorful, pretty pieces of Bahamian currency, unlike the officious-looking U.S. green. "I think I'm covered," I said. She had risen from her chair and had crossed the room to pick up a briefcase. I got up and met her halfway to the door.

"You're all set." She handed me the case. Then she put her hands on my shoulders and stood up on her toes to give me a quick kiss, a fraternal peck on the corner of my mouth. "Thanks. I appreciate it." She smiled, then her hand went to her mouth. "Oh, wait, I almost forgot." I watched, puzzled, as she went to a bureau, got the camera case that was on it, and handed it to me.

"This is almost as important as the briefcase. A friend of my father left this in his room last week when he was here. Please give this to Mr. Smith; he'll see that it's returned."

"Okay. Will I see you when I get back?"

"I don't know. You can spend the afternoon in Miami if you want. But I'll try to get free tonight. Dinner?"

"Sure. I guess I'll see you then."

"Good. Have a good trip, and thanks again." She gave me another obligatory kiss, performed automatically but almost too self-consciously.

In the hotel limousine, I decided I didn't like the setup. For a month or so now, I had lived in a fog, letting my emotions run unchecked without bothering to understand what they were or where they came from. The gray cells were slow and underused. The thought processes were muddied and dulled, and I had not tended to track well on any but the simplest of problems. But something told me that the situation was not quite right. Something was out of sync, and it nagged at me.

At the Nassau airport I bought my ticket and luckily got a seat on the 10:45 flight to Miami, not an easy thing at the end of the tourist season. I had an hour to kill, but decided to wait at the gate. All passengers traveling back to the U.S. are shunted through customs into a large waiting room complete with snack bar and rest rooms. On my way through, customs asked the usual questions and made a cursory inspection of the briefcase and camera case. Anything to declare? No. New camera? No. Open the briefcase, please. Yes, sir. Okay, you may go ahead. I found myself a reasonably secluded corner in the waiting room and settled in for the duration.

I had no inclination to examine the contents of the briefcase. Marty's business did not particularly excite me, and I had no reason to paw through her papers. But the camera case intrigued me. I had caught a glimpse of the contents when it had been inspected by the customs man, and I wanted a closer look. So I unlatched the top of the rectangular leather case and peeked inside. It contained a relatively new, sophisticated camera body, a fat, stubby 600 mm zoom lens, another shorter lens, a couple of rolls of film, bill of sale, and some odds and ends. It was a basic collection of very good equipment, and I didn't resist the temptation to play with it.

The zoom lens screwed easily onto the body, but when I pulled off the lens cap and looked through the viewfinder, I saw nothing. I frowned, took off the lens, checked the mirror and shutter positions in the body, screwed the lens back on, took another look, and saw nothing. Something must be wrong with the lens, I decided. I was annoyed. Something this expensive and sophisticated should work. I rummaged through the camera case and found a jeweler's screwdriver. I began loosening screws and finally got the lens apart. The guts had been ripped out and replaced with cotton. I pulled at some of the cotton and found a good-sized piece of what looked like rough, unpolished crystal. This was no chunk of rock salt I was holding; it was an uncut diamond.

I quickly stuffed the cotton back into the lens and dropped it into the camera case, then sat back to think. The rock would probably yield anywhere from a two to five-carat stone. And there was room in the camera lens for maybe ten or twelve rocks. I was supposed to meet a guy in Miami with the unlikely name of Robert Smith and unwittingly give him untold thousands of dollars' worth of uncut diamonds. If something went wrong, I was the patsy. I didn't like suddenly discovering that I was a smuggler. It didn't even appeal to my sense of larceny and greed. I smelled a setup, but it made no sense. At least I now knew what cargo I was really carrying. I didn't know what I was going to do, but I knew I would not do what was expected of me.

It was 10:24, time to do something. I carefully repacked the camera case, then made my way across the room to a courtesy phone on the wall. I made a call, then looked around the lounge while I waited. The waiting room buzzed with conversations as tanned, happy people traded vacation stories. Tennis rackets stuck out of every other carry-on bag. Casual slacks, open shirts, blazers, loose flowing skirts, and floppy-brimmed straw hats abounded. Children with peeling noses ran up and down through the rows of chairs. The snack bar did a brisk business in soft drinks even though the room was air-conditioned. Once past customs, there was no way out of the waiting room except onto an airplane, unless . . .

The page came over the loudspeaker a moment later. "Emerson Ward, please come to Eastern Airlines' ticket counter." I grabbed the briefcase and the camera case and had my plane ticket and ID in my hand as I sauntered out of the waiting room past the customs officials. I waved my ticket and passport, told them I'd be right back, and kept walking toward the ticket counters.

"I'm Emerson Ward," I said as I walked up to one of the agents at the counter. "You paged me?"

The girl looked at me, then at the papers in front of her, then around at the other personnel behind the counter. She turned back to me and asked to see my ticket, looked at it, compared it to a manifest, then walked over to a man who appeared to be a supervisor. They conversed for a moment, then she came back and returned my ticket to me.

"I'm sorry, sir. There must be some mistake. We didn't page you. Your tickets are in order, and I can see no reason why we would have paged you." She smiled sweetly.

"Oh," I said. I let my face fall, feigning confusion, then brightened. "I'll bet I know what it was. My wife must have called and tried to have me paged. You see, I'm just going to Miami for the day and my wife mentioned that she might want the camera today if I didn't need it. Could I leave this here with you in case she comes out to pick it up?"

"Certainly, sir. And what was the name again?"

"Emerson Ward. I really appreciate this." I handed her the camera case, and watched as she wrote my name on a tag, taped it to the case, and put the case under the counter.

"Okay, you're all set, sir. Have a pleasant flight."

"Thanks very much."

On my way back to the lounge, the same customs official who had checked me through earlier briefly glanced at my ticket and passport and waved me on.

The flight to Miami was too short. In that period of time I could resolve nothing, could come to no conclusions. There were only questions. Someone had gone to extraordinary effort to avoid paying duty on the diamonds, I thought wryly. The whos, whys, and wherefores all eluded me. And I wondered about Martha. Had she known? I reconstructed the morning's conversation and decided that either she hadn't known or she was a superb actress. But I wasn't sure. I had glommed onto Marty Culbertson like a fish sucking for oxygen, and had depended heavily on her for emotional security for the last month or so. But the relationship had changed subtly, and I was no longer sure of what I felt for her.

There were too many unknowns. It occurred to me that I was being naively and dangerously stupid about the whole thing. I had acted on impulse, momentarily outraged that someone was using me. Blind luck had led me to discover what I was carrying, and I had let a childish impulse motivate me. "Temporary insanity" I would plead when they chunked my feet into a bucket of half-set cement. "It's all a horrible mistake," I would wail when they wired my wrists and lifted me over the gunwale to drop me into the depths somewhere off the coast of Florida. I had cast myself in a starring role without reading the script or meeting the other players. It was like strolling nonchalantly into a jungle cave without a flashlight or weapon and with a total disregard for the fact there might be lions, jaguars, snakes, and worse inside. The only thing dumber than what I was doing now is charging someone who is holding a loaded gun. I've done that, too.

The four miles between me and the sun-dappled azure of the ocean below suggested it was too late for remorse. I closed my eyes and let my mind go, playing out all the conceivable scenarios. When I'd run them through, and had done some mental rehearsing, I pushed it all to the back, filing it for easy reference, then opened my eyes and looked for something to distract me for the rest of the trip.

I had gotten a seat in first class. The section was half empty, but I guessed it would be full on the leg from Miami to New York. I found my distraction in the two flight attendants. Looking slightly bored behind the smiles that stayed firmly in place as if painted on, they stood talking to a couple of junior executive types sitting a seat ahead and across the aisle from me. I tried to decide along with them who was going to make the first move, who was going to suggest dinner in New York. I was almost ashamed of my cynicism because of the nagging feeling I had not yet confronted that such hostility was the result of something drastically wrong with my personal world, not theirs.

The cabin bell rang, and the stewardesses went forward to prep us for landing. I felt fear now, but it was a familiar feeling, one that I had not experienced for months, the kind of feeling that gives everything a sharp edge and makes each breath taste alive. The wet trickle under my arms and the steady thumping in my chest were strangely comforting.

We descended, a giant misshapen spoon into a blue custard sky dotted with fluffy meringue clouds. Miami Beach lay sprawled below, its sand, steel, glass, and cement glittering from this height, a white expanse networked with a blue patchwork of swimming pools. The beach itself was littered with dots of color in constant motion. It was hard to imagine the concept of individuality applying to those indiscernible spots massed below. I hadn't been to Miami in a long time, but I had heard it had become like an old dowager whose makeup seems to look attractive from a distance, giving the impression that she still is as she once was. The reality, the closer inspection, is disappointing. I was glad that I would not be making a closer inspection.

The plane touched down and taxied to a gate. A few of us disembarked. Most passengers were going on to New York. I fleetingly wished I was one of the many, but I'm not that fond of New York. Inside the terminal, I looked around. The sudden attack of paranoia seemed unfounded. I took several deep breaths. One of those white phones beckoned, politely offering me its services, a courteous courtesy phone. I made my way through the crowded departure lounge toward it, trying very hard not to contemplate the possible consequences of the game I was playing. But I would finish the foolishness I had started, if only to prove to myself that I could save myself from my own stupidity. I made my call and waited, heard the page for Robert Smith moments later, then heard a clicking on the receiver as another white courtesy phone somewhere in the terminal was patched into mine.

"Mr. Smith?" I inquired politely.

"Culbertson?" came the reply.

I frowned. "Is this Mr. Robert Smith?" I asked again.

"Yes?" The voice was now guarded.

"Mr. Smith, Martha Culbertson sent me. Is there somewhere you would prefer to meet?"

"Marty sent you? Who are you?" I sensed the suspicion in the voice and I didn't want to lose him.

"Yes, sir. She was extremely busy today, so she asked me if I would fly up here to meet you. I'm an employee of the hotel, but since I don't know you, Ms. Culbertson suggested I page you. I just got in."

"All right." There was relief in the voice, but I also sensed a note of irritation, of tension. "Where are you now?" I told him, and he directed me to a bar in the terminal. I suggested he look for me—my height is easy to spot, even in a crowd. Five minutes later, he met me at the entrance to the bar as I was walking up. He was a short, full-bellied, bald man, and he nervously chewed a fat cigar butt as he led me to a booth in the cool, dim interior. He already had a drink on the table, and he latched on to it as soon as he slid into the booth. As I slid in across from him, I took mental notes to be considered later—the yellow flowered pants, white sport shirt open at the collar, navy blazer. He was pink, not tanned, and in the light outside the bar I had noticed that he was sweating even though the air-conditioning was sufficiently cool. I pushed the briefcase across the table to him. He started to open it when a waitress came by the table to check on us. He started to wave her away, then looked at me.

"You want a drink?" he asked gruffly after a moment of indecision.

"No, thank you. I guess you might say I'm on duty."

He turned back to the girl. "Give me a tab when you get a chance, honey." Then he opened the case and quickly pawed through its contents. He looked at me, confused.

"What the hell kind of joke is this? You were supposed to be returning a camera, right?" There was suspicion in the voice again.

"Ms. Culbertson asked me to tell you that the camera hadn't been fixed yet," I lied. "She said to tell you that she was terribly sorry, but that she didn't have time to call you. She will get in touch with you as soon as it's ready. Anyway, she wanted me to deliver these papers to you."

"Oh, for chrissake! You're kidding, right?"

"No, sir." I said it firmly, with conviction.

"So what the hell am I supposed to do? I gotta have that camera." He brought a pudgy fist down on the table, rocking his drink, to emphasize his point. "The damn thing was supposed to be ready no later than today. Everybody down there knows how important it is. Somebody screwed up. I'd like to know who."

"I wouldn't know," I said coolly. "I work for the hotel; I'm not involved with the family's private affairs." There was just enough huff and sarcasm in my voice to set him back. He started and blinked at me, realizing that he had overreacted.

"Hey, I'm sorry I jumped on you." There was a nervous edge to his voice. "I know you haven't got anything to do with it. I just don't know what could have gone wrong, you know?"

The waitress showed up with the check. Smith looked at it, then opened the billfold and riffled through it.

"Damn," he said, laying the wallet on the table. He slapped his front pockets, then felt his jacket pockets, obviously not finding much. "Oh, well," he muttered, and pulled a credit card out of the billfold, handing it to the waitress.

"So anyway," he said to me when the girl was gone, "this thing was pretty important, and I hope you can understand why I got a little angry. Hope I didn't hurt your feelings?" I shook my head. He was rambling, trying too hard to smooth things over. I relaxed and looked congenial, letting him think everything was okay with me.

The girl came back with the check to be signed. The light was bad, but I had mentally snapped to attention and my eyes had been on the card since the tip tray had hit the table. By the time he had picked up the card to slip it into his billfold, I was almost positive that the name on the card was A. Portolucci.

"Hey, what's your name, anyway?" he asked as he stuffed the wallet back into his pocket.

"Jim Lord," I said automatically.

"Yeah, well, Jim, I appreciate the trouble you went to get me these papers. You tell Marty to give me a ring when that camera's fixed, okay?"

"I'll do that." He had slid out of the booth, and I followed his lead.

"You have a nice flight back now," he said, then headed for the door. I waited until he had disappeared, then slid gratefully back into the booth. I waved the girl back to the table and started my own tab.

*   *   *

The trip back to Nassau held more questions than the trip to Miami. But I did not consider them immediately. Like a recalcitrant child, I had deliberately disobeyed Marty's orders and had gotten away with it. I was delighted with myself. I positively chortled with glee at the thought that I had fooled the bad man, that I had fooled the customs man, that I had fooled those who would fool me. A thrill, a tingly chill ran through me at the thought that in a small way I had once again cheated the ultimate nemesis of us all, Death. They had not chunked me into wet cement—yet. I had somehow wedged open a door that had slammed tight weeks before, closing off a vital part of the me I had grown so accustomed to and fond of over the years. I still could not see clearly through that doorway. I was not yet sure what pieces of me lay beyond it, but I was pleased with myself.

The announcement to fasten seat beats for our descent into Nassau jarred me back to reality. I had taken a step I could not retract. Someone had called the last play very carefully, but had expected no opposition. I had stumbled onto a piece of the play, had read it as well as possible, organized a hasty defense, ran interference, and had recovered the fumble. I now had the diamonds, but was damned if I knew why. My self-congratulatory pat on the back suddenly seemed premature. I had come off the bench without knowing what the rules were or who my opponent was. I faced a lot of unknowns at one hell of a disadvantage. My only option was to try a little razzle-dazzle, throw the ball around the backfield for a while, force the opposition's hand, and key on their actions.

Nassau held no magic for me now. The cabbie got an extra five for playing cruise director and making the twenty-minute drive from the airport last more than thirty minutes. The expensive camera lens died on the operating table on the way. The stones went into a coat pocket. The camera case and contents went into a shopping bag. Confidence in my

personal security and safety went out the window. The slight
bulge in my pocket made me feel frangible and insignificant.
People have been known to kill for less. But at the same time
I felt a smugness that no one knew the degree of wealth and
power that lay hidden in my pocket. I had a momentary,
insane compulsion to brag about it.

At the hotel, I put the shopping bag in the hotel safe, and
signed a receipt. Then I called Marty's room on the house
phone. She wasn't in. I left a note for her: Mission accom-
plished; hero returned; gone into town on shopping spree to
celebrate; will meet you for dinner. I composed it carefully,
trying to pretend I had never opened that camera case. Then
I went up to my room to shower and change.

I moved slowly, forcing myself to relax. I put on a fresh
pair of khaki pants, a loose, long-sleeved, collarless shirt,
and a pair of sandals. I transferred the stones to a small
plastic bag I found in my toilet kit and put it in the pocket
of a windbreaker that I slung over my shoulder. I took a cab
over the causeway and into town.

Nassau actually offers few advantages over Miami. It is the
political and commercial hub of the hundreds of Bahamian
Out Islands and the center of Bahamian problems. Recognizing the importance of the tourist trade to the economy, the
government has spent a great deal of energy and resources
on public relations since the islands achieved independence
from Great Britain. On the less accessible Out Islands where
the communities are smaller and more closely knit, there is
little strain between tourists and natives. The natives recognize the benefits of catering to the tourist trade. And many
of the foreign property owners are generous in their commit-
ments of time and money to fund-raising and community
affairs projects on behalf of the natives. But in the small city
of Nassau, there is a more acute awareness of an imbalance
in the distribution of wealth, one that has existed for cen-
turies.

Paradise Island is a world unto itself. The old British estates outside of Nassau now house resort hotels and elegant restaurants, and are still frequented by rich and richer. In the city itself, "over the hill"—that part of town formerly separating poor blacks from rich whites—hasn't changed much. After years of colonialism, the residents of Nassau now see some of the worst examples of capitalistic hegemony. Foreign businesses taking advantage of the liberal Bahamian tax laws steal, take, build, buy, and ravage, often giving little in return. Cruise ships disgorge hordes of loud rude people in search of souvenirs of their five-hour stay in port. The underlying atmosphere in Nassau, away from the glitter of Paradise Island, is of political and social unrest. It is not apparent to the casual tourist, but as I wandered the streets, I sensed suspicion and distrust that I had never felt on any of the Out Islands. It was not a strong feeling, but it made me a trifle uneasy. And the crowds of people were beginning to grate on my nerves, so I stopped wandering and went in search of the post office.

I needed a phone and didn't want to use the one at the hotel. I had no idea who the bad guys were, but the diamonds I had in my pocket seemed to have something to do with the Culbertsons. I suddenly wanted to become as inconspicuous as possible. In the post office I placed a person-to-person call to Brandt. I didn't really expect him to be in on a Friday afternoon, but he answered on the fifth ring.

"Emerson who?" he asked after the operator had clicked off.

"Go suck an egg. What are you doing home?" I asked, now grinning.

"Why are you calling me?" came the retort.

"That's not an answer."

"I'm tending my garden and taking some sun. If you're smart, you'll plant your bulbs early this year. Where are you?"

"I'm in the Nassau post office."

"What in heaven's name are you doing on Long Island?"

"Nassau, Bahamas."

"Oh. What are you doing in the Bahamas?"

"Taking some sun, but not, regrettably, tending my garden. And, of course, talking to you. Listen, I need a favor."

"Aha! I knew there must be some reason for this call. I couldn't imagine you being motivated to call me by feelings of remorse."

"I need some information," I said, ignoring his remark. "First, dig up whatever you can about the financial status of Culbertson Hotels. I don't want a rehash of the annual report; talk to your banking buddies, see if there are any behind-the-scenes mutterings about anything. Then, see what you can find out about Bertrand Culbertson's personal finances. Same thing—get me whatever dirt there is."

"What's going on down there?" He had heard the serious-ness in my voice.

"I'm not sure yet. I'm trying to find out."

He pressed for details, but I didn't have any.

"Okay, you understand what I need to know?" I asked when he finally realized that I couldn't tell him anything.

"Sure, I've got it. Hey, how will I contact you? Where are you staying.?"

"I'll get back to you, say, Monday afternoon. That should give you some time to find out something. Besides, I'm not sure where I'll be."

"All right. I'll see what I can do. Take good care." There was concern in his voice.

"Thanks."

He hadn't asked about Marty, for which I was grateful. My feelings for her were jumbled and confused. There was some-thing very wrong in our relationship, and I didn't know what it was. I wasn't sure whether to believe that she'd had anything to do with the deal that was supposed to have taken place in

Miami that morning. I didn't want to think anymore. My head hurt.

A small pub down near the waterfront served as sanctuary, supplying a cool, dim interior that relieved the pressure of the day's heat and a cold St. Pauli Girl that soothed a parched palate, nattering nerves, and a queasy stomach. After two beers, I was ready to consider lunch. The menu offered a variety of conch dishes. Conch is a popular staple in the islands, for reasons unknown to me. The Bahamian dishes in which it is a base—fritters, salads, and chowders—are all delicious, but conch meat itself is tasteless and tough. Eating conch is akin to munching on rubber bands. I tried variations on the theme half a dozen times before I gave up. On two of those occasions, conch and I had a violent disagreement, and I lost both times. Nothing else has even come close to making me as thoroughly sick. I passed on the conch and decided on grouper. It was very good.

When the edges of my vision began to fuzz slightly and the feeling of contentment began to turn to lethargy, I paid the bill and got on my feet before it was too late. The light and heat outside assaulted me, causing me momentarily to consider waiting out the day in the seat I had just left. But for some reason I was fidgety. There was a churning in the pit of my stomach. I didn't like waiting for someone to discover my little charade and make the first move. It was my move, but I wasn't ready.

I found myself walking the waterfront, and stopped to take it all in. Boats of all sizes and shapes filled the harbor and spilled out onto the deeper blue of the Caribbean, the farthest just white dots trailing white froth across the blue expanse like tiny comets. The hotels of Paradise Island glittered in the sun across the harbor like the coins and jewels that had probably been spent to build them. It was a Baccarat day, with the sun shining through an atmosphere of crystal clarity, making water, sand, glass, steel—anything reflective—spar-

kle and glisten with flashes that danced and rippled in constant motion.

I sat on a dock piling and let my thoughts drift and float.
If I took my mind off the problem, I thought, I might suddenly
be struck with a solution. I let myself get caught up in the
day, the movements of water, air, light, boats, people, the
sounds, the smells, the warmth, the colors. Unconsciously,
my fingers traced the semismooth irregularities of the stones
in my pocket. They seemed unreal.

Judging from the sun, it was about six o'clock. It would
be dark in another hour or so. The afternoon had slipped
away from me, indifferent to my plight. I walked toward the
causeway over to Paradise Island. It was a pleasant walk
except for the apprehension knotting my gut that grew stronger
as I neared the hotel. I felt conspicuous again, paranoid. I
recognized no one as I passed through the lobby to the elevators. I had the elevator to myself, and when I got off on
my floor, the hallway was empty. I flopped on my bed, trying
to calm my jangling nerves. I had done a foolish thing, and
now I was afraid of getting caught. I couldn't possibly find
out anything before the deception was discovered. And it was
none of my damn business. Why had I impulsively chosen
this mystery to solve, this windmill to tilt at. Was it some
personal inadequacy? Guilt? A death wish? I had failed Jessica, and now I was making amends by getting involved in
something that would probably kill me. My judgment was no
longer trustworthy. My instincts had grown too rusty.

I regulated my breathing and concentrated on the ticking
of the small clock next to the bed, slowly letting my mind
empty, until finally, I fell into an uneasy sleep.

VII

I SAT UP abruptly, fearing I had been asleep for a long time, then got up slowly when I saw it had been only fifteen minutes. I washed my face and freshened up, then decided to shave and took another five minutes. When I came out to put on a clean shirt, a piece of paper on the dresser caught my eye. It was a note from Marty asking me to meet her in the bar downstairs at about eight o'clock. I tossed it into the waste-basket and finished dressing. I transferred the plastic bag to the pocket of a blazer. As I was slipping into a pair of deck shoes, I thought I heard a sound from Marty's suite. I stepped to the adjoining door, but hesitated, uncertain about con-fronting her. I wanted a drink and a chance to read her before I decided what to tell her concerning the events in Miami. That thought prevented me from knocking on the door, but for some reason I quietly opened it a crack and listened.

I heard a man's voice, muffled yet understandable, but when he paused I could hear no reply.

"Yes, sir," the voice said. "It's all set. She's down at the bar now. We'll make our move in about five minutes." There was a pause, then, "Yes, the note is just as you wanted it." Another pause. "Yes, sir, we'll contact you as soon as she has been safed. We know our part, don't worry. I don't think there will be any problems." A shorter pause. "All right. I'm on my way."

I heard the small click of a telephone receiver being re-placed and carefully pulled the door closed and pressed my ear to it. I thought I heard the hall door to Marty's suite being shut, but waited an extra thirty seconds with bated breath, listening. There was no sound, so I slowly and quietly opened the connecting door until I had a reasonably unrestricted view of her sitting room. It was empty. Blood sang in my ears, and my heart pounded as I headed cautiously for the bedroom. Had someone been there I never would have heard him over the thumping in my chest. But there was no one. I felt relieved, but my relief was almost overwhelmed by fear and concern, fear of discovery and concern for Marty.

I found the note on the dresser, but resisted the impulse to pick it up. I suddenly felt as if I were trapped in a scene from a bad television script. The note was addressed to Bertrand Culbertson. In letters cut from pages of a magazine and pasted on the paper it asked for one million dollars' ransom for the safe return of his daughter. But the pieces of the conversation I had heard only minutes before suggested that she had not been kidnapped yet. I found I was moving without having been aware of it.

Almost instinctively I stepped quickly back into my suite and locked the door. I checked the hall before going out, and headed purposefully for the elevators without appearing hasty or desperate. The elevator took forever to arrive, then was agonizingly slow getting to the lobby. The cocktail set was out in full force. I sauntered toward the bar. One saunters when one is nonchalant. I did not feel nonchalant, but hoped I appeared so. I started to go into the bar, then hesitated, exercising caution. I felt foolish. I hitched up my pants, strolled in, then quickly headed for a dark spot at the end of the bar. I scanned the room and finally spotted Marty at a table on the far side. A man sat next to her, chatting. She didn't seem to mind. Perhaps she knew him.

The bartender asked me what I wanted to drink. I ordered a tall Myers's rum and tonic and put money on the bar. I deliberated, caught in an internal conflict. Something more than the man's presence at Marty's table prevented me from approaching her. To tell her that she was about to be kidnapped seemed preposterous. She would laugh it off, or make a scene, but she certainly wouldn't take me seriously. My drink came. I took two big slugs. Just when I was beginning to wonder if it was all a joke, the numbers started to fall.

Marty suddenly slumped over the table. The man next to her looked consternated and leaned over as though to ask her what was wrong, putting his arm around her shoulder. She didn't move. The man looked up, glancing around the room with concern on his face. Apparently spotting someone he knew, he waved his arm for help. Another man stood up from the bar and quickly moved to the table. They exchanged a few words, then each took one of Marty's arms around his shoulders and lifted her to her feet. Her chin sagged on her chest, head lolling, hair spilling down, half hiding her face. They had undoubtedly drugged her drink, but an apparently overserved lady at cocktail hour would not appear abnormal, nor would anyone pay much attention to the two chivalrous gents helping her. It was a clever snatch, and I was suddenly frightened; they were very ballsy fellows.

Whatever they had put in her drink had hit her hard, but hadn't put her out. She was able to shuffle her feet in an attempt to walk as they half carried her to the door. I let them leave, tossed down the rest of my drink for courage, then followed discreetly. Their passage through the lobby drew casual, disinterested glances. The desk clerk glanced up; I heard him ask if he could be of assistance. One of the men said he thought she would be all right, but that he would call a doctor if she wasn't better soon. The desk clerk nodded and went back to his work. My admiration, and fear, of the pair went up a notch. I pushed away my feelings of helplessness. I hung back by the desk, waiting. Finally I followed Marty and her escorts toward the elevators and fell in behind them.

They got in an open elevator and a couple quickly stepped in as the doors were closing. But I was too late. I impatiently hit the elevator call button. The indicator above the elevator stopped on 2. I hit the call button again, and stepped back to watch the indicator slowly blink out the floor numbers until it stopped on 6. The couple had asked for the key to room 612. I swore under my breath and sprinted for the stairwell. There would be a back way out, a fire exit. I cautiously opened the stairwell door, sticking my head through to listen for them. Nothing. I slipped through the door and down the stairs to the back exit, using the same procedure with that door. Then I saw them, about fifty yards away, making their way through the parking lot.

I started to follow, but hesitated when they met a third man. A shaft of light from a streetlamp cut across the man's face, and suddenly I was paralyzed. I had seen that face standing over me in my darkened living room, watching me as I lay helpless. Their voices were indistinct, but I had no desire to get any closer. After a moment, the third man nodded, then abruptly turned and strode quickly across the parking lot with the fluid grace of a big cat. The others moved on.

In my tan blazer and light-colored trousers, I was too visible, so I gave them a big lead. I waited until the big man was out of sight in the other direction, then began to follow Marty and company. My only worry was that they would get into a car. Instead they surprised me by heading for the beach. I had thought they would continue the gamble they had taken in the hotel and stick to more populated areas—a foolish notion. A second thought suggested that they knew what they were doing a hell of a lot better than I did. When they reached the beach, I dropped back, and slowed my pace to match theirs.

The threesome stopped suddenly. I was too far away to see what they were doing, but I was downwind, and the light breeze carried sounds well. I *could* see that though the two men still held Marty's arms, she was bent almost double, and I heard what sounded like retching. It was a good sign. She might get rid of some of the stuff they had put in her system. The fresh air might help, too. I could think of no way to get her out of this without her cooperation, and if it took two men to help her walk now, then I wouldn't be much good to her by myself.

"Puke your guts out, sweetheart," I muttered. They were moving again, and I started after them, still mumbling under my breath.

They had made a good choice taking the beach. The sand was soft and deep, making walking difficult, causing me to falter occasionally. The three ahead of me simply looked like overindulgent partygoers, the best of friends, having a nice little arm-in-arm stroll in the moonlight. Revelers would have made more noise, but they appeared innocuous enough. They were good, damn good, and the realization sent another chill through me. The thought of simply following them and reporting their whereabouts to the police never occurred to me. I had subconsciously mounted my swaybacked steed and was riding off to save my lady. I ignored the small voice that kept calling me crazy.

Finally, we came upon one of the hotel marinas, and I quickened my pace to close the gap. I was still a hundred and fifty yards away as they walked out onto a dock toward the slips. The marina was full, and I was afraid I might lose them once they got in between the superstructures of all those cabin cruisers, so I sprinted the distance to the pier. After a moment's hesitation where the pier branched off into the myriad of slips, I finally spotted them about fifty yards away heading for the gangplank of a large cabin cruiser. Halfway down the slip, Marty seemed to start coming out of her stupor and began squirming in the men's grasp. I moved instinctively, trying to put aside all thoughts for my own safety, but suddenly could think of no good reason why I should risk my life to save this particular damsel in distress. The thought almost stopped me dead in my tracks, but I was too late. I was already into my act.

I was at the top of the slip, moving toward them, mouth open, face slack, eyes droopy, trying very hard to walk a straight line. They were trying to wrestle Marty up the gangplank, but turned when they heard me coming. I had their attention now. There wasn't a glimmer of recognition in Marty's face, which was both good and bad. I had worried that she would give me away, but now I wondered what kind of condition she was in.

"Good evening, gentlemen—and lady." I spoke slowly, enunciating carefully. I made a sweeping bow and pretended to almost fall over. "Did you . . . um . . . come to join me for a little nightcap?"

The man on Marty's left loosened his grip on her arm and took a step toward me. "You've got the wrong boat, fella."

They were off guard—tense, but off guard. I took another step forward and looked at the boat, feigning bewilderment.

"Wrong boat?" I scratched my head.

One more step was all I needed, and I took it as he started to reply. I never heard what he said. I made the last step sort of a lurch, then charged full speed, putting my shoulder in the stomach of the man on Marty's right, flipping him up and over the rail onto the deck. I let my momentum carry me into a spinning snap-kick that caught the other man in the chest, sending him backpedaling off the end of the pier into the water with a satisfying splash. I grabbed Marty's arm and half dragged her up the slip gangway before she understood what was going on and tried to use her feet.

Time went into slow motion. I could hear nothing but the screaming and pleading inside my brain, "Let's go, let's go! Come on!" An internal switch had been thrown from fight to flight, and my adrenaline-charged system could have done the hundred-yard dash in less than ten seconds. But as if in a nightmare, my feet felt like they were mired in quicksand. Marty was not yet cooperating. I supported over half her weight. Her feet touched the dock only every other step. And still the screaming went on inside my head, "Please, God, make her move her feet! Come on!" We were on the main dock, with a clear shot to freedom. I couldn't hear any sounds of pursuit, only the incessant screaming in my mind, and that was suddenly punctuated by an explosion that stopped time altogether for an instant.

Time started up again in very slow motion. Marty spun away from me, stumbled, fell, seeming to float ever so slowly toward the dock. And I floated toward her, trying to move faster. I took one step—it was like trying to walk underwater on the bottom of a pool—and then another, and I was at her side. I went down on one knee, grasped her, and pulled. She faltered, then slowly got up. And as the echoes of the explosion faded away, time picked up speed. We were running again. I heard a half-whispered shout behind me, just one word—"Idiot!"—and I jumped off the dock into the sand, then turned to catch Marty as she jumped. I heard her gurgled scream when my hands grasped her waist. I pulled my hands away and then I knew. Marty's right side was bloody. The man had called his partner an idiot, not me. His partner had pulled a nasty gun and fired a nasty bullet that made a nasty hole in Martha Cranston Culbertson. I had been merely frightened before. Now I was panicked. I drew big gulps of air and quickly took stock.

Marty was alive. The bullet hadn't hit anything vital. That was point one. Point two: she was in shock, and still drugged. That was both good and bad; at least she hadn't felt anything except direct pressure on the wound, so perhaps she could travel. I heard someone still floundering in the water, meaning we had a lead of sorts. The gunshot would attract attention, which would temporarily distract Marty's two playmates. They

would think first of their own safety, as we also would. I took
Marty's arm—her left arm—and gently pulled her to her feet.
I looked around desperately, searching for an idea, and when
I saw it my panic disappeared, replaced by the more familiar
fear and an icy calm.

"Come on," I whispered gently. Marty clung to me as I
led the way down the beach to a group of glass-bottomed
dinghies pulled up on the sand. Quickly and quietly, I managed to launch one, get Marty into it, where she collapsed
in a heap on the bottom, and clambered in myself. I got it
turned around and pulled hard on the oars three times, letting
it glide back toward the slips. The little boat slid under the
pier, and I stood up and grabbed the edge of the dock above
me with my fingertips. I pulled us along, ducking in among
the big boats in the slips. There was no sound of pursuit: the
gamble had worked; the kidnappers must have thought we
were on shore somewhere. At the end of the marina, I gave
one last push off the pier, sending us gliding out into the
dark of the harbor.

Out on open water, almost midway between Nassau and
Paradise Island, I stopped rowing and let the boat drift. It
occurred to me that I had no plan, no place to go. Marty lay
unconscious in the bottom of the dinghy. She needed a
doctor—more likely a hospital—but I didn't dare take her
into Nassau. The guy who had shot at us had to know that
he had hit Marty, though I thought he had been trying for
me. They would certainly check the hospitals if they didn't
find us before that. I shook my head, trying to understand
what the hell I was doing at the oars of a glass-bottomed
dinghy, with a dying woman for cargo, in the middle of Nassau
Harbor, with no place to go.

The tide was ebbing, and the boat was drifting out of the
harbor to the open sea. I didn't intend to drift aimlessly until
we starved to death like shipwreck survivors, but I was
damned if I was going to start rowing without knowing where

or why I was rowing. I gazed into the night. What, I wondered, was the man who had broken into my house doing in Nassau? And who was he? The day's events now had me truly confused. None of it made any sense. I wanted to believe I had hallucinated everything. But in my pocket was still a small fortune in diamonds, and a bleeding Marty still lay silently crumpled in a small bundle at my feet.

The water was calm, reflecting light from Nassau and a bright three-quarter moon. I spotted a boat heading out of the harbor in our direction, and I sat up and paid attention, praying they had not yet thought to look for us here. As it drew closer, I saw that it was a trimaran under power—one of the island charter boats—and I relaxed. I watched it curiously. It was a large boat, perhaps fifty feet, reminding me of the one I had cruised on a few years before when I had found Jessica in the islands. I grabbed the oars to position the dinghy close enough to hail the trimaran as it passed by. As it drew abreast, I counted six people on deck.

"Ahoy!" I called. The trimaran was throttled down and put in neutral.

"Yo!" came the reply. "What can we do for you?"

"I have a hurt woman with me. She needs attention. Permission to come aboard?"

"Come alongside and identify yourself," said the man at the wheel. I assumed he was the captain; the others kept quiet, staring. I brought the dinghy alongside the sailboat. Hands reached down to hold the gunwales, keeping it steady, so I could turn and stand up to speak to the captain.

I introduced myself and indicated Marty's body curled up at the bottom of the dinghy. "I could use some help," I added.

"Derek Jones," the captain announced, sticking out his hand. I was relieved to feel his solid grip. He started giving orders, and within minutes Marty was in a bunk belowdecks being tended by Derek and one of the women. The painter of the dinghy had been fastened to a cleat, and the first mate,

Derek's wife Amanda, had taken the wheel and put us on course. I had been given a drink, and had done what I could to help Derek and the volunteer nurse, then had gone topside to wait for Derek. He appeared shortly. We went forward to the bow to chat in private.

"She needs a hospital."

"I know."

"I should turn this crate around and take you back to Nassau, but I have a responsibility to my passengers, too."

"I wondered why you were out this late."

"We took a vote, and the passengers decided they wanted to try night sailing. It's good clear weather, nice moon, so here we are. What in God's name were you doing out here in that dinghy?"

"Escaping," I said simply.

"So I gathered. I really should report this and take you back to Nassau."

"You can't. Please." He was my only chance.

"Why the hell can't I? There's a bloody bullet hole in that lady down there." His voice was angry, but it wasn't directed at me. He fidgeted for a moment. "Who is she anyway?"

"Martha Culbertson."

He frowned, then the name connected. "You mean the hotels? That's bloody beautiful. You better tell me the whole thing."

So I gave him the story, leaving out only the diamonds. I didn't want to worry him unnecessarily.

"Where are you headed now?" I asked when I had finished.

"Governor's Harbour. We land sometime tomorrow afternoon." He looked at me, and I searched his face, silently asking. "Oh, all right, but I have to take it up with the passengers. They're paying for this cruise."

"Thanks."

"Don't thank me yet, mate. I'll be back in five minutes with a yea or a nay. Cross your fingers."

It was more like ten minutes, but when he came up to the bow he had his thumb up.

"What did you tell them?"

"I told them that I didn't completely understand what was going on, and that for personal reasons you hadn't gone to the authorities, but that you seemed to be on the level. I only had to lie twice. Not bad, eh? I added that you would be getting off in Eleuthera tomorrow so wouldn't present much of a bother. They're secretly thrilled to death, and I think delighted you're on board despite the circumstances. This is the most excitement they've had the whole cruise."

"Thank them for me, will you?"

"I'm sure you'll find a way. They're a good lot—quiet, well mannered, and pleasant, thank God. You'll get a chance to talk to all of them. We've set up four-hour watches at the helm and with your friend. If she dies on me, I swear I'll have your head."

"Fair enough. When do I stand watch?"

"First watch at twenty-two hundred hours, second at oh-two hundred, third at oh-six hundred. I was about to go off watch and entertain the passengers, but your arrival seems to have taken care of that, so I guess I'll stay on. But there's nothing other than my own rules that says the captain can't have a drink. Join me?"

"Delighted."

Some people might think that the romantic aspect of chartering a sailboat in the Caribbean—the sun, the sea, the laid-back life-style, the lushness of the islands and the women—would almost ensure that a man like Derek Jones would stay single, footloose, and fancy-free. But his wife Amanda was the perfect match. She was as competent a sailor and a better cook by half. She was a large, strong, attractive woman in her early forties, an Irish country girl. It was the strength and gentleness in the eyes, behind the plain features, that made her attractive. She was quiet, and though Derek appeared to run the ship, they actually shared responsibilities. She was at the helm now, and I was sure that Derek had conferred with her before consulting the passengers about what to do with Marty and me. Amanda ran the operation— oversaw reservations, itineraries, provisions, and supplies— and had the final say in most cases. They were well suited to each other. Amanda and I had not exchanged more than a hurried greeting when I had come on board, so when Derek and I settled with our drinks in the cockpit, I extended my gratitude to her.

"Glad to oblige," she said warmly.

"Amanda, luv," Derek broke in, "I've decided to stand watch, and have assigned Emerson and Mrs. Morley to stand watch with me. Would you mind seeing to the others and looking in on Emerson's friend and see that I haven't botched her treatment too badly?"

"Aye, aye, Skipper." There was a twinkle in her eye as she turned to swing down the companionway into the main cabin. Derek and I sat in silence for awhile after she was gone. The aroma of Derek's pipe drifted pleasantly in the night air. I settled back with my drink, listening to the gentle throbbing of the diesel engine beneath my feet, searching the night for answers to the questions that swirled in my head. I finally broke the silence.

"How did she seem to you, Derek?"

There was a long pause before he answered. He stood at the helm, looking forward, pipe clamped in his teeth. Finally, he took the pipe out of his mouth and turned to look at me.

"I don't know," he said quietly. "The bullet went all the way through, and it seems to be a clean wound. But I don't know what the internal damage might be. She didn't seem to be hemorrhaging, but she may be. The bleeding seems to have stopped, but I don't know how much she already lost. And there's always the danger of infection. We did what we could, but she needs attention soon. I gave her a shot of morphine, so she'll not feel any pain."

"And the other passengers?" I wasn't really sure what I wanted to know, other than to have his assurance that they wouldn't make trouble or that I wasn't making trouble for him.

"They seem to have a great deal of sympathy for you both. I think that story you concocted helped sway them in your favor. Running into us was one hell of a stroke of luck for you."

"I can't thank you enough." Derek wasn't hinting that I owed him, but I felt I did. He was simply trusting me on good faith. And when I had explained to him what had happened, he had accepted my suggestion of what to tell the passengers.

I told the others that I had been at a party on a cruiser in the harbor, and that Marty was the owner's wife. She and her husband had gotten into a violent argument and I had happened in on it. Fearing for the lady's life, I had stepped in and tussled with the gent. In the ensuing confusion, I had flipped the dinghy over the side and had entreated Marty to get in while I kept her murderous husband at bay. After I had gone over the side after her, the husband had pulled a pistol and taken potshots at us and one of the slugs had hit Marty. It was corny enough to sound plausible.

Derek and I fell into silence again, disturbed only once when Amanda came up to the cockpit to bring us coffee. I didn't know what I felt. It had all taken on a surreal quality, like a conversation you hear when half asleep, unable to separate dream from reality. The little gray cells in my head were trying to link all the day's events in a neat little package, but the thoughts moved too quickly; the pieces refused to fit into the screenplay my mind kept rewriting. Toward the end of the watch at midnight, Amanda came back up.

"She's awake now," Amanda softly said to me. "She's confused but seems right in 'er 'ead. Go to 'er."

I nodded and started for the companionway, but Derek's voice stopped me.

"Emerson, you can send Mrs. Morley up here to finish her watch, and tell her, by all means, to bring a drink and her husband with her if she wants. The breeze is picking up, so I think we'll have her under sail in a few minutes. It should be a pretty sight in the moonlight."

I swung down into the cabin and headed for the extra stateroom Marty was staying in. Mrs. Morley met my knock, and I relayed Derek's suggestions and my thanks for playing nurse. She was a nice, matronly sort in her late fifties, early sixties, who seemed to have great sympathy. She patted my arm on the way out, murmuring, "There, there, she's fine— everything will work out all right."

But Marty didn't look fine. She was pale, her face had a greenish pallor, and the blue-gray eyes were dull and lifeless, with dark circles forming under them. But she was aware, cognizant, trying to give me a small smile.

"Pain?" I felt my eyebrows go up. She closed her eyes and shook her head. I sat on the edge of the bunk and took her hand in mine. In a moment she opened her eyes.

"Where are we?" she asked. It was barely a whisper.

"On a sailboat. With friends."

"What happened?"

"Somebody tried to kidnap you."

She frowned. "I can't remember. Tell me."

I started with what I had seen in the bar, when she stopped me.

"Wait a minute. Those men weren't trying to kidnap me. They were helping me." She paused. It was an effort for her to speak. "I remember suddenly not feeling well, and then being taken outside for some fresh air."

"Marty, they drugged you."

"It's not possible. Why would they do that? I know them all."

"You *what?*"

"They work for the hotel. They wouldn't kidnap me."

"But I found a ransom note in your room."

"Maybe someone was planning to kidnap me, but it couldn't have been those men. How could they hope to get away with it?"

"Wait a minute. What about the third man in the parking lot?"

"Third man?"

"Sure. Big fellow with a round face and small eyes."

She paused. "Oh, you mean Vince Johnston?"

It was as if she had punched me in the solar plexus, knocking the wind out of me; I felt the blood drain out of my face and I couldn't breathe. My mind raced in confusion.

"What was he doing there?" I managed to ask through gritted teeth.

"I'm not sure."

"How do you know him?"

"He's involved in some deal with my father. Look, it doesn't matter anyway. I'm sure Vince wasn't trying to kidnap me." She closed her eyes and grimaced with pain. Maybe it was the morphine confusing her, but it didn't ring true. She was hiding something. I couldn't imagine what connection Vince Johnston could have with Bertrand Culbertson.

I didn't like the half-baked suspicions that had started to form in my head. They flashed in and out of my consciousness like cockroaches scuttling across a kitchen floor when the lights are suddenly turned on. There was a long silence as I let a question form in my mind and surface like a bubble released from the muck at the bottom of a pond.

"Marty, did you know what was in that camera case?"

She frowned, confused. I had changed the subject. I reached into my pocket, pulled out the bag of stones, and showed it to her. She still frowned, then her mouth opened as she looked at it and she gasped.

"Where did you get that?"

"You knew about the diamonds?" The churning was back in the pit of my stomach.

"Yes. I mean no . . ." She was frightened now. "How did you get them? No one knew . . ." She hesitated.

"You set me up." I didn't want to believe it.

"No, I . . . no one was supposed to know." Her voice was high and plaintive, like a child caught in the act.

"You *used* me."

"No, it wasn't like that. Emerson, please." The voice was placating now, and I wanted to believe that she was innocent, but I couldn't let it go. She had known. "Listen," she continued, "it had to be done. I had to protect my father. We had to do something." She was struggling to cope, fighting the drug in her system, trying to find a way to explain. But it wasn't coming out right. I couldn't make sense out of what she was saying, and I knew it was partly because she was trying to cover up something. Suddenly her eyes opened wide in fright.

"If you have them, then . . ." She couldn't finish, but fell back and closed her eyes. After a moment, she gathered the strength to speak. "Someone must have been after the diamonds, must have thought it was a double cross when you didn't deliver them."

"What were they for? What was the payoff?"

"I can't tell you." She almost screamed it. "Why did you mess it up? They'll probably kill us."

"They won't kill us. Because they weren't after the diamonds. The man who shot you made a mistake. He blew it. They were after a ransom, but not the diamonds." I heard my voice. It was calm. I didn't know where it was coming from. I was more confused than ever, but I felt an assurance that I was right. But I also felt sick, shocked, unable to accept the emotional impact of what she had done, unable to determine why she had done it.

"Give me the diamonds," Marty whispered.

"I don't think so. I don't know what your little game is, but I think I'll just hang onto them for a while. You're in no shape to do anything with them."

"Damn you! I've got to make sure they're delivered to the right people. I should have known you'd screw things up. I should have known from the beginning."

I looked at her curiously. "Sorry. If you won't tell me what's going on, I'll just have to find out for myself."

She stared at me, and in her eyes was hate, and fear. Because now she knew little more than I. Someone *had* tried to kidnap her. And despite the morphine, she knew she was hurt badly, and she knew someone had tried to kill her. She was a pitiful sight. I didn't tell her the bullet had been intended for me. I suddenly felt sick. She had used me, and I couldn't forgive her for that. But someone else had been using her, and because of my interference, she had gotten a bullet in the back. Someone was playing for very high stakes, and still she clung naively to some conviction that she could play the game.

"Get some sleep," I said finally. She closed her eyes, exhausted.

When I got topside, I became aware that we were listing, and I could no longer hear the diesel. Derek and Amanda had put up the sails, and the sight was truly incredible. The two couples had joined the captain and his wife in the cockpit, and I stopped for a moment to chat and to report that I thought Marty was probably asleep by now. Then I excused myself and made my way up to the bow. Between each of the three hulls were slung webbed nets to prevent anyone from falling overboard. I flopped into the one between the main and starboard hulls and lay on my stomach. Burbling and hissing, the hulls carved white froth out of india ink, sending it spraying and splashing out over the glassy surface to be reabsorbed after our passing as though it had never been. I watched, mesmerized, then finally turned over onto my back to look up the curve of the sails to the top of the mast and beyond to the stars. The mast gently swayed far above, and I was rocked with the same rhythm in my cradle. Moonlight glinted off the aluminum mast and off the shrouds and stays, little droplets of light winking and cascading in the dark. And I felt a strange sadness that was almost a relief. I had created a rift between Marty and myself that I knew would never close. I wanted comfort, affection, love, and I had blindly believed she would give me these things. I had felt something was wrong with us and had exposed her betrayal. But I still didn't know why. Everything blurred into indistinguishable shapes, blobs of black and white in a changing pattern as the boat rocked. I felt a pain that as yet had no source. And it was as large and deep as the pool beneath me.

I didn't hear Amanda come up to the bow, but I felt her presence. When I looked up, she was squatting on the main bow, clasping her shins, chin on her knees, looking forward. In a moment, she turned to look at me.

"I didna mean to disturb ye, Emerson. Yer pain is none of my business, and I wouldna have come had I known." She spoke softly, soothingly. "'Twill all work out for the best, ye'll see." She paused. "Ye're a sensitive man, but a strong one. Ye'll do what y' have to, what's best."

"Thank you," I managed to say. Perhaps she had some intuitive sense of what I needed to hear even if she didn't know the reasons for my pain. Wherever they came from, her words touched me, and I was grateful.

"I'll not ask any questions. Come, I'll fix ye some coffee with brandy." She rose and held out her hand. I scrambled out of the safety net, taking her hand, and followed her aft.

It was a long night, and I didn't sleep much. I stayed on deck most of the night, occasionally curling up on the cockpit cushions for a nap. And every once in a while I checked on Marty. Someone was with her at almost all times, but she didn't wake. Toward morning, she became feverish, tossing and turning in her sleep, opening the wound. Amanda and I changed the dressing and checked with Derek about giving her another shot of morphine. He said to wait as long as possible. So we watched and waited, and when she half started out of unconsciousness at dawn in obvious pain, we gave her another shot. She slept peacefully again.

VIII

THE DAY DAWNED bright and clear. Amanda and I had the watch, and we had to shield our eyes as the sun rose, huge and red, slowly at first, then seeming to rise faster and faster, turning orange, then yellow. It was quiet except for the constant hissing and slapping of the hulls cleaving the small swells, a sound that barely touched the conscious mind. There was no movement belowdecks. Those not already in their bunks had gone gratefully to them at dawn. Derek slept in a chair in Marty's stateroom.

At the end of our watch, I went to rouse Derek and found him already up and having breakfast in the galley. I reported all quiet topside; he reported no change in Marty's condition. Then he went up to relieve Amanda, and I went to look in on Marty. She was sleeping fitfully, and her forehead was hot to touch. I stood for a moment looking at her, feeling helpless, wondering what had brought us here, saddened by the thought that neither of us was here for the right reasons. It was someone's cruel idea of a joke. We certainly weren't meant for each other, but we had been thrown together for some reason, I felt.

As I left, Mrs. Morley was making her way to Marty's stateroom, stifling a yawn, a cup of steaming coffee in her hand. We exchanged a few words, then I went back to the galley. I had some toast and coffee, then refilled the cup and took it up to the cockpit. Derek watched me silently from the helm, sipping slowly from his own mug as I settled into the cockpit cushions.

"Why don't you turn in?" he asked after a moment. "You look bushed."

I shook my head. I was exhausted, awake only by sheer force of will. The fatigue that washed over me made my body feel heavy, my head light.

"Really, Emerson, there's no reason for you to stay up. Get some sleep."

"Later," I said. He shrugged his shoulders.

"Have any plans yet?" he asked a minute later.

"Do you know if Dr. Gilbert still lives in Governor's Harbour?"

"Roland Gilbert? Sure, he's still there."

"I know him," I said after some hesitation. "From last time." I paused as memories of the last time I had been down here, of the doctor on Eleuthera, of Jessica, swirled murkily in my mind. I shut them out. "I'll see if he's willing to care for Marty for a while. Then I guess I'll just play it by ear."

Derek was silent. I stretched and tried to stifle a yawn, and as I lay there lulled by the sounds of water and wind I fell asleep.

I woke to the sounds of voices and movement in the cockpit, momentarily confused as sleep slowly left me. I sat up and looked around, getting my bearings, remembering. The sun was almost directly overhead. Mr. Morley was at the helm, and the other couple—I forget their names—sat across from me. They all stopped talking and looked at me as I sat up, then resumed their conversation as I yawned and rubbed my eyes. I excused myself and went to check on Marty. Derek and Amanda were both in her stateroom, and they looked up with a start when I opened the door. They were changing her dressings, and seemed to have been in conference.

"How is she?"

"Her fever's worse," Amanda said, not looking at me.

I watched them finish with the bandages. They paid no attention to me, and when they had finished cleaning up, Amanda pushed past me without meeting my gaze.

"I'll go see whose turn it is to watch 'er," she said as she left. I looked questioningly at Derek. He got up and came toward me.

"She's bad," he said, "but there's not a bloody thing we can do. She needs more attention than we can give her here."

"Amanda?" I asked with raised eyebrow.

"She wants to send a distress signal and have a helicopter pick her up. She's afraid the woman won't make it; she's superstitious about people dying aboard her boat. Don't worry, I convinced her that we'll make land in plenty of time, but I'm damned worried, too." He paused. "Well, come on. Let's go see where we are."

Derek pored over the charts in the main salon, and then explained how he approximated our position. Amanda brought us lunch, and we talked some more. The afternoon dragged on. A pall had fallen over passengers and crew. Though it had gone unspoken, news of Marty's deteriorating condition was known by everyone, and there was little conversation or cheer from anyone for the rest of the day. The sight of land toward late afternoon made us all breathe easier.

By the time we cruised into the harbor, Derek had everyone scurrying around the decks in preparation for docking. The landing and docking were almost flawless, and as soon as bow and stern lines were made fast, I hustled ashore, leaving them all to contend with furling the sails and the rest of it. I found a cab almost immediately and woke up the sleepy driver by offering him a Bahamian ten-dollar bill if he could get me to Dr. Gilbert's small villa in half the usual time. He earned the ten.

Gilbert remembered me, for which I was grateful, and when I had given him the gist of it, he immediately took command, asking me only the important questions, getting ready to go as he did so. He called his wife into the room in between questions to me and gave her succinct instructions to carry out while we went to get Marty. Within just a few minutes of my arrival we were ready to leave.

"Oh, Mary?" Gilbert said to his wife on our way out. "Call Anna and tell her to bring things to spend the night."

We took Gilbert's car. He still looked like an English country gentleman, a little older perhaps—more slackness in the skin around the throat, deeper lines in the face around the eyes, a few more white hairs. I still trusted him.

"Mary's a good woman," he said as we started off. "Fine wife. Excellent nurse."

I nodded agreement.

"Well, Mr. Ward," he continued, "calamity seems to be your specialty. Either you're a womanizer with a penchant for the frail ones, or you're a humanitarian who constantly finds himself precipitously in the middle of it, so to speak." He paused to glance at me, but I don't think he expected a reply. "You obviously haven't told me half of it."

"The only things you need to know are that this woman is in no danger as long as no one knows where she is; that the bullet she took was intended for me and I plan to stay away from her so nothing further happens to her; and that neither one of us is wanted by the law." I paused. "Dr. Gilbert, we have met on only one other occasion, but on that occasion I found you an extremely competent doctor, and I think you found me a surprisingly trustworthy person. Would you consider it presumptuous to assume that we are essentially the same people we were a few years ago? Because that's the assumption I made when I decided to come to you."

"I find that reasonable," Gilbert said after a moment. "But I'll agree to your request for, uh, discretion on one condition."

I bit my lip. "Okay."

"If I feel that this patient needs hospitalization, or is beyond help of any sort, the authorities will have to be informed. But if I think I can help her without hospital facilities, you have a bargain."

"Thank you." I breathed an audible sigh of relief. Gilbert glanced at me and gave me a small smile.

Derek and I lifted Marty into the back seat of Gilbert's car. He had given her a cursory exam on the boat and had reluctantly decided to take her home and care for her there. He had praised the care she'd already received. When we'd gotten her out to the car, Gilbert took me aside.

"I assume you want to get on with whatever it is you have to do," he murmured. "There's no need for you to come back with me. Mary and Anna will help me with her."

His display of trust took me by surprise.

"Well, go on," he said impatiently when he saw my hesitation. "We'll take good care of her."

"Thank you. I'll be calling you to check on her."

"You do that. And come back and tell me about it someday." With that, he turned and got into the car.

I went back aboard ship, shook hands with the men, kissed the women, thanked them all profusely, and beat it before anyone could get maudlin. I was halfway up the dock when Derek caught up with me.

"Emerson," he said, putting a hand on my shoulder, "I just want you to know that though we're all relieved to have Martha in someone else's care, we're all sworn to secrecy. I'm glad we could help."

"Thanks. You may have saved her life. Tell them I've never sailed with a better crew. I owe you a big one."

"Forget it. Take care, and good luck." He gripped my shoulder, then spun on his heel and was gone.

My only consideration was to get away from Marty, from everyone we'd come into contact with. If calamity was my specialty, when it fell again I didn't want any more innocents around me. Marty had gotten herself into this mess, but I had helped precipitate matters, and I didn't want anyone else to get involved. I found a garage and rented an Austin jeep for a week. Then I went in search of a quick bite to eat, and spent almost half of my remaining cash on dinner and a couple of beers to take with me. I climbed into the little jeep and drove.

It was dark now, and once I was away from the lights of town, my headlights cleared a path through the blackness that kept closing in behind me. I had no place to go, no plan, so I just drove north on a whim, feeling the warm breeze, hearing the night sounds of island creatures, letting my mind wander. And I was suddenly tired of me, tired of the shenanigans of Emerson W. Ward, self-appointed knight-errant and romanticist. Trustworthy, I had said to Gilbert. And perhaps too trusting. I had seen the harsh realities of life too many times to still have this fantasy that the world is a bright and shining place full of wonderful people. Perhaps my chosen role was not wrong. Maybe I had just lost my perspective. Things had looked very different since Jessica had died. The way I functioned had changed in the two months since her death. Jessica . . .

I had been unable to accept her death. But now, driving through the night on the island where it had started, a door that I had slammed shut suddenly opened, and tears welled up in my eyes. I loosed the pain, the memories, and the despair from the closet where I'd hidden it all. I grasped at all the fragmentary memories of Jessica and loved her, and I felt her loss, felt my pain and anger and frustration rip through my being. And I finally began to accept. I let her go, let go of the illusion that it had not happened, that someday she would come back to me. And slowly, the pain lessened, leaving me exhausted and numbed. I drove automatically, not thinking, until much later, with a few short splutters, the car ran out of gas.

I pushed in the clutch and guided the car onto the shoulder, letting it roll and come to a gentle stop. I put it back in gear, set the hand brake, switched off the ignition, and hid the keys under the seat. Then I cursed the damn thing, startling some birds sleeping in the brush, and started walking. I walked for perhaps half an hour until I was exhausted. The sound of water breaking on shore was close by to my right, so I stumbled off the road, pushing my way through the scrub toward the sound. It was not far to the small beach, and when I reached it, I collapsed on the sand and slept.

I was working the problem. It was not yet dawn, and the morning was still, the sea calm. The beach was tinged pink with predawn light. The palms didn't even rustle. The nightmare that had awakened me was almost forgotten; instead the memories of the past few days occupied my mind. As the sun rose, my mind grew clearer. I stood and stretched, then made my way back to the road and started walking north. The anger that had filled me became focused. I felt rage at the unknown someone who'd ordered Marty's kidnapping. I felt rage at the two who had drugged her, and more rage at the one who'd shot her. I was furious with Marty for using me and for setting me up. But most of all, I was furious with myself.

I finally understood what I had done. Accepting Jessica's death had been the key that had unlocked the whole can of maggots that had been eating my insides. I had been unable to face the pain of Jessie's death. I had been afraid of falling apart, afraid that I didn't have the emotional strength to deal with the pain, so I had locked it away, pretending it didn't exist. And I had gone looking for someone else to take it away, to take care of me, to fix my life. Martha Cranston Culbertson had come along, and I had clung to her like a leech, sucking emotional support, expecting her, as Brandt had said, to "kiss it and make it better." But subconsciously I had known all along that I was the only person who could fix it and make it better.

Freudian theory may come closest to the mark. I had been

hurt, hurt badly enough to feel that I couldn't deal with the pain. I had gone looking for an emotional Band-Aid and a sympathetic mommy to apply it. Marty had done an excellent job of mothering. She had come into my life and had immediately taken control, dominating, manipulating, conniving, cajoling. I had fawned, accepting in desperation and in constant fear that she would withdraw her attention if I misbehaved. But grown men don't need mothers. They need love and caring, but not mothering. And subconsciously I had rebelled, repulsed by my childishness. I had been uncomfortable with Marty because I had relinquished all control over my life to her. But deep down I had hated myself.

I remembered the last time we had made love, only a few days ago. We had not been close since coming to Nassau. Something in her manner had put me off, had made me not want to bring up the subject. But that night, we responded to each other as though some curtain between us had lifted. Our touches became more fervent, sensual, excited, until finally we were joined. We established a slow, lazy rhythm, and we were both reaching a kind of plateau when I sensed that she was receding. Her responses suddenly weren't the same, though she continued to keep pace. I could barely feel or sense her presence. I didn't know what was lacking, but I was at the point of no return—and not just physically. I could sense that she no longer wanted to finish what we had started, but something made me want to push the moment, to unlock whatever door it was she didn't want opened. I thrust harder and felt her tense and start to pull back. I held her closer and she met my thrusts with her own, savagely, vengefully. When I began to climax, it was almost painful, and as I did I felt her orgasm beginning, then felt her try to suppress it, pulling back against my embrace. But it was too late for both of us—she reluctantly rode out her climax.

Then I hadn't known what it was. I had simply felt a sadness. Now I knew that it had been her strange reluctance

that had made that moment so painful. Whatever had bound
us during those first weeks was gone for her. But still I had
clung to her. I had sanctioned her to think for me, to feel for
me, and couldn't understand why I still bled and hurt. Now
I couldn't understand why Marty had singled me out. A need
to dominate? Penis envy? With that thought, I laughed. Emerson Ward, Amateur Psychologist.

I was angry that I had been so easily caught in my own
trap of self-pity, but I was relieved that I had not completely
lost touch with myself. I could regain control. I could heal
the self-inflicted wounds; the one caused by Jessie's death
was already starting to close. It was a relief to have Marty
out of my life. There were still questions to be answered
before she could be written off, but she was emotionally dead
to me now, and to do what I thought I must required having
no emotional attachments to her. Letting her go was easier
when I replayed our relationship. I don't think she was a bad
person. We had used each other; I just hadn't used her to
my best advantage.

An advantage was what I needed. As I walked, ideas began
to take shape in my mind, built with imaginary scenarios and
conversations formulated from bits and pieces of information
and impressions that popped randomly from memory. Perhaps
with Brandt's information about Culbertson I could devise a
plan. As though working on a jigsaw puzzle, as pieces were
tried and gradually fit into place, I heard cheerful humming,
an occasional snort of derision, a smug chuckle, and more
humming—coming from me. These were familiar sounds. I
was alive and thinking. With a self-congratulatory pat on the
back, I welcomed myself back to the world.

By midmorning, I reached the Glass Window, the narrowest
point on Eleuthera. The rocky island coral, only a hundred
yards or so wide, drops off sharply to the sea on both sides.
To the east, the Atlantic Ocean swells roll in, battering the
cliffs, occasionally breaking over the top to wash across the

road and into the calm of the Caribbean to the west. Within a half hour, I was standing on a small strip of sand, looking across a narrow channel separating Eleuthera from the tiny neighboring Harbour Island. The walk around the wide bay to the ferry that goes from North Eleuthera to Harbour Island is a long one. I considered swimming the short distance, but finally decided to walk. It took another two hours to reach the ferry dock.

The ferry ride was short and pleasant. I hopped off as soon as we docked and went in search of a cab. The island is only a little more than three miles long and half a mile wide, but I'd had enough walking. Most of the hotels are on the ocean side and close to town, but I opted to try my luck at a small place on the harbor side south of town called the Tamarind Bay Club. I'd stayed there before, so I knew the owners, Roy and Denise, and I liked the setup. The rooms were all small private bungalows, and the food was the best on the island. My luck was good; they had a room. I knew I must look god-awful with a three-day stubble of beard, wearing clothes that I'd slept in, so I told them I'd just come in on a sailboat and hadn't bothered to get my gear yet. I borrowed a razor from Roy, got my key, and headed straight for a shower.

Getting clean never felt so good. I scrubbed myself twice, letting the hot water play on muscles sore from walking. After shaving and rinsing out my clothes, I flopped down on the bed and instantly fell asleep. It was dark when I awoke, and I felt disoriented. I groped for the phone and called the front desk to find out what time it was. It was 7:30, so I asked for room service and ordered food, lots of food. It had been a day since I'd eaten, I realized, and I was famished. While eating, I made a mental list of things to do in the morning. Finally, I pushed away my plate, slid naked between the cool sheets, turned out the light, sighed contentedly, and slept again.

Morning was well established when I snapped open my

eyes and looked around the room. The day sounds of birds
and water and people, which had melded surrealistically into
my dreams, now became real and intelligible as the images
in my mind faded. I sat up and half turned to reach under
the pillow, allaying a suspicion before it fully formed. The
bag was where I'd put it before falling asleep. I pulled it out,
swinging my legs out from under the sheet to sit on the edge
of the bed, and dumped the contents on the pillow: a dozen
uncut diamonds, wallet with credit cards, sunglasses, and
six Bahamian dollars. After taking inventory, I carefully put
it all back, and went into the bathroom.

The face that greeted me in the mirror could have looked
worse. I splashed cold water on my face and rinsed out my
mouth, scrubbing my teeth with a forefinger, then combed
my hair with my fingers. I shook out my clothes and put them
on, grateful that I wouldn't have to wear them for long. I
reclaimed the bag and the room key from the nightstand, and
left in search of a ride to town.

It had been years since I had been to Harbour Island, but
everything was comfortingly familiar. Even the potholes in
the road to town seemed not to have changed. I had gotten
a ride with Roy, and we swung past the cemetery, around
the corner past the library, and headed up the hill toward
the post office. I had him drop me on a corner, and walked
a block to find a shop. I bought clothes, toiletries, and a
shoulder bag to put it all in. I wore one of the new outfits,
stuffing the old clothes in the new bag, and headed for the
post office.

I had the woman behind the counter place the long-distance
call for me. I held my breath while it rang, praying that
Brandt was home. He picked it up on the third ring, and I
waited while he accepted the charges and the operator got
off the line.

"Emerson?" His voice was faint but clear.

"Brandt, I can't tell you how glad I am to hear your voice."

"Where are you?"

"I'm on Harbour Island. Off the tip of Eleuthera."

"How did you get there?"

"I'll tell you later. Let's try to keep this short. I need some money. Could you wire, say a thousand dollars? If you need money to cover it, you know where my emergency funds are hidden. Wire it to me at the post office."

"Sure. What's going on down there?"

"I'll explain when I get back. I'll be flying in sometime tomorrow."

"Okay. The money should be there this afternoon. I did some research on Culbertson. I'll tell you about it when you get back."

"Thanks. See you soon."

I hung up and asked the woman to place another call for me. I called the garage in Governor's Harbour where I'd rented the jeep and told them I'd run out of gas and that they could pick it up because I wasn't going to use it anymore. I paid for the call, then told the woman that I was expecting a money order to be wired and would be back later to pick it up. Then I headed toward the waterfront, stopping at the Royal Bank of Canada on the way. I asked to speak to an officer, and introduced myself, explaining that I was a guest at the Tamarind Bay Club. I showed him my ID and credit cards, and told him that a money order was being wired to me and I hoped he would be able to cash it for me. I also said that I would want to rent a large safety-deposit box when my funds arrived. I was genial. I was politic. I was earnest and serious and businesslike. In passing, I dropped a hint that I was desirous of confidentiality. He was eager to help, glad to oblige, and grateful that I had chosen his bank to do business with.

I had enough cash left for a couple of beers, so I strolled down the waterfront to the local tavern and plopped down in a chair on the small porch that overlooked the harbor. I put my feet up on the railing and settled in for a long wait. It was quiet on this side of the island. The tourists were on the beach on the other side. The natives were taking midday siestas. Most of the charter fishing boats were out, so the main dock was quiet. The ferry was not running; the morning group of departing vacationers had gone, and the afternoon influx wouldn't come for a few hours. Across the street, an old man slept on a bench in the shade of a tree at the water's edge. Two mangy dogs lay in the sand at his feet, lazily scratching at the flies that buzzed around them.

It was so peaceful, I wondered why I had this compulsion to find answers, to finish what someone else had started. Why couldn't I let the matter drop? I had freed myself. Marty meant next to nothing to me now. I could simply pay Dr. Gilbert for his services and let Marty fend for herself when she recovered. There was no need to involve myself further. But I felt a need to screw up someone else's life, someone else's plans, as badly as mine had been screwed up. I puzzled over that for a long time.

Much later, I went back to the post office to pick up the money order, then returned to the bank to cash it. I signed the papers for the safety-deposit box and carefully locked away the diamonds. I was counting on the fact that someone would soon be very anxious to find out where they were. Then I stopped by a travel agency to buy a ticket home and finally went back to the hotel to get a rum punch and watch the sun disappear below the horizon in a blaze of oranges and pinks and purples.

IX

I FERRIED OVER to the airstrip on North Eleuthera the next morning and took a puddle jumper from there to Freeport, avoiding both Nassau and Miami. Just because you're paranoid doesn't mean they're not out to get you, I reasoned. I doubted that anyone would or could connect me with the disappearance of Marty and the diamonds, but I wasn't taking any chances. A direct flight from Freeport got me into Chicago midafternoon. I had only the shoulder bag, so I bypassed baggage claim and hurried out of the terminal into a cab. I'd never seen a more welcome sight than the skyline of my town unfolding in view as we drove downtown.

My little house greeted me with a look of forlorn emptiness, accusing me of having been gone too long. I quickly unpacked and changed into a T-shirt and a pair of gym shorts. I slipped on a pair of sandals and padded into the kitchen for something to eat. The refrigerator yielded a beer. I took a long pull while investigating the possibilities for lunch. It didn't look promising. I finally took a can of tuna and a can of mushroom soup down from the cupboard, and while the soup was heating I chopped some green onion into a bowl with the tuna and stirred in some mayonnaise and lemon juice. The bread was stale, so I decided on crackers that were a little less stale.

I sat at the kitchen counter and munched thoughtfully. I stared out the window and watched a sparrow hop to and fro on the back terrace in search of its own lunch. When I finished eating. I uncapped a fresh bottle of beer and took it into the living room.

It was quiet, too damn quiet. There was a click and a muted humming from the kitchen as the refrigerator compressor rumbled to life. The air conditioner in the back bedroom whirred distantly. A car whizzed by outside. The floorboards creaked familiarly, but unnaturally loud as I prowled from room to room, looking for something that wasn't there. The house had never seemed so empty. It suddenly felt too big for even my ungainly bulk. I couldn't sit still, and I moved impatiently like a solitary ice cube rattling around in an empty ice tray, cold and diminished, looking for some vestige of Jessica's presence, some lingering echo of her laughter.

She had filled my house, had made it comfortable and cozy—a home. Her smile had illuminated dark corners, and her soul had warmed every room. I imagined my house missed her as much as I did.

I put a jazz tape in the stereo and turned up the volume, trying to fill the empty space. The world was now thoroughly shut out; I was safe and secure in my house. It had been so easy to walk away from all that had happened, as if it had never existed. The sound of the single gunshot, the feel of Marty's blood oozing through my fingers, the sight of sails against the moon, the long, lonely walk down an endless tropical road—they were all elements of a bad dream that was already fading from memory. It just didn't feel right to be so quickly transported to a world that was just as it had been left, untouched by all that had touched me.

The serene sameness of the house, the quiet street, the lake sparkling in the sunlight two blocks away—somehow all of it seemed like a denial of how I felt, of what I had been through. Nervous tension filled me, and the loud music pulled at my jangling nerves causing muscles to twitch in syncopated rhythm. I stalked restlessly until I could stand no more, and finally went to the den and yanked open the closet door. I pulled out the exercise mat and the thirty-five-pound dumbbells.

First, I did sit-ups, setting a tempo with the music, up and back, up and back, until the muscles of my abdomen burned and knotted with effort. I could feel the tendons in my neck stand out and blood throb in my temples as I strained past the one hundred mark. After fourteen more I couldn't raise more than my shoulders off the mat. I fell back and panted.

After a moment's rest, I stood up and hefted the dumbbells and began pushing them with the same rhythm, shutting everything out of my mind. First military presses, then pulls, then bench presses, then curls, fifty of each with a steady one-two, two-two, three-two, four-two, huff-puff, huff-puff, huff-puff . . . Finally came the deep knee bends with the weights on my shoulders, an added seventy pounds. My knee joints cracked and groaned and my calf and thigh muscles quivered with the strain. Sweat rolled off my forehead into my eyes and trickled down my chest. After about forty-five of these my left knee gave out, and I sat down hard on the mat, jarring my teeth.

The tape shut itself off, and I sat in the silence listening to the thudding in my chest grow calm and quiet, just staring into space. As though from a distance, I heard myself take a deep breath and exhale with a sigh, bringing me out of my reverie. I got up slowly and headed for the shower. I was, I decided, almost ready to talk to Brandt.

The stinging hot water rinsed away most of the remaining tension in my body, and I let the steamy spray play over each sore muscle in turn until they all glowed with warmth. I pulled on a pair of loose, cotton drawstring pants, and an old faded blue Chemise Lacoste, and padded barefoot into the kitchen. I felt better. I still didn't feel right, but I felt better. The aggression would have been better spent putting someone's head through a wall—at least I would have gotten more satisfaction out of that—but I didn't know which way to turn.

I picked up the kitchen phone and dialed Brandt's number.

"Hi, I'm home."

"So you are."

"Cocktails? My patio?"

"Sounds fine. Shall we say ten minutes?"

"Delightful." I grinned as I hung up the receiver. Despite my feeling of displacement, it was good to be home, and even better finally to have someone to talk to about the things that had been eating at me for months.

I hummed a nameless tune as I hunted in the kitchen for food and drink, cheerfully banging cupboard doors open and shut. I found an unopened box of fresh crackers hiding in a corner and I set up a tray with the crackers, celery, a chunk of cheddar cheese, some cream cheese, and a tube of anchovy paste. Then I sliced some lime and built two large Myers's rum and tonics. By the time I carried everything out to the patio, Brandt was letting himself in through the back gate.

"Halloo!" his voice boomed across the patio. He strode toward me with a wide grin on his face. He grabbed my outstretched hand, pulled me to him, and with his other gave me a big squeeze. "As painful as it is for me to admit," he said with his hand still on my shoulder, "I have missed your dour countenance and your irksome moods. You look good," he added, holding me at arm's length. "Island life must agree with you."

"Sunshine agrees with me," I chuckled. "Sit down. I fixed us drinks."

"Aha!" He positioned himself on a chaise close to the tray. "You must have known I skipped lunch." He spread cream cheese on a celery stalk, squirted some anchovy paste on it, and crunched hungrily.

The sun moved out from behind a high-rise building to the west of us, casting a deep golden light and long shadows across the patio. The warm softness of the air and the angle of the sun foretold summer on the way. Brandt raised his glass.

"To friendship," he said softly.

I had wanted love. I had wanted to be in love, to experience that once-in-a-lifetime thrill of trusting someone implicitly, completely, of placing the whole of me at someone else's feet, knowing I would be accepted as a precious gift despite my flaws. I had wanted to share totally with someone, to share my joys and perspectives, to learn of someone else's, to experience through another's life and love for me. Jessica could not give me what I sought, and Marty would not. And I realized that Brandt's caring, ever-present and unquestioning—another sort of love—had brought me through time and again, had enabled me to face the aloneness of the solitary life I had chosen. Though neither of us felt complete, we had more than most. I raised my glass and gently clinked it against his.

"To friendship," I repeated. He smiled warmly, as if at peace with the world. We relaxed, sipping our drinks, feeling the weight of the late afternoon sun lighten as it dipped toward the horizon.

"So," he finally broke the silence, "tell me what happened, what you have been doing."

"I'm not sure where to start," I said hesitantly.

"At the beginning, of course," he said gaily, then saw my exasperated look. "All right, let's start with where's Miss Culbertson?"

I should have known he'd ask that first. "She's in Governor's Harbour, on Eleuthera, recuperating, I hope, from a bullet in the side."

"What?" Brandt was suitably shocked.

"I'm like a magnet," I sighed. "First, I attract the ladies, then the bullets start whizzing around us like bees. Up to now, I've had the good fortune not to get stung. They, on the other hand, have not been so lucky. I'm beginning to wonder why women and violence seem to go hand in hand. Perhaps it's my karma."

I tried to make light of it. As well as Brandt knows me, he has never gotten used to the sordidness that is part of my life. He is both mortified and thrilled by it. It offends his sense of propriety to know that that other world impinges so closely upon his own sheltered world, and that I, his closest friend, traverse so easily from one to the other. At the same time, a secret self, I suspected, wanted to take part in my adventures, to live in the same twilight that sometimes envelops me. He is not naive, merely myopic, but I often felt the urge to isolate him, to protect him from that other world. I had the good sense to be afraid of that world, but he, like a child, would be morbidly fascinated, too curious to be scared until it reached out and bit him. I wanted to save him from that.

"Tell me what happened." I could see the excitement in his eyes, the need to be drawn close to the precipice and peek at the danger that lurked over the edge.

I closed my eyes, took myself back in time to the week before, and began.

It was dark when I finished, and we were almost done with the third round of drinks. The photosensor had automatically turned on the patio lights, and now mayflies and moths flitted and hovered close to the bulbs. A pale half-moon rose ghost-like over the housetops, brushing the tops of the trees in the yard. Without the sun, the patio bricks quickly lost the day's heat, and the air grew cool, almost chilly enough for a sweater.

"How could she do that to you?" Brandt asked after a long silence.

I waved away his remark. "Because I let her. Anyway, it doesn't matter now. What bothers me is whether I'm letting my imagination run away with me. Maybe I'm creating melodrama where there is none. Tell me what you learned about

Bertrand Culbertson. I want to see if any of these jumbled pieces fit."

"All right." Brandt drained his drink. "I won't bother telling you what lengths I had to go to for information. Bertrand Culbertson is either very unlucky or very stupid. Unlucky, I think, because he's done all right by the hotel chain. He's not as shrewd as his father was, but he hasn't made any mistakes running the corporation, not major ones, anyway. So, let's assume he's not stupid—at least, we can assume that he has good advisers. But his personal finances are something else.

"First of all, Culbertson got tapped by his wife in a sticky divorce six years ago. The settlement was very large. She lives in Carmel—expensive house, servants, quiet but elaborate and frequent parties, good taste in clothes and jewelry and cars, not loud but very lavish tastes. Anyway, she's been draining him for years. Not enough to hurt, but enough to annoy.

"Culbertson's bad luck started in seventy-four when he took a bath in sugar futures. He repeated the performance in seventy-six with coffee futures. That information comes from reliable sources down at the Board of Trade. He doesn't like publicity, so most of his financial dealings are done through fronts, making it hard to link his name to any specific investments. But I was able to trace his name on one deal a few years back. Seems he threw in with a developer and a group of investors on an apartment/shopping center complex. For reasons that are unclear, the bank foreclosed—he dropped around six hundred thousand on that one. And there are rumors of other losses. But no one seems worried. He has no bad debts. His financial dealings, though kept quiet, all seem to be aboveboard.

"However, I did some research on his position with Culbertson Hotels and did some quick accounting. By my calculations, the money he is pulling out of the company in salary, bonuses, profit sharing, et cetera, doesn't come close to covering the losses he seems to have suffered in the past few years. That might not mean anything, though. He could have sources of income we know nothing about, and, he undoubtedly does. But I get the feeling that something isn't right."

"What makes you think so?"

"I'm not sure. Maybe it's just that he's so secretive I suspect the worst. I didn't have much time, but I did an awful lot of checking, and I can't figure out where he got the money to cover those losses. He hasn't sold any of his stock in the corporation. His ex-wife hasn't stopped giving parties. It doesn't smell right."

"The corporation is doing all right?"

"Growing by leaps and bounds. About ten years ago, it began successfully diversifying into restaurants, a fast-food chain, some resort properties. They've upgraded meeting and convention facilities in a majority of the hotels, so have weathered recessions very well so far. Culbertson stock has nearly doubled in the past five years. No, there are no problems there."

"What if," I mused, "what if Culbertson embezzled funds from the corporation to cover his personal losses and is looking for a way to put the money back before it's discovered?"

"You mean the diamonds?"

"Sure, why not? Why would Culbertson—assuming it was his idea, not Marty's—want, or need, to smuggle diamonds, especially uncut diamonds? To avoid paying duty? No, I would imagine that he'd be able to buy uncut stones on the black market through his international connections at a relatively low cost, and sell the cut stones at a much higher price here."

"That makes sense. But why the kidnapping attempt?"

"Hell, I don't know. Someone stood to gain from grabbing Marty. After all, the ransom note asked for a lot of money.

What's curious is that the man behind the kidnapping was Vince Johnston."

"What?" Brandt looked at me quizzically.

"It's a small world," I sighed. "What I don't understand is Marty's belief that Johnston had nothing to do with it. She seemed to think he and her father were business associates."

"Wait a minute. Didn't you say that Vince met Marty and those two men in the parking lot?"

"Yeah, so?"

"Isn't it possible that Vince *didn't* know anything about it, that he just happened by and recognized Marty? Those men may have told him what you suspected, that they were just taking her out for some air because she didn't feel well."

"I suppose it could have happened that way," I said after a pause. "None of it makes any sense. There are too many variables, and all we're doing is playing 'what-if' games. Until we establish some concrete motives, we could suspect any number of people for any number of reasons. And the most frustrating thing is that I don't know what to do or where to start looking for answers. Ever since I got home this afternoon, it's as if nothing ever happened. It all happened somewhere far away to someone else. It must have. If it had happened to me, I would know whom to fight, whom to point a finger at. It doesn't make sense."

Brandt was silent.

"Besides," I said as a thought occurred to me, "why would Culbertson go to the trouble of smuggling diamonds if he needed money? Why not just sell some of his stock?"

"He doesn't want to lose control of the company. If he, or rather the family trust, ever held less than fifty-one percent, some company would gobble him up. Too many vultures looking for merger material right now."

"That's true." I pondered silently for a moment. "Come on, let's go in. It's getting cold." I stood up and turned for the door.

"I'll have one more cocktail," Brandt said as he followed me inside, "and then go home to bed."

I was a child again, huddled in the corner of a sailboat cockpit, trying desperately to meld with the cushions and become invisible in the dark. The boat sailed under full moonlight with no one at the tiller. It stayed on course, ploughing gently through the small waves, sails full with a light breeze. There seemed to be no one on board, but the child was frightened by the feeling of a presence somewhere near, despite the fact there was nothing but black ocean on all sides. The child's eyes moved to the leeward rail to watch the white froth pushed up and out to splash back into the sea as the hull knifed through the water. Then his eyes traced a stay, following it up to the point where it attached to the mast, and from there past the top of the mast to the moon beyond. As he watched, the moon took on features—a mean mouth and eyes that were too close together. A sudden noise brought the child's eyes down to the cabin gangway, and with rising fear he watched a man's form slowly climb to the deck. With horrified fascination he saw the man loom larger and larger until his head blotted out the moon. The light cast a spectral halo around the man's head, but his features were in darkness. As the man moved closer, the child could finally see that his features were the same as those of the moon.

The child bolted in terror, trying to escape, but knowing there was none from a boat in the middle of the ocean. The man grinned in the moonlight and took a lightning-quick step back and to the side to intercept the child. As the child tried to run past, the man brought up his arm and tapped the child on the temple with a dark object he held in his hand. The child stopped dead in his tracks, stunned and paralyzed by the blow, then shook his head to clear it, and swung his fist with all his might. His fist glanced harmlessly off the huge man's thigh, but the child swung again and again, trying to move him aside. The man tipped back his head and laughed soundlessly, then brought his arm up in a quick, fluid motion, again tapping the child on the side of the head. Blinded by tears of frustration and fear and paralyzed once more, the child stood rooted to the spot, then watched in horror as the man struck him again and again. Each time the object landed on an arm or leg or shoulder, the child felt a shooting pain and saw a cut open at the point of impact and slowly ooze black blood. The child could not move, and grew weaker as each blow opened another wound and let his life drip away.

I lurched out of bed in an effort to break away from the dream, and woke bathed in sweat on my hands and knees on the floor. I pulled myself to my feet, blinking away the last tendrils of the nightmare, and realized as I moved that all my muscles were stiff and sore from exercising the day before. It felt as if someone had hammered them with a mallet. The clock said it was nearly 5:30 A.M. I decided against going back to sleep. Instead, I pulled on a sweat suit and a pair of sneakers, slipped out the back door, and headed for the lake.

When I got to the beach, I stopped and did some stretching exercises to work out some of the kinks, then started a slow jog north. When I got to the North Avenue beach, I slowed to a walk, feeling a little looser. There was a light fog rising four or five feet off the lake, drifting in cottony billows. The sun peeked over the horizon, tinging the eddying fog with pink. It was a beautiful spring morning, and my dream was soon forgotten as I walked briskly up to Fullerton then turned toward home, passing other early-morning joggers on the way. I ran the half mile from North back to Division, then walked the few blocks to the house, catching my breath.

After showering and getting dressed, I went out for a newspaper to see what had been happening in my absence. I made a pot of coffee and sat at the kitchen table to read and drink. It was all old news—new players, but the same old games, a scandal here, a murder there. With unemployment high and a long, hot summer looming, the mayor prematurely announced summer plans to "fest" everyone to death with Neighborhoodfest, Italianfest, Jazzfest, Chicagofest. . . . School wasn't even out yet, and teachers were already talking about new contract negotiations in the fall. The Police Department was accusing the mayor's office of hampering an investigation into dirty dealings on the part of one of the mayor's committees. The mayor's office was accusing the Police Department of hampering an investigation into drug dealing by a group of the men in blue. Some things never change.

I was on my second cup of coffee when the phone rang. It startled me—I couldn't think of anyone who would call this early. I picked up the kitchen extension.

"Emerson? It's John Pearson."

"John, how are you?" I couldn't keep the surprise out of my voice.

"Where the hell have you been? I've been trying to get in touch with you for a week."

"Sorry, I've been out of town."

"Well, I'm glad I finally got hold of you. I'm in Chicago on business and I'd like to sit down and talk."

"Why don't we have dinner this evening?"

"I'm booked on a flight back to New York this afternoon and I really should get on it. Could we do lunch somewhere?"

"Sure."

"I've got some meetings this morning that I can probably get out of by twelve-thirty or so."

"I'll make reservations and meet you then." I gave him the name and address of a place on Rush Street.

I called Brandt to see if he was free for lunch. He was. I poured another cup of coffee, took it to the den, and started going through the stack of mail that had collected while I was gone. I sorted it into piles—junk mail, pay-now bills, pay-later bills, magazines. The junk pile was by far the largest. I sifted through it to see if there was anything interesting, then threw it all out. I went through the pay-now bills, writing checks and stuffing return envelopes. I filed the pay-later bills. Then I started to leaf through the magazines, but my attention kept wandering. I wondered what John Pearson wanted to talk about, what he had found out. I was more than curious; I was anxious, and waiting patiently was difficult.

I was still fidgety, so I cleaned the house. The woman who came in once a week would have a fit—there was nothing left for her to do except the kitchen floor. I stopped short of that. Finally, it was time to go.

I walked and still got to Harry's early. I sat at the lower-level bar and ordered a Bloody Mary. There was no one else at the bar. Harry's Café is primarily a saloon, with lots of open floor space around the lower-level bar, and high cocktail tables with bar stools spaced around the square upper bar. The interior is dark wood with lots of shiny brass fixtures and sparkling cut-glass interior windows and mirrors to offset it. The lower-level bar is black and green marble, and the floor is black slate. When the place fills up at night, which it usually does, it's hard to appreciate the effort that went into the decor.

Brandt arrived a little after twelve-thirty and joined me at the bar. He had just gotten his drink when John Pearson walked through the door, right on time. We stood up to greet him.

"Emerson," he said, giving me a hug, "it's good to see you again." He turned and shook Brandt's hand. "Brandt, I'm glad you came along."

We got a table along the south wall that was bright and cheery. The dining area is on the building's periphery, along two walls, and the atmosphere at lunch is calm and pleasant compared to the nightly revelry of the beautiful people, the young affluent singles looking to become couples, if only for the night. They come to party, consuming vast quantities of white wine, Stolichnaya, and Perrier, and to hunt for prey, occasionally ducking into the bathroom to sniff cocaine, emerging to renew the hunt, and the party, with increased energy.

We ordered a round of drinks and left our menus unopened. When the drinks arrived and the pleasantries about the comparative weather in New York and Chicago had been exchanged, John got a thoughtful look on his face and began to speak.

"I wanted to tell you an interesting little story," he said with a wry grin. "I didn't get back to you earlier, Emerson, because it has taken me almost this long to put together all the pieces." He paused to take a swallow of his drink.

"Vince Johnston did not leave Jessica penniless. Although she could have had anything she wanted from me had she told me, she still had a small trust fund I set up for her as a child that Vince didn't know about. She also had a few other scattered investments. She was a shrewd woman. Sometimes I think she felt driven to compete with me just as a son might have. I never expected it from her; she was simply an achiever, as much for herself as for me, I think.

"Anyway, she developed a scheme to get her money back. As you know, she knew the ins and outs of the stock market as well as anyone can know something that unpredictable. She did a lot of homework, and picked a company to invest in. It was a small company in a good cash position, but not with too much growth and very tightly controlled."

"What company is that?" Brandt interrupted.

"Drescher Construction."

"Mmm, I've heard of it."

"Anyway," John continued, "Jessica began buying stock in the company, a little bit at a time. To pull off her scheme, she needed far more capital than she had, so she enlisted the aid of a number of my friends. Damn them, not one of them uttered a word to me about it. She bought in at four dollars a share in relatively small lots, as I said. She always bought anonymously, through different brokerage houses, carefully covering her tracks. The company didn't have all that much stock outstanding, so as the number of shares dwindled, the price per share kept climbing. She didn't care; she kept buying.

"In the meantime, from what I understand, Vince Johnston had lost most of the money he stole from Jessica. About the time the stock hit thirty dollars, Jessica had practically cornered the market—she owned almost all of the outstanding shares. And at the same time, a funny little man I know from one of the brokerage houses approached Vince on behalf of an anonymous client. I had to threaten the man with financial ruin to get him to tell me this part of the story. He went to Vince and offered him fifty thousand dollars for a thousand shares of Drescher that had a market value of thirty thousand. Vince had seen how the stock was performing, and though he was cautious, he was even more greedy. He had just been offered twenty grand, free and clear. He sold short, not knowing he couldn't buy a thousand shares at any price."

John paused as the waiter stopped at the table. We ordered another round of drinks.

"Selling short," Brandt remarked, "often is not worth the risk. My daddy once told me, 'He who sells what isn't his'n, pays the price or goes to prison.'"

"Well, Vince paid the price," John said. "A week after Vince had sold short, the market price skyrocketed to eighty-nine and the S.E.C. stepped in and suspended trading. A few days later, the funny little man went back to Vince and did some dickering, and negotiated a settlement of two-fifty a share—times a thousand shares—that's two hundred and fifty thousand dollars in cash. Jessica had burned Vince and burned him badly."

"What about Jessica's holdings?" I asked. "How did she get away with it?"

"Oh, she made out fine. That's why she told you there was more in addition to the two hundred and fifty thousand in the suitcase. You see, she started unloading the stuff in earnest a few days before the S.E.C. stopped trading. The large volume of trading because of the blocks she was selling is what made the price begin to skyrocket. She was out of the market completely the day before trading was suspended, with a ton of profit for herself and her investors."

"Whew!" Brandt sighed. "That's a hell of a way to take a bull market by the horns. But the boys at the S.E.C. are a clever bunch. They may just find out what happened."

John smiled slyly. "I'm not sure they will in this case. Even if they do, it will take an awfully long time, and they still probably won't unravel half of it. Anyway, the stock is trading again—at around sixteen, I might add—and things have quieted down considerably."

"Well, now we know where she got the money," I said quietly. "The question now is where did Vince Johnston get the money?"

"Yes," John mused. "If Johnston was that broke, where *did* he get the money to pay off Jessica's sting?"

"What's even more interesting is that Vince knew Jessica stung him."

"What?" John exclaimed. Both he and Brandt turned to look at me. "It's not possible. There's no way he could have found out."

"You did, and somehow he did, too."

"Oh," Brandt said, as though a thought had just occurred to him. "It wasn't . . . he didn't . . . ."

"Yes," I said, figuring out what he was trying to say. "It was Vince who broke into my house that night looking for the money. I don't know how he found out, but he must have followed Jessica and figured I had the money."

"I don't get it," John said.

"Sorry, John, I only just found out. I had never met John-ston, but I saw a man when I was down in the Bahamas last week who was identified to me as Vince Johnston. It was the same man who broke into my house the night Jessica died."

"The man is vermin!" John blurted out. "He has absolutely no scruples!" Brandt and I looked quizzically at him. He had turned two shades of red and squirmed uncomfortably in his chair. "I'm sorry," he said after a moment, "it's just that I have to admit that this is not the first, uh, indiscretion that Johnston has committed. Or the second, for the matter.

"I don't know how to say this, but Vince had me in a rather indelicate position some time back. Shortly after Jessica mar-ried him, Vince came to me and threatened to expose a family secret that I thought would hurt Jessica if she found out. I told him I had no money, which was true—Maudie's legacy was all tied up in trusts, and my business hadn't been doing well. Johnston persisted, so I finally gave him ten thousand dollars and told him to go away.

"I had no idea he would force Jessica to sign over her inheritance. I thought he'd be satisfied with my money." His voice quavered, and he had a look of despair on his face. The guilt probably ran pretty deep.

"What's the terrible secret?" I asked softly. Ten thousand dollars' worth of secret made me very curious.

"I'd rather not talk about it." He set his jaw, and I knew I wouldn't get anything more out of him.

"Well," I sighed, "it sure would be interesting to find out where Vince got that money."

"Let me see what I can do." John was suddenly eager, as though trying to make up for some shortcoming—perhaps to Jessica? "I know some people who may be able to help. I have this strange urge to find out everything I can about Vince Johnston, to learn all his nasty habits, his wishes and dreams, and then slowly to ruin him in the most painful manner I can devise."

He spoke with a bravado that I'm not sure even *I* felt, as much as I had come to despise Johnston. My first encounter with him had been painful, and frankly, the man frightened me. There was something out of kilter about him. It suddenly occurred to me that John Pearson was a very nice, but very naive man who had never really come to grips with reality. I knew from long-ago conversations with Jessica that his business had been financed by his wife, who had loved him dearly. And though he had played the role of protector and provider, he'd done it out of a sense of self-esteem, not necessity. I liked him, but I sensed that his perspective of the world was shaped by newspapers, books, and television, not experience.

We ordered lunch—cold poached salmon with a cream Dijon and dill sauce and cold green beans vinaigrette, and a carafe of white wine.

"Were you down in the Bahamas on business or pleasure?" John asked, taking a bite of his salmon.

"Pleasure to start, but it turned into something more."

"Oh? Something to do with Vince Johnston?"

"That's part of it. I don't understand what he was doing there."

"I think what's more curious, Emerson," Brandt chimed in, "is that there seems to be a link between Vince and Bertrand Culbertson."

John was taking a sip of wine and suddenly choked, sending him into a fit of coughing. Brandt and I turned to him in consternation, and our waiter rushed over to offer assistance. John waved him away as his coughing subsided.

"I'm all right," he spluttered, trying to get a breath. "Just went down the wrong way." The waiter hovered around John's chair, wiping up the wine John had spilled, asking him again if he was all right. John finally regained his composure, but his color still looked bad. His face was pale and drawn.

"What I don't understand," John said when the waiter had gone, "is why Jessica didn't tell me what had happened. Johnston should have been thrown in jail and left to rot for what he did to her."

"John," I said gently, "would you have testified to what Vince had done if you were Jessica? She *lived* that nightmare, she didn't need to relive it. Getting even was the only means she had of punishing Vince without being publicly humiliated as she had been privately."

"I suppose you're right," he said sadly.

Oddly, I felt a strong affinity for John Pearson, and sensed he felt it, too. We had shared the love of someone very special, and with Jessica gone, all we had left were our memories of her. Jessica was the bond that cemented a friendship between us.

When it was time for John to leave to catch his plane, he grasped my hand in farewell and held it for a long time without words. Then he quickly said good-bye to Brandt, and when he turned to walk out the door, I thought I saw a tear in the corner of his eye for the girl we had lost. It was ironic, after all Jess had been through, that she'd made the phony stock option work, but she hadn't had an option on death.

I settled the check while Brandt got our coats, and we strolled north on State Street. Brandt had been strangely quiet through most of lunch and seemed to be brooding about something.

"Odd," he said finally as we reached the corner of my street.

"What is?" I stopped and turned to face him.

"John sure changed the subject quickly when I mentioned Bertrand Culbertson." He scratched his head, then turned and wandered off toward home, leaving me standing on the corner, wondering.

X

I SAW THE BLURB on a back page of Monday's *Wall Street Journal*, but for some reason it didn't register. I don't even think I really read it. In the process of catching up on the news, I was looking intently for any hue and cry over Marty's disappearance. But I didn't expect to see her name in the *Journal*, so I didn't pay any attention to that little tidbit. For all my trouble I was rewarded with no news of a kidnapping or a disappearance; Martha Cranston Culbertson wasn't newsworthy, it seemed. I had already checked four other papers, as far back as Saturday, the day after it happened. Nothing. It shouldn't have surprised me. Marty never had been kidnapped; I had seen to that.

So my mind turned to other thoughts. My mind works in convoluted ways. Not two days before, I had been complaining to Brandt that there were too many suspects and not enough concrete motives even to begin figuring out what was going on in the world of Culbertson hospitality. Suddenly, I found myself inventing more suspects and motives to muddle the problem. I had no other answers, so I clung tenaciously to a new conviction.

I folded the newspaper with a sigh. There is too damn much change in the world. They say that change is the only constant, and that without it people would stagnate and die. We huff and puff in a desperate run to keep up with the times, to be current and on top of things, until one day we find that all the running has brought us face to face with grinning Death instead of cheering crowds at a finish-line tape. And we wonder why we exert all that effort. There is no trophy, no glass of Gatorade or pat on the back from those we run with. All that way, we miss the sights. All that exists is the black asphalt with the white stripe down the middle. Once in a while, time should just stand still for a bit so we can catch our collective breath and take a look around to see what else there is.

I sighed again, realizing it's even harder to stop time than it is to keep up with change. My own attempts to resist change required as much effort as the race to keep up with it. Each time I reevaluated my life, seeking some sense of purpose, I measured how much I changed, and it was inevitable, the changes were measurable no matter how hard I tried to remain the same.

I called Brandt to see if he remembered the name of the law firm that had handled the Culbertsons' divorce. He did, of course. I went to the desk in the den and took out my file of business cards. Every time I have any kind of business meeting or walk into someone's office, I take a card—I never know when I might want to be somebody else. I also had boxes of leftover business cards with my name on them from one company or another. All the other cards were filed by profession—banker, dentist, doctor, dry cleaner, lawyer, public relations type, sales rep, and so forth. I pulled out the stack under "Lawyers," and culled through it to see if I had a card from the firm Brandt had just told me about. There it was, with embossed brown lettering on a rich, cream-colored stock, crisp and clean. My temporary name, the card said, was Lawrence J. Atkins.

I called Brandt back to confirm my hunch that all client contact would have been handled by a managing partner of the firm, and to find out exactly where, in the Carmel area, Mrs. Culbertson's house was. I knew he was curious, but he didn't press me for details.

I dialed the California number Information gave me, figuring it would be a house line, not a private one, and suddenly realized on the second ring I didn't know what to say.

"Culbertson residence," a female voice answered.

"Um, is Mrs. Culbertson there, please?"

"No, I'm sorry. May I take a message for her?"

"This is Lawrence Atkins, her attorney in Chicago. It's very important that I speak to her. Is there somewhere she can be reached?"

"You're from Chicago? She is in Chicago now. You could try to reach her there."

"Would you happen to have her number handy?"

The voice rattled off the phone number and cheerfully bade me a good day. I hung up feeling somewhat relieved. I wanted to see the woman in person, and had thought I'd have to go to Carmel. Seeing her in Chicago would be easier, and much less expensive. I sat back for a moment, mentally rehearsed my approach, and dialed the Chicago number.

"Hello?" This female voice was a little deeper, more melodious.

"Is Mrs. Culbertson in?"

"This is she."

"Mrs. Culbertson, this is Lawrence Atkins with Putnam, Abbott." I fingered the card in my hand. "I have some important matters to discuss with you, and wondered if we could make an appointment today."

"You'd rather not discuss them over the phone, I take it."

"I would prefer seeing you in person. I'd be delighted to come there if that would be more convenient for you." I sounded polite but earnest.

She hesitated. "Just a moment, Mr. Atkins. Let me take a look at my appointment book." I could hear papers riffle in the background, then she came back on the line. "I should be free at about three o'clock this afternoon."

"Shall I come up then?"

"That would be fine." She gave me the address, and said the doorman would be expecting me.

The address on Walton was a newer high rise just west of Michigan Avenue. I waited at the front desk while the doorman announced me, trying to work some of the stiffness out of my shirt collar. I had put on the navy wool pin-striped suit, starched white shirt, yellow silk tie, and camel hair topcoat, none of which had been worn for months. I had grabbed a leather attaché case and had stuffed some papers and manila file folders in it for effect, hoping I looked the part of a lawyer. The doorman waved me on up, and I entered the elevator, still pulling at my collar, feeling slightly giddy from lack of oxygen.

Her apartment was on the twenty-eighth floor, and I was pleasantly surprised. I had expected one of those buildings with no more than four apartments per floor, each a half a block long with rooms so large you can get lost in them. Hers was a sunny studio with a great lake view, tastefully furnished so that even the bed did not look out of place in what doubled as the living room.

Marian Culbertson struck me even more forcefully. She wore a smartly tailored light gray wool suit that showed off a figure belying her age and a white silk blouse with a high, ruffled neck. Her dark blond hair was naturally sunstreaked and tied into a loose bun. Her only jewelry was a strand of pearls. She had to be a few short steps past fifty, but easily looked fifteen years younger, the only hint being the myriad of tiny lines around the eyes made deeper by a lot of time spent baking in the sun and what I came to realize was an easy smile. Most striking was the same square jaw and wide-set gray eyes that Marty had. It was almost like looking at an older sister, and I had to turn away and look out at the lake to keep from staring at her.

I had given her the business card at the door, and she looked at it while closing the door behind.

"Magnificent view," I murmured, turning back to face her.

She looked at me curiously, sizing me up, and I thought I detected a hint of amusement on her face that puzzled me.

"Would you like some tea, Mr. Atkins?"

"Yes, please. I'd love some."

"Please sit down." She sat on the couch in front of a coffee table that held a sterling tea set. I sat across from her in an easy chair, and set the briefcase on my lap. She poured for both of us, added milk and sugar to mine.

"Now, what can I do for you, Mr. Atkins?"

I took a sip of my tea and placed the cup down on the table. "I'm sorry to bother you," I said, opening the attaché case and ruffling through its fake contents, "but I'm new to your case and I thought I should see you in person." I paused, then continued hesitantly. "It seems that there is a discrepancy in, ah, the amount of money you're receiving from your former husband, and the amount stipulated by the terms of the settlement."

"Bull," she said quietly. The exclamation, coming from that picture of elegance, startled me, then gradually seemed to fit her character. "You really *don't* know anything about the terms of the settlement. But perhaps that's because you're not Mr. Atkins." She said it with that same faint look of amusement.

I was stunned. I had not been as clever as I thought.

"One point two million dollars," she said abruptly before I could protest, "in four yearly installments. That was six years ago." I started to object, but she waved her hand peremptorily. "Oh, come, come. I don't know who you are, but you're certainly not Lawrence Atkins."

Her eyes said she wasn't bluffing. She knew, somehow. "What gave it away?" I asked with a very red face.

She smiled broadly. "No less than a junior partner can afford to take enough time off in a sunny climate to get the kind of tan you have; no less than a senior partner or managing partner would have made the appointment with me; and practically no lawyer makes house calls unless it's for a social visit, not business reasons."

I thought for a moment, flabbergasted. "You mean you only suspected?" I asked, feeling even more embarrassed.

"No, I knew," she said delightedly. It didn't give me much comfort. "I called the firm. Lawrence Atkins is sitting at his desk; his secretary told me he had scheduled no appointments this afternoon."

I groaned. I was definitely losing my touch. Dumb is one thing; deliberately stupid gets you killed.

"Why did you keep the appointment?" I asked, suddenly realizing that she had not thrown me out.

"I was curious," she shrugged. "I wanted to find out who you are and why you would want to masquerade as someone else just to see me."

"But I could have been anybody—a burglar, a rapist, a con man." Her nonchalance had me confused.

"You still could be any of those things. You're certainly a con man." She smiled again, and I was riveted by how much she looked like Marty, and someone else, too, though I couldn't put my finger on who. The impression was disconcerting. "So? Who are you?"

"What? Oh, Emerson Ward," I said, frowning.

"And what do you do, Emerson Ward?" She said it slowly, as though talking to a child.

I had to laugh. She had nailed me dead to rights, but had not been angry about my deception. I had wanted to dislike her, I discovered, but had found her the opposite of my expectations. She was warm, friendly, and curious—not imperious and brusque. I suddenly liked her a great deal. Because she looked so much like Marty, I think I had subconsciously expected her to *be* like Marty. She wasn't, though in some ways they seemed nearly identical—the way she moved, the way she stood, and her expressions, both verbal and facial. I laughed, and she laughed with me, easing my embarrassment.

"I'm a writer of sorts," I said when I could talk again.

"Of sorts?"

"When I feel like it, or when I need the money."

"And when you're not writing?"

"Oh, I do other things." I shrugged.

"What kinds of things?"

"Favors for friends mostly. This and that."

"You're certainly mysterious." She took a sip of her tea. "Why did you want to see me?"

I mulled over the options, and decided to be at least half truthful with her.

"Mrs. Culbertson, I have reason to believe your former husband is being blackmailed."

"And you think it's me." Her smile faded.

I nodded. "Let's say it could be you. You live in high style, and there's no love lost between you and your ex-spouse."

"My business is no business of yours, and I have no need to defend or justify myself to you. But I will set you straight." She had a look of distaste as though she was not used to confessing anything. "The settlement I got from my husband was intended to hurt him because he hurt me. It didn't bankrupt him, it only stung him a little, which was the intent. First of all, with that kind of money, why should I suddenly get greedy? Second, I don't need it.

"What you don't know about me, Mr. Ward, is just about everything. My family had a substantial amount of money, which was left to me and my sister. Six years ago I took that and the first installment of the settlement and started my own art gallery, something I'd always wanted to do. I parlayed that one little gallery into four—three on the West Coast and one here in Chicago. I have a good eye, and I know what people will buy and what price they'll pay for it. I'm not being immodest; it's the truth. Since the galleries have been doing so well, I've even had time to do some painting, and it's beginning to sell as well as the other artists I represent. That's one of mine." She pointed to the far wall.

I got up to look more closely at the painting. It was from inside a forest, all muted greens and yellows and browns, with a rough path through the middle, and just beyond the artist's sight, sunlight fell into what was probably a little clearing. That shaft of sunlight beckoned the imagination, suggesting something magical and wonderful just around the next bend in the path. She was right: it was a good painting, absorbing and pretty.

"I'm sorry." I turned around slowly. "It's very good."

"What's your interest in Bertrand, anyway? Did he hire you to find out who's blackmailing him?"

"No, nothing like that." I shook my head. "Let's just say I found myself in the wrong place at the wrong time. I think someone was using me as a go-between for a payoff from your ex-husband, only I wasn't supposed to find out. It's all too damn confusing. I'm just thrashing around trying to make some sense out of what's been happening to me lately. I don't really care what happens to your ex, but I do care about what happens to me."

She looked at me curiously. "That's a little selfish, isn't it?"

I shrugged. "Were you close to your daughter?" I asked, abruptly changing the subject.

"Not as close as I would have liked," she said hesitantly. "She was always 'Daddy's little girl.' She has the same lust for power that Bertrand has, something I didn't care all that much for, so she took after him, looked up to him. Why do you ask?"

"I think she's into something way over her head."

"How have you suddenly become such an expert on my family, Mr. Ward?"

"Mrs. Culbertson—"

"Marian," she interrupted. "Since you know so much about us, we might as well be on a first-name basis."

"Marian," I conceded, "I don't know if you remember, but I met Marty at a party in Lake Forest many years ago. She was being molested by two of the guests . . ."

There was sudden recognition in her eyes, but she hesitated again, then nodded. She seemed to be about to say something.

"Recently," I continued, "she and I . . . dated, so we got to know each other fairly well."

"I see." I think she saw perfectly well. She looked appraisingly at me. "Well, I guess I can see why she did."

Suddenly, in a small hand gesture, a slight shift of position, the way she held her head, and the way she looked at me, I saw the merest hint of an invitation. Not an open invitation, but a posture that said she might be interested, that she could be persuaded if the approach was discreet and tactful. I was tempted. She exuded a sensuality that was feathery light, almost intangible, one that blended with her graceful and elegant charm. She was as indirect as her daughter was direct, and something in her gentle manner reminded me strangely and abruptly of Jessica. The hollow cavern in my chest yawned, black and aching, the temptation was gone. The experience with Marty had shown me that I wasn't ready to let anyone take Jessica's place. Not yet.

"Marian," I said, thinking of Marty, "I don't know why you've been so patient with me since I tried to deceive you. You deserve a better explanation of why I'm here, but I really don't have any answers."

"Emerson, is it? Emerson, you're still here because I haven't made up my mind about you."

She already had, unless I misread the signs, but I mentally conceded that she was accepting me on faith. I hadn't said or done anything to offend her. One simple mistake, I imagined, could cost me dearly. She may not have had a craving for power, but she obviously knew how to use it.

"I should tell you, somebody tried to kidnap Martha. I don't know who or why, yet." Her eyebrows went up a notch, but she waited to hear me out. "I blundered into it, and helped her get away, but she was shot while we were escaping. She'll be all right," I added hastily, "but she was hurt pretty badly."

"You seem to have very little time for writing what with all these 'other things' popping up," she said quietly. "Where is she?"

"In the Bahamas. I'd rather not say where. I took her someplace she'd be taken care of, and where she won't be found if someone's still looking for her."

She hesitated, then nodded. "All right. Obviously there's nothing I can do to help, but Martha probably wouldn't accept my help anyway." Her lower lip quivered. "You know, of course, that Martha isn't my natural daughter."

"What?" Her revelation took me by surprise.

"She's adopted, and though I've always loved her as my own, she's always run to her father when she's needed help. Daddy's little girl . . ." There was a trace of bitterness in her voice.

"But she looks so much like you," I said, still dumbfounded.

"She's my sister's child. My sister died when Martha was very young, and her father didn't think he'd be able to take care of her on his own. Martha was so enamored of 'Uncle Bertrand' at the time, it was really her choice to come live with us. We eventually adopted her. But I shouldn't be telling you all this." She gave a small shake of her head, as if to clear it of old and painful memories. "Tell me what I can do to help."

"You might be able to help solve this problem I've got. Tell me a little about your ex-husband. Do you still care for him?"

"Part of me does. I think that's why I wanted to get even with him during the divorce, if that makes any sense."

"You mean if he hadn't meant anything to you, you wouldn't have cared about the settlement."

"Right. The divorce hurt me, so I fought back with the only weapon I know of that could hurt him—money. I suppose I don't care as much now. I've gotten over the hurt."

"What kind of man is he?"

"Bertrand? Slimy as an eel and twice as slippery. Does that surprise you?" She poured herself some more tea. I declined a second cup. "I knew that when I married him. He has none of the finesse his father had, but he has his admirable qualities. I chose to ignore his dark side. He was handsome—still is—and gracious when he remembered himself. What attracted me most was his strength. He went after what he wanted and took it. There's a certain magnetism about that kind of raw power, that self-assurance. He convinced me, without too much trouble, that I was what he wanted and that no other woman would do. I guess deep down I always knew he would wield that same power over other women. And during our last few years together, I realized I just wasn't all that interested in his life anymore. I was more interested in what *I* wanted out of life. So we got divorced."

She looked sad for a moment, thinking about it, then turned her attention back to me. "What else do you want to know?"

"Who would want to blackmail him?"

"Any number of people, for any number of reasons. Bertrand made a lot more enemies than friends. I'm sorry I can't be of more help than that." She paused. "You see, Bertrand uses people to get what he wants. He has a strange charisma that binds people to him and makes them do his bidding until they drop from exhaustion. He did it to me—for a time. Some of those people must be angry about the way they were used, angry enough to want to get back at him. Though I don't envy anyone the task; he can be a formidable adversary." She shivered.

"Marian, you've been very helpful and very kind," I said, "but I shouldn't take any more of your time."

I rose to put on my coat. She saw me to the door. I took her hand and thanked her again, then turned. She put a hand on my arm to stop me.

"Take good care of Martha, will you?" she said softly.

I felt small and sad as I walked to Brandt's house. Perhaps it was empathy for Marian Culbertson, a warm, charming woman who had been deserted by a family that neither wanted nor needed her. Perhaps it was because she had deserved better in the first place. But I knew I didn't have to feel sorry for her. She would be fine. She had a life of her own, and some guy who deserved her would come along some day to keep her company. I really felt sorry for myself, for the me that did not have a woman like that on my arm.

"I miss her," I told Brandt as he fixed us drinks.

"Her who?"

"Jessica." I took a swallow of the Glenfiddich on ice he handed me, and was silent for a minute. "Count Maid Marian out of it," I said finally, thinking aloud.

"What?" Brandt looked curiously at me.

"I went to see Marian Culbertson today on the hunch that she may have been squeezing her ex for more than just alimony." I told him the rest of it, trying to explain my feelings about her. "I just wish I knew what was going on. Is it a personal vendetta against Culbertson? Does it have something to do with the hotel chain? Is it a—"

"Wait a minute," Brandt interrupted. "That reminds me of something I just saw somewhere. Hold on a second." He scurried off. "Aha!" he said when he emerged five minutes later with a triumphant gleam in his eye. He waved a copy of *The Wall Street Journal* under my nose. "I knew I'd seen it somewhere."

I took the paper and read the short article he pointed at.

THREATS AGAINST WORKERS
STALL HOTEL RENOVATION

MIAMI, Fla.—Restoration of the old Sandbeach Hotel in Miami Beach has been postponed for an indefinite period because of alleged death threats against construction workers at the site, Miami sources say. The construction site has been picketed recently by members of the Hotel Workers Union, but it is not known if there is any link between the pickets and threats against construction workers. Drescher Construction Co. officials called the work stoppage, claiming numerous complaints of harassment at the site by employees.

Culbertson Hotels, which owns the Sandbeach, unveiled plans for a major renovation of the once-posh hotel when Dade County officials began discussing the possibility of legalized gambling in Miami. The hotel had fallen on hard times in recent years before being bought by the Culbertson chain.

A spokesman for Culbertson Hotels refused to speculate as to the cause of the threats being made against the construction crew. Hotel Workers Union officials were unavailable for comment.

"So?" I was irritated by the fact that it was the same blurb I remembered seeing, but hadn't read.

"So . . ." Brandt mused for a moment. "Remember the trouble here in Chicago a few years back when the Marriott was being built? Marriott decided that the hotel was not only going to be built by nonunion labor, it was going to be run by nonunion personnel."

"Sure. There were pickets on-site off and on from the time construction started until after it was finished and the hotel was opened."

"Right. And how do you think Marriott managed to open its doors?"

"They paid off the unions." The light was beginning to dawn. "Maybe."

"Maybe yes, maybe no, but there was only token resistance at Marriott, very few pickets, and not much press because there was very little trouble. It seems probable that somebody accepted an under-the-table gratuity in return for not making trouble."

"Okay," I pondered, "you're suggesting that Culbertson was trying to buy off the Hotel Workers Union in order to keep the Sandbeach nonunion."

"That's my guess. The diamonds could have been meant as a payoff to keep the unions out of Culbertson's hair, and now they're stalling the project because the payoff was never made."

"It fits. But how do we go about confirming it?"

"Would the names of the union leadership help?"

"I suppose they might. From what I understand, though, it's run almost directly by mafiosi types."

"I know. I have a friend in the Justice Department who owes me a favor. I could probably get him to give us a rundown on the important players."

"Gee, I'm not sure I want to get tangled up with any Syndicate people." I saw his look of disappointment; he wanted to do something. "But I guess it wouldn't hurt to find out."

He brightened immediately. "I'll put in a call first thing tomorrow morning."

"Good. Now let's get something to eat."

Neither of us felt like cooking, so we went over to Twin Anchors, a neighborhood bar in Old Town, for steak. Twin Anchors is a hole-in-the-wall with a worn linoleum floor and an old oak bar, which serves the best ribs anywhere and a fillet that you can cut with a fork. It's always crowded on weekends because Sinatra likes the ribs so much he patronizes the place when he's in town—the fans are ever hopeful of catching a glimpse of him. When we had finished the blood-red steaks and mopped up the garlic butter with our french fries and polished off our third beer, we said good night.

The phone woke me up the next morning before seven. I rolled over and picked it up on the fourth ring.

"I've got the list of names," Brandt said excitedly. I mumbled something so he would know I was awake, and he began to rattle off names. He made it through five, along with the office each one held, when I stopped him.

"Hold it. What was that last one again?" I sat up, fully awake now.

"Albert Portolucci. Why?"

"Bingo," I said softly. "Hurry over here. We've got some planning to do. We're going on a little fishing trip."

I hung up and headed for the shower before he could protest, and by the time I had dressed, I heard his knock at the front door. I sat him down while I made a phone call to reserve some plane tickets.

"What on earth are you doing?"

"Portolucci is the connection, don't you see?" I said excitedly. "He's the guy I was supposed to deliver the diamonds to in Miami. So we're going to go back down to the islands to see if there are any big fish to be caught."

We talked for almost an hour, turning over the alternatives. I didn't want Brandt involved unless we could find a safe way to handle the situation. Trapped animals tend to bite. By eight-thirty we had the beginnings of a plan; by nine we had packed and were on the road; and shortly after ten, we sat in the first-class section of an Air Jamaica jet on its way to Nassau.

At five that evening, we were sitting in deck chairs at the Tamarind Bay Club, sipping rum punches, watching the sun glint off the water between Harbour Island and North Eleuthera.

"Deceiving, isn't it?" Brandt said, looking out over the

harbor. "It looks so sparkling and clean."

I nodded knowingly. The dancing water, in its multiple shades of blue, was alluring and inviting. But on the ocean side of the island, where the coral reefs nearly break the surface, one has to beware of morays, stingrays, and barracuda. On the harbor side, where the water is relatively deep and all the fishing boats dump their refuse, one has to beware of the predatory schools of sharks feeding on garbage and small fish, especially at night.

It was late the next morning before we caught a ride into town. We had talked for hours after dinner, planning and rehearsing, and both of us had slept late. I dropped Brandt off at the post office so he could make the all-important phone call and told him to meet me at the bank later. I headed for the main dock to look for a charter boat captain named Reuben.

I had gone deep-sea fishing with Reuben a few times on that vacation years before, and remembered him as a grizzled, gruff old black man who operated his boat single-handedly and who was reputed to be the best fishing pilot on the island. I took a chance on Reuben still being there, and after asking for him, a small boy directed me to his boat. He had just come in from a half-day charter and was washing down the afterdecks with buckets of water. I hailed him from the dock.

"Hey, Reuben."

"Yeah, mon?" He turned to look at me.

"Are you free tomorrow morning?" I pulled a wad of cash out of my pocket. He spotted it and moved closer to the rail to look up at me. His expression didn't change.

"Got some people say they want to go out tomorrow." He shrugged his shoulders.

I squatted down so our eyes were almost level. "They make reservations?"

"Just said they were thinkin' 'bout goin' out, that's all."

"What's your rate for the day?"

"Three hundred." His eyes flicked to the money and back to my face. "Bring your own lunch. I bring whatever you want to drink."

"Here's a hundred." I peeled off a few bills. "That's to reserve the boat. I'll pay a full day's rate on top of that if we have any luck tomorrow."

"Okay." The money disappeared into his pocket. He hadn't blinked an eye. "How many?"

"Three of us."

"What do you want to drink?"

"Beer—St. Pauli Girl."

"Sure, mon. Bad year for yellowtail. Okay for wahoo, though."

"One other thing, Reuben. Do you have a dinghy?" He nodded. "With an outboard?"

"Sure, mon. Got a fourteen-foot Whaler. New outboard, too."

"Good. We'll want to take it along. See you tomorrow morning."

I could feel him watching me as I walked up the dock toward the bank, but when I turned to look, he was busily swabbing the decks.

When Brandt met me at the bank I introduced him to the officer I'd met earlier, explaining that we were business associates and that he would be using the safety-deposit box I'd rented. Either one of us was to have complete access to the contents of the box in case one of us was called away on business. We signed the necessary papers and walked back out into the tropical noonday sun. The pavement practically bubbled under the soles of our sandals as we strolled down to the waterfront. I pointed out what I thought were strategic positions, and explained what I thought would be the sequence of events the next day. Brandt was quiet and thoughtful, asking few questions. He seemed to be caught in some personal dilemma, and I let him work it out for himself.

We found a cab down near the yacht club and rode back
to the Tamarind Bay Club. While Brandt went to the bar to
order us something tall and cool, I went in search of Roy. I
found him at the front desk getting ready to leave for town
to pick up some arriving guests.

"Roy, would it be all right if Brandt Williams and I used
the runabout this afternoon?"

"I can't really spare anyone this afternoon. Did you want
to go snorkeling?"

"No, no snorkeling. I know you prefer an extra man in the
boat for that. We just wanted to take a tour of the harbor."

"Well, all right. You know how to run it?"

"Promise. We both have merit badges in boating."

"Okay," he said, laughing. "Stay in the harbor, though.
The currents in the cuts are tricky. And try to have it back
by five."

"Thanks. We'll be careful. Oh, one other thing—will you
tell Denise that three of us are going out with Reuben tomorrow and ask her to have lunch made up for us."

"Sure. Have a good time."

I couldn't find Brandt in the bar. The bartender finally told
me he thought Brandt had been heading for the water when
he left, so I sauntered down to the pier to see him lazing
comfortably in a deck chair.

"We're set for this afternoon," I said, pulling up a chair
next to his. He paid no attention, and I looked to see what
had caught his interest. I shrugged and turned back to face
him.

"Why don't we run through some of the details," I suggested.

He put a finger to his lips and slowly turned to look at me.
"I am contemplating a nearly naked lady, a sight made even
more scintillating by the fact that she is not entirely naked,
and you barely glance her way. Can you not appreciate the
luster of her flawless skin, the perfection of her evenly golden

tan, the molded contours, the sun-streaked hair? Must you think about details?"

He smiled broadly, and I knew that whatever crisis he'd faced was over; he'd made a decision. I know him well enough to suspect that he'd been trying to fit our plans into his own sense of morality and fair play.

"Did you bring the tape recorder?" I asked, taking a sip from a Myers's and tonic.

"No. I thought the cassette recorder might be too bulky, so I went to a duty-free shop in the airport while you were getting the tickets and bought one of those micro-dictation units. It looks kind of like a transistor radio, and fits in a shirt pocket."

"You're acquiring an absolute flair for this sort of thing," I said admiringly. "How did the phone call go?"

"Okay. He's coming. I gave him explicit instructions just like we rehearsed—fifty thousand in unmarked hundreds in a plain briefcase. I told him that if he wasn't alone the deal was off, and that we would know if he wasn't alone."

"The money's the only thing that worries me. I don't want to get caught with it without having a legitimate reason for having it."

"I took care of that." Brandt saw my curious stare and pulled an envelope out of his pocket.

In the envelope was a crisply folded letter on thirty-pound buff stock with a very well-known corporate logo embossed in the upper left-hand corner. The letter, addressed to "To whom it may concern," authorized Brandt Williams and his associates to negotiate on the signer's behalf in the sale or purchase of "development property," and entitled Brandt to the "standard" finder's fees, payable in cash, et cetera, et cetera. The signature was not only impressive, it was authentic.

"I typed it up before I left the house yesterday," Brandt said. "The old boy signed a few blank sheets of stationery for me once in return for a favor because he knows I won't abuse his signature."

"You're amazing," I marveled. "Come on, let's get some lunch."

After we'd eaten, we headed back down to the dock. The runabout was in good shape, and was thoughtfully provided with electric start. We checked the gas supply, kicked over the outboard, and cast off the lines. I took the helm and idled away from the pier, then throttled up until the boat was planning. As we headed north past town, I pointed out some of the sights I remembered, shouting over the high whine of the engine. I skirted around the shallows north of town, a broad expanse of pale-blue water contrasting sharply with the darker turquoise of deeper water. The shallows become sand flats at low tide, extending a quarter mile out from shore. At high tide it can be excellent territory for bonefishing, a pastime as exciting and as sporting as fly casting for trout. Silvery and faster than lightning, schools of two- and three-foot bonefish can hardly be seen in the glinting shallow water against the white sand bottom. But there is little doubt of their presence when one hits the lure on light monofilament line.

I took the boat in a wide arc, heading in close to shore once we were past the shallows. We cruised past the north cut—a channel between Harbour Island and a series of smaller islands curving north that links the harbor with the Atlantic. We bounced in the chop created by swells that flowed through the cut from the ocean. Then I throttled back to get a closer look at the small islets we were approaching.

I ignored the first islet. It had a small, sheltered beach and was a favorite picnic spot for boaters. I was looking for something more secluded. We found it on the third island we came to. It was little more than a chunk of coral rising out of the sea, probably only a hundred feet long in any direction. But the scrub-tufted rocks rose some fifteen feet high in a ridge down the center, hiding us from the ocean on the other side. And there was a small cove in which to anchor the runabout.

I killed the engine and glided in with Brandt watching the water depth from the bow. He threw the anchor overboard and snubbed the line tight on a cleat. Once we were sure the anchor was secure, we rolled up our pants and slipped over the side into the shallow water. We kept our shoes on— stepping barefoot onto sea urchins nestled on the bottom is painful, and the coral that makes up those rocky islands is sharp and jagged. On shore, we split up, looking for a suitable hiding place. Within a minute or so, Brandt called out, and I backtracked to find him in the rocks. He had discovered a natural shelf in a small outcropping of rock just above eye level.

The diamonds had been retrieved from the bank and now were sealed in a plastic bag inside a small box. I wedged the box into the space, then checked to determine if it could be seen from any angle. It seemed secure and well hidden, but in a moment of temporary paranoia I scrambled to the top of the ridge and surveyed that part of the harbor still in view to see if any boats were near. The last thing we needed was a curious fisherman to come nosing around. We were alone, so I climbed back down. We waded back out to the boat, weighed anchor, and started back toward town.

"I told him to take the first scheduled flight in," Brandt shouted over the noisy outboard. "That should get him here about ten. But he might send someone on ahead on a charter."

"I'll check in the morning," I yelled back. "Good thinking."

He gave me a half-smile and leaned back in his seat, silent and pensive.

I didn't sleep well. Nightmares kept bringing me to half-wakefulness. I kept hearing that echoing gunshot, but instead of Marty, it was I who felt the bullet, causing me to spin and fall in slow motion. Finally, I snapped awake after one bad dream and sat up to light a cigarette. Daylight was not far away, so I didn't try to sleep anymore. Brandt snored lightly in the next bed. Birds tittered outside the open window—breakfast table chatter. The air didn't move. It felt damp, smelled musty, tasted salty. I pulled on a pair of shorts, stubbing out the cigarette and lighting another, then quietly let myself out to walk down the slope to the water. I had a strange, intangible feeling of dread but didn't try to understand it. I simply waited.

XI

BY EIGHT-THIRTY we were ready to go. I had taken a swim and had decided to stay salty. When I had gotten back to the room, Brandt was up and just stepping out of the shower. We had a quick breakfast, collected our picnic hamper from Denise, and now we waited for Roy to get the car and take us into town. He dropped us at the main dock, and Reuben was waiting for us. We chatted with Reuben for a few minutes, telling him that we didn't expect to get under way until after ten. Then Brandt and I took a walk to review last-minute preparations.

"I want you to camp out here," I said to Brandt, pointing to the bench under the tree at the water's edge. "Let him walk past you. I'll be watching the people who get off the ferry, and if he's alone, I'll signal you when I want you to move."

"All right. Then I take him to the bank."

"No, I've changed my mind. I want you to have the brief-case, and I don't want him out of my sight. Here's what you do. See the bench on the corner? The next street up, where the bank is? Okay, I'll be on the flying bridge of the boat, so I'll be able to see up the street to the bank, but I can't see inside it, and I don't want him to pull any stunts. When I signal you, go after him. Catch up to him, but be casual. Talk to him, pretend you know him. Keep walking. Take the briefcase from him, then sit him on that next bench and tell him to wait while you go to the bank."

"What if he insists on coming with me? What if he won't stay put on the bench?"

"Tell him, first thing, that you're both being watched very carefully through a twenty-power scope by a man with a high-powered rifle, and that if he makes one mistake, there will be a bloody hole in him large enough to put your fist through."

"You needn't be so graphic," Brandt said with some distaste.

"*You* should be. I don't want to take more chances than we have to. And I want you to impress upon him that he would be wise not to take chances, either."

"All right. So, I go to the bank, check the briefcase to make sure the money's there, have the case put in the vault, then bring him back to the boat for a fun day of deep-sea fishing."

"Right. I don't think he'll object. But he may get nervous on that bench, even though he can watch you all the way, so don't take too much time with the briefcase. I think he'll want to find out where the diamonds are. Once you're on the boat, reassure him, talk with him, try to draw him out. Remember, we're trying to get a confession out of him. I think by the time you retrieve the diamonds, he should be ready to tell you the whole story. Have you got the tape recorder?"

"Yep." He tapped his shirt pocket.

"Okay, unless you can think of something we've missed, we might as well get into position and wait. I don't want him to surprise us. Set?" Brandt nodded. "Good luck."

We shook hands and I strolled back to the boat. I was counting on Brandt's ability with people to draw the man out while I stayed in the background unless I was needed. I wanted to keep our prey off-balance and unsure of himself. I wanted him to think he was simply being blackmailed. If he was convinced that all we were after was his money, he wouldn't suspect that we really wanted to put him in jail.

On the boat, Reuben cut up bait, readied poles and reels

and hooks, and puttered around checking things. We chatted amiably; rather, I chatted and he gave me an occasional amiable grunt. I suggested tactfully that we head out the south cut and work our way north. It would not do to offend the island's best pilot, but as long as we suggested rather than ordered, Reuben would take us wherever we wanted to go; we were paying for it. I said that I would not be fishing, and I would be happy to help him if he needed it. I asked questions about the boat, about the radio, about weather conditions, trying to sound casually curious. It wouldn't hurt to know how to pilot the boat in the event of an emergency. I asked if he had a pair of binoculars I could use.

"Sure. They up on de bridge."

"Reuben, what do you do if you hook into a shark?"

"Most times, mon, when they hit de bait, they cut de line. Lose a lot of good hooks dat way. If it be a small shark, and it don't cut de line, we gaff him near his tail, lift him out de water, cut off his tail, then cut de line and let him go. If it be a big shark, and he be messin' with de bait all day, I shoot him if I can. Where they be a shark, there won't be no fish. And sometimes, a hungry shark will follow the sound of de boat, scarin' away all the fish. Then I'll shoot him if I can. Otherwise, I leave 'em alone. No sense messin' with them if they don' mess with you." He shrugged. I'd never heard him say so much at one time.

"Then you have a rifle?"

"It's up on de bridge, too. You want to see it, I show it to you later, mon."

"How about the Whaler? Is it ready to go?"

"Sure. Don't know why you want it, though. Can't fish when you towin' a boat. Lines might get tangled up."

"Once we're through the cut, why don't you throw bumpers over the side and tow the dinghy alongside?"

He shrugged again. The curly gray beard hid his expression, but his dark eyes were curious. He looked at me for a moment, then turned away, so I ambled over to the ladder leading to the flying bridge and climbed up. It was time to keep an eye out for the ferry.

The short airstrip had been closed for years because it is almost too short even for STOLs, so the only ways to get to the island are by seaplane or boat. I had been watching for planes, just in case, and no boats had arrived at either the main dock or the yacht club dock that I knew of. I found Reuben's binoculars and quickly scanned the harbor, then focused on the ferry dock over on Eleuthera. It was too far away to really make anything out, but I could see figures moving around like ants. I turned to sweep the waterfront, panning slowly, pleased with my vantage point. Brandt loomed large in the lenses, sitting calmly on the bench, looking out at some children playing in a rowboat close to shore. I panned left along the waterfront, then slowly raised the glasses, scanning up the street to the bank. I had an unobstructed view. Satisfied, I lowered the binoculars and sat in one of the folding chairs Reuben had set up on the bridge, considering the day—a cloudless sky and a light breeze taking some of the sting out of the sun's heat. It would be nice out on the water. A speck of white against the blue of the harbor water caught my eye. I raised the binoculars. It was the ferry. I turned to catch Brandt's attention. He acknowledged my wave.

It took the ferry five minutes to finish the trip and tie up at the end of the cement pier only twenty-five feet from Reuben's boat. There were few passengers—two islanders, a young tourist couple. Bertrand Culbertson was the last one off. He was alone—a big man, bigger than I had expected, a couple inches over six feet. He wore a navy blazer over an open-necked sport shirt, casual slacks, deck shoes. The clothes hung well on a frame that looked in excellent condition for a man in his late fifties, making him look more formally dressed than the casual attire suggested. Steely gray hair

framed a ruggedly handsome, well-tanned face. A hawkish
nose gave his face a hard, hungry look. The briefcase was
in his left hand. He looked around to get his bearings, his
eyes coolly searching, taking stock, then he strode casually
down the pier. I saw Brandt stiffen to attention, glancing
briefly in my direction then turning his gaze out to the water
until Culbertson had turned off the pier onto the street and
past him. I had looked carefully to see if anyone on the dock
made a move to follow him, and when I was satisfied that no
one had paid any attention to his arrival, I looked back at
Brandt. He was watching for my signal. I checked Culbertson's progress, then gave Brandt the go signal.

I picked up the glasses to watch as Brandt approached him
from behind. My stomach knotted in anticipation, adrenaline
flowed, my chest felt tight. Culbertson had taken the bait.
Brandt had come up beside him, matching his stride, and
had put a hand on his shoulder. Now they stopped and turned
to speak face to face. They talked for a moment, then resumed
walking, Brandt's hand back on Culbertson's shoulder, as
though they were old friends. When they reached the bench
on the corner, I could see Brandt talking and gesturing toward
the bank. Culbertson handed him the briefcase and sat on
the bench, casually crossing his legs, but never taking his
eyes off Brandt. Brandt was in the bank for four or five
minutes, then suddenly reappeared and joined Culbertson. I
called down to Reuben to tell him that we would be ready to
cast off in a few minutes, then continued to watch the pair
as they came toward the boat. When they were halfway down
the pier, I clambered down to get the mooring lines while
Reuben fired up the engines from the main helm. Brandt let
Culbertson precede him onto the boat so he could flash me
a thumbs-up while Culbertson's back was turned. We had
agreed that he would not acknowledge that he knew me, that
I would pretend to be Reuben's crew. When they were aboard,
I cast off and Reuben headed for the south cut.

It was half an hour before Reuben smiled and nodded, indicating that he had found his spot, seemingly no different from any other spot within a three-mile radius. But when I pointed that out to him, he tapped the side of his nose with a confident look and said, "Dey be fish here, mon." He throttled down, letting the boat drift under minimum power, turned the helm over to me, and scrambled down to the deck. First, he pulled in the skiff that bobbled in our wake and lashed it, fore and aft, along the port side. Once he was satisfied with the way it rode alongside, he turned his attention to baiting the hooks on two of the three poles chonked in their places in the gunwales. Then he took the rods one at a time to cast the bait, handing them to Brandt and Culbertson with explicit instructions on how far to let the line out, how to set the drag, and what to do when either one got a strike. Culbertson had been quietly fuming with impatience ever since we had gone through the cut, and when Reuben started baiting hooks, he seemed almost ready to explode. But when Reuben placed the butt of Culbertson's rod into the swivel cup of the fishing chair and impatiently motioned to him, Culbertson shrugged his shoulders, took off his coat, rolled up his sleeves, and swung his bulk into the chair. Reuben uncapped beers for them, then climbed back up to the bridge to take back the helm. As he eased the throttles to a sedate trolling speed, he instructed me to be the spotter, to warn him if either line got a strike, and to keep him informed of the direction the fish were fighting so he could pilot the boat in a way to make the catch easier. I swung a deck chair around to face aft, slung the binoculars around my neck, then climbed down to the deck to get a Coke for Reuben and a beer for myself before settling in. Culbertson had given me a couple of curious glances on the way out, and as I came out of the cabin with the drinks, he turned in his chair to give me another one. I met his gaze, gave him a half-smile, and wished him luck.

We trolled in a northeasterly direction, cruising slowly, lolling in the small swells. I moved the chair out of the shade of the canvas top stretched over the flying bridge and baked in the hot sun. There seemed to be little discussion between the two men in the chairs on the deck below, but I wished that I could hear whatever they said. I was uneasy. I didn't like Culbertson's interest in me. He had turned twice more, craning his neck to stare up at me coolly, without expression. I guessed that he must have come to the natural assumption that I was Brandt's accomplice. But I sensed that he was thinking a whole lot more than that, and it bothered me. I couldn't tell where the nagging doubt was coming from. There was nothing Culbertson could do, nowhere he could go, but his presence was electric, filling the atmosphere with tension. I felt like I had cornered a hungry lion that might well choose to ignore the odds pitted against it. The danger signals were all there: "Approach with extreme caution." But I pushed the thoughts out of my mind, chagrined by my nervousness. Surely I was overestimating Culbertson's capacity for nastiness despite Marian Culbertson's warning. He could not be the same sort of man as those he hired to do his dirty work.

After half an hour or so, Reuben again throttled back and turned the helm over to me. He went down on deck and had them reel in both lines to check the bait and let the two men get up and stretch. He gave them a five-minute break to use the head and get more beer, then he put fresh bait on the hooks and sat them back down to let their lines out. Reuben steered us in an almost westerly direction this time, and through the binoculars I noted with some pleasure that our course would bring us close to the north end of the island. Midway through the next half-hour shift, Brandt got a hard strike, but the lack of resistance as he reeled it in suggested a barracuda. Reuben confirmed my opinion even before we could see it, and as Brandt reeled it in close to the boat, Reuben went down to the deck to bring it in. When it was close enough, Reuben leaned over the side and gaffed it with a four-foot gaffing hook, bringing up a three-foot barracuda. He whacked its skull with a short wooden club and slid it into the catch box in the transom, carefully avoiding the toothy jaw. Culbertson had reeled in his line as soon as Brandt had gotten his strike, like he was supposed to, and Reuben checked his bait and rebaited Brandt's hook, then threw both lines back in. At the end of the half hour, Culbertson hooked into a beautiful bull dolphin, and had a good twenty-minute fight bringing it in. When Culbertson had it in close, Reuben threw the engines into neutral, and I joined him on the deck to watch him gaff it and pull it up over the side.

We had drawn close to shore, and while Reuben wrestled the still flopping fish into the catch box, I saw Brandt check our position and look at his watch.

"Say, Reuben?" Brandt said, launching into his pitch. "It's about time to eat. What do you say we take a break for lunch?"

"Sure, mon. Whatever you say."

"I told Mr. Culbertson I would show him the harbor area, as well as property on the island," Brandt continued. "As long as we're this close to shore, would you mind if we anchored in close to the cut? Then I could take the skiff and give Mr. Culbertson a quick look at this end of the harbor before lunch."

"It's okay with me. You payin' for de boat whether you fish or not."

Reuben took the boat in, piloting from the main helm, and found a calm spot near the cut. I manned the anchor, dropping it on Reuben's command, then waited for his second shout a moment later to snub the line on a bow cleat. The anchor dragged for a moment, then held as our momentum slowed. Reuben cut the engines. Then Brandt started the outboard motor on the skiff and Culbertson climbed in. I came aft and unhitched the bowline while Reuben did the same with the stern line. Culbertson reached out to push off, and they putt-

putted away toward the channel. Brandt turned to throw me a last knowing glance. I crossed my fingers.

I got a sandwich out of the cooler, uncapped another beer, and went to join Reuben in the shade of the main cabin. He had brought his own lunch, a grease-stained brown paper bag that held a few cold conch fritters. He ate them with relish, sucking the grease off his short, spatulate fingers, wiping his mouth with the back of his hand. A few crumbs stuck in his beard.

"Culbertson is thinking of buying property down here," I said by way of explanation. I took a bite of my sandwich, not sure I really wanted to eat. "He owns a big hotel chain, you know. He's thinking of building a small resort, either here or over on Eleuthera. Man sure seems to have a lot of money."

Reuben grunted his replies and looked indifferent, so I took my sandwich and went up to the flying bridge to sit in the sun. I picked up the binoculars and panned slowly, starting at the tip of Harbour Island on my left, and going right, scanning the channel, then the little islands. The first island was dead ahead; the third was three or four hundred yards off the starboard bow. There was no sign of life on any of them. I wondered why in hell we had decided to let the transaction take place out of sight. I began to worry. The nagging doubts came back. I had made a dumb mistake. Maybe Culbertson wouldn't prove how dumb it was. Ten minutes passed, then twenty. They should have been back. I trained the glasses on the channel. Five more minutes passed, then the skiff suddenly sprang into sight. I sighed with relief, and looked up as Reuben climbed up to the bridge behind me.

"They're on their way back," I told him.

I focused the glasses back on the skiff. The little boat bounced around in the lenses. I pulled my chair forward and rested the binoculars on the rail to steady them. I could now make out the two figures in the skiff. They drew closer.

Culbertson was at the tiller. Brandt was in the bow, facing aft, away from me. He wasn't sitting right. I couldn't get the glasses to settle down. My hands were shaking. They drew closer. A little over a hundred yards maybe. Brandt was hunched over, his head bowed. Something was wrong. The alarms in my head went off. But I couldn't tell . . . something in Culbertson's right hand, down low. Fifty yards now. I was up on my feet, going for the watertight aluminum case under the wheel that held the rifle. I saw Reuben's startled expression as I undid the first latch, then heard Culbertson's shout.

"Don't go for that gun, Ward!" he yelled. "Or I'll blow a hole in your friend!"

I froze. Reuben froze. A great dread boiled up out of my stomach. I took great, silent gulps of air, forcing tingling adrenaline to my limbs, containing the dread in my bowels. The air went silent. Culbertson had cut the outboard, and was gliding toward the starboard side.

"Both of you, stand to starboard with your hands on the rail," he commanded. We complied instantly. He watched us carefully even as the skiff came alongside and gently bumped the boat. I saw the short-barreled revolver now as he switched it to his left hand in order to grasp the gunwale of the larger boat. He must have kept it hidden in an ankle holster under his trousers.

"Gentlemen, I'm an excellent shot with either hand, and I can't miss at this range," he said, pointing the gun at Brandt. "So please don't move suddenly."

I followed the direction the gun was pointing with my eyes, and noticed the blood, the matted hair over Brandt's left ear. He was unconscious, propped up with an oar. Culbertson pulled the skiff alongside the boat with his free hand, never taking his eyes off us. Finally, when he was almost even with the transom, he stood up and stepped onto the boat, holding the skiff's painter. He switched the gun back to his right

hand, and tied the painter to a stern cleat, then stood back
in the center of the deck.

"All right. Now you can come down here slowly and give
me some help," he said with an audacious smile. "You're
first, Ward."

I did as he said. My mind was in a turmoil. How had he
known? Had Brandt slipped up? Had I? How could I have
blown it so badly? How could I have made the mistake of
giving Culbertson an opportunity? I was afraid. I thought I
had covered all the bases, and now my confidence was
shaken. Brandt was obviously hurt badly—a concussion at
the least. I had to push away the fear or there would be no
hope of saving the situation. My feet touched the deck, and
Culbertson waved me over a couple steps. Reuben was right
behind me.

"Now," Culbertson instructed, "I want you to get your
friend out of the skiff and into the cabin. Slowly and carefully,
gentlemen. We wouldn't want to hurt him, would we?" His
sneer scraped my nerves raw.

I glared, hatred replacing fear, then turned to get Brandt.
I grasped him under the arms and Reuben took his feet. It
wasn't easy maneuvering in the small boat with a dead weight,
and we almost tipped over the skiff, but we finally managed
to hoist Brandt onto the deck. We carried him into the cabin
and laid him on a bunk. Culbertson had us tie him in with
some extra line, and when he was satisfied, he herded us out
of the cabin and had us stand near the transom. Then he
climbed up backward to the flying bridge, using only one
hand. It was awkward for him, but not as awkward had he
let us go first to try to kick him off the ladder when he followed.
He motioned Reuben to join him, instructing me to go forward
to pull the anchor. I didn't know if Reuben would be of any
help to me—I hadn't been able to read what was going on
behind those dark eyes. So I followed orders and hoped that
Culbertson would make a mistake. Reuben fired up the twin

diesels, and as soon as he put them in gear, giving me some slack, I started pulling in the anchor. When it was on deck, Culbertson told me to come up. Reuben swung the bow around and pointed it out to sea.

"Now, why don't we just take a little cruise?" Culbertson said when I joined them on the bridge. He stood to starboard and motioned me forward. I stood to port. Reuben was at the helm, directly in front of Culbertson.

"What do you plan to do now?" I asked. "Kill us, I suppose?" I half leaned against the port rail, arms folded across my chest.

Culbertson chuckled. "Of course I'm going to kill you. Once we're out of sight of land, we all go back down to the cabin. I tap you lightly over the heads, open the sea cocks, and down you go—a tragic accident at sea. I don't know, maybe an engine caught fire, and the fire could not be put out. I panicked and jumped overboard, then managed to climb into the skiff. I don't know what happened to the rest of you, I'm in such a state of shock. But, stricken with grief, I assume you must have gone down with the ship."

Out of the corner of my eye, I caught a glimpse of Reuben looking in my direction. I sensed that he was ready, waiting for some cue from me. It gave me encouragement. I had to distract Culbertson and hope for an opening. He was keeping the gun leveled at me, and that might have been his first mistake.

"So, the diamonds really were a payoff to the union," I said, "so you wouldn't be locked into a labor contract."

Culbertson was momentarily startled, then he smiled broadly. "Yes. It would have worked out very well, too, if you hadn't butted in. I can still make it work now that I have the diamonds back. Damn unions," he continued disgustedly. "The power they have—brute force is all it is. What do they know about taste, class, superior service?" He lapsed into a brooding silence, but he had answered my question.

"Why drag your daughter into it?" I asked.

"I didn't *drag* her into it. Martha would do just about anything for me."

"Including getting herself killed?"

"What? She's dead?" There was a touch of legitimate concern in his voice.

"Not yet."

"You know where she is." It was a statement, not a question. "Tell me."

"Why should I?"

He shrugged. "It makes no difference. When she shows up, she shows up."

He was not concerned enough, and I didn't believe he was that callous, at least not where his daughter was concerned. Something didn't ring true. He knew something that I didn't.

It was my turn to shrug. "I guess you have all the angles figured. It's too bad you weren't so smart with your business deals. Then you wouldn't be out in the middle of the ocean trying to shore up your crumbling empire."

The eyes glinted, and the nostrils of the hawkish nose flared. A vein in his temple pulsed. His face flushed. He was nervous and on edge. The pressure must have been getting to him for a long time. I thought furiously, looking for a way out. I knew I could throw him off balance, but I had to find a way to take advantage of it. I caught another glance from Reuben. He could hear what was happening.

"Where are the diamonds?" I asked abruptly. Again, he was startled. I needed more time, had to cool him down, distract him. I didn't want to provoke him yet.

"They're safe," he smiled, patting his pocket.

I looked casually around the bridge, pretending thoughtfulness, but carefully taking stock. A wall enclosing the bridge came to midthigh, and had a cable safety rail on top of that. There was nothing up there that wasn't fastened down except a life ring on the wall behind Culbertson's knees. The aluminum case with the rifle had been thrown overboard as soon as Culbertson had climbed to the bridge.

"You're asking a lot of questions," Culbertson said accusingly. His face darkened.

"Nothing else to do while we wait. Humor me. A dying man's last wish—to have knowledge he can't use."

Culbertson chuckled, confident again. "Why not?"

I shifted position, slowly and openly. I sat on the low rail, hands on the ledge supporting some of my weight. "You know, Culbertson, a couple of things still bother me. For instance, why is Vince Johnston working for you?"

The question brought him up like a pistol shot. He stared at me with a mixture of surprise and hatred on his face. "What the hell do you know about Vince Johnston?"

"I know him by reputation." I was startled by his vehement reaction. "He's not what you'd call a savory character."

"Fucking bastard," he spat. "I'll take care of him, too, in my own time, in my own way."

He fidgeted restlessly. I was afraid I had provoked him too much, so I said nothing for a moment. I was puzzled. There was a stronger link between Culbertson and Johnston than I'd thought, and that worried me. But I would have to let it wait until later—if there was a later.

"How about me?" I asked, trying to distract him again. "How did you know me?"

"My daughter," he said, his expression lightening. "Such a trusting girl. She told me about you." He paused to reflect.

While he was talking, my fingers had gripped the ledge, curling over the lip, and they had found something interesting. It seemed to be a length of pipe. I froze as Culbertson returned his attention to me.

"Martha told me you described yourself as 'tall, gangly, loose-jointed.' When I saw you, I didn't think it was some odd coincidence—I understand you've been spending some time with Martha in Nassau. I figured you must be the famous

Mr. Ward, whatever you are." He paused. "She thought you
were blackmailing me," he continued with an amused look.
"That's why she was stringing you along, to keep an eye on
you."

I didn't grasp his meaning at first, and the remark never
had a chance to sink in. I had leaned over slightly, stretching
my fingers to examine this thing they had found. Reuben had
been watching me discreetly, and now I saw a little smile on
his face. Then I had it. It was a boat hook, and I laid odds
on it being mounted in spring-loaded clips. I casually leaned
forward farther still, until my fingers had a grip on the boat
hook. Culbertson blithered on.

"You know, your friend had me on the run for a while. I
thought you must know more than you obviously do. I
thought—"

He didn't get to finish his sentence. I had gotten a good
enough grip that I thought I could pop it loose, so I gave
Reuben an almost imperceptible nod. He hit the throttle and
spun the wheel around. The sound of the engines starting to
rev caused Culbertson to whirl around toward Reuben, and
in that instant, I popped the boat hook out of its clip and
lunged toward Culbertson, swinging as I came. The boat's
abrupt change of direction threw both Culbertson and me off
balance, causing his first shot to hit Reuben in the shoulder
instead of the heart and my first swing to miss entirely. The
bullet's impact swung Reuben around, knocking him back
against the control panel, and he slid unconscious to the
deck. My second swing caught Culbertson's wrist, sending
the pistol flying over the side. I went sliding into Culbertson
and lost the boat hook in the scuffle. He got to his knees
before I could untangle myself and popped me a good one
on the cheekbone, glazing my eyes and numbing the side of
my face. Then he was up, and he cut the ignition, yanking
the keys out of the instrument panel and heaving them out
to sea. I was halfway up by then, seeing only hazy images,

when the sudden loss of power sent me tumbling forward. I clutched at Culbertson's trouser leg and he went down hard. He lashed out with a free foot, connecting squarely with my forehead at the hairline, fuzzing my vision again, and sending a dull ache all the way down to my toes. My grip went slack, and he scrambled free, turning to climb down to the deck.

He was going for the skiff. I knew it instinctively, I knew it consciously, but my body wouldn't respond. I couldn't stop him, couldn't move. I roared with frustration. And the sound echoed through the caverns of my mind, bouncing from one synapse to another, triggering flashes of fragmented images— Brandt, Reuben, Marty, a lone child in the dark, Jessica crumpling to the floor in front of a shattered window, blood, all the hurt caused by people like Culbertson. And all my sand castle virtues were washed away by a sudden tide of onrushing rage. I suddenly knew that stopping him was no longer enough. I had to kill him.

It all happened in an instant. Something rolled over my knuckles as the boat yawed. It was the boat hook. I grabbed it and flung it with blind fury. The blunt end struck Culbertson just above the left eye as he was disappearing from view. He screamed in pain, both hands going to his face in reflex, and he fell backward off the ladder. As I scrambled to my feet and went after him, he lurched to his feet, blood streaming from the cut over his eye. I moved warily away from him.

Now I stood between Culbertson and the stern where the skiff was tied. He watched me intently, then tried the direct route straight through me. His eyes gave him away. I took a half step to my right and doubled him over with a solid left to the midriff, then sharply brought up my left knee, breaking his nose. I stood over him, thinking he was finished. With speed I didn't believe possible, he straightened, butting me in the chin. My jaw clacked shut with a loud snap, loosening some teeth and sending skyrockets through the top of my head. He moved quickly and punched me in the face with two short jabs. I got my hands up and hunched my shoulders, waiting for the next blow, but it never came.

He suddenly seemed to reconsider his strategy, and abruptly turned and scampered forward along the side of the cabin. I followed slowly, wondering what he was up to. The cabin rose a good four feet above the deck, and because of the flying bridge and an overturned dinghy lashed to the top of it, Culbertson had already disappeared from view. I made my way forward until I reached the foredeck. An open hatch beckoned, and I stood motionless, trying to decide what to do. A flickering shadow in the corner of my vision made me instinctively throw up my hands and turn. Culbertson was standing on top of the cabin behind me viciously swinging an oar in a good imitation of Jack Nicklaus pretending my head was a golf ball. The oar smacked into my palms, rapping my knuckles across the bridge of my nose, bringing tears to my eyes.

Culbertson was heading toward the stern. By the time I caught up with him, he had untied the skiff. I grabbed his belt and yanked hard. Culbertson backpedaled and went down with me on top, fingers clawing for a grip on the vulnerable throat. He wedged a knee into my chest and pushed, sending me flying backward to crack my head on the transom. Everything went momentarily black, and when I could see again, he loomed hugely above me, swinging the wooden billy club. I twisted my head, and the club came down on my collarbone, snapping it like a matchstick. I heard myself scream. Culbertson dropped the club and climbed on the transom. He was going to dive in after the skiff that was drifting away. I ground my teeth against the pain, willing myself to my feet, cursing a blue streak for added motivation, desperately searching for a weapon of some sort.

The rage within me blossomed, changing from chrysalis to winged demon, metamorphosing me from a human being driven by many needs to another sort of creature with only one all-consuming need—to hurt, to maim, to kill, to avenge all the suffering I had seen in the satisfaction of sending a soul to hell. I spotted the gaffing hook propped in the corner. Etched in my brain in freeze-frame action are the single step that took me within reach and the fluid grab-and-swing motion with my good arm just as Culbertson was starting to dive. The hook connected. I slid back and collapsed in a heap on the deck.

I was afraid that I had not finished him, afraid that he would pull himself dripping over the gunwale to end what he had started. But I couldn't move. I lay huddled, spent and full of pain. Culbertson should not have hurt me so badly. I had been in good condition, and I am not small. I had grossly underestimated him. When someone nudged me with a foot, I yelped in fright. I looked up and saw Reuben standing over me, holding his wounded shoulder. Relief flooded my system. I struggled to sit up.

"Is he gone?"

"Gone, boss. You got him good," There was a small smile on Reuben's face, and new respect.

"Can you see him? We have to get him."

"Yeah, he still be floatin' out there. What you want to fish him out for?" Reuben frowned and looked puzzled. "He be good shark bait."

"We have to! Come on. I'll explain later."

Reuben went into the cabin and came out with an extra set of keys. He started the engines from the main helm and brought the boat around in a slow arc. I stayed aft and kept my eyes on Culbertson's body bobbling in the waves. The gaffing hook stood straight out of the water like a marker, and Reuben idled the boat right up next to him, giving the engines a shot of reverse to bring us to a stop. I grabbed the handle of the gaffing hook as it came by, holding on until Reuben came aft to help me. We looked ridiculous—two one-armed men wrestling with a carcass—but we managed to haul Culbertson's body on board. Reuben deftly slipped the gaffing hook out of Culbertson's guts and dipped it over the side to rinse it off. The sight nauseated me. The front of Culbertson's shirt was stained red. The sightless eyes stared skyward, an expression of horrified surprise on the dead man's face. I leaned over, firmly clamping my jaw, and fished in his pocket, pulling out the diamonds still sealed in the plastic bag. I went through his other pockets and found Brandt's tape recorder. Amazingly, it still worked, but when I rewound it and punched the play button, the voices were too garbled to understand.

"What now, boss?" Reuben asked me as he put away the gaffing hook.

"Culbertson was a very rich and influential man. If people find out I killed him, even under the circumstances, there will be hell to pay. There will be an investigation, and we could all be charged with manslaughter, or even murder. It's likely they'd take away your boat. And I hate to think what they might do to me. Letting people know what really happened would louse things up for me. Do you understand?"

"Sure."

"You heard him admit what he did. I'm not sorry I killed him. My friend and I were trying to prove what he did so that he would be put in jail. But even with proof, I'm not sure we would have been able to put him away. Men like Culbertson can buy their way out of trouble. It's better this way. But we can't let anyone know what happened. As it is, there will be an inquest and we'll have to have a good story ready to stay out of trouble."

"You want to make sure he stay gone for good?"

I nodded.

"Okay, boss. I see what you mean 'bout letting him go. He might drift up on shore and be found. I surely don' want no trouble. I'm not sorry you killed him either. Man like that don' deserve to breathe God's air. I got some old anchor chain we can wire 'round his waist. Send him to de bottom where de sharks and 'cuda pick him clean. Okay wit you?"

"Okay with me."

While I was in the cabin getting the chain and some wire, I checked on Brandt. His color was not good, and his pulse was weak and thready. I lifted his eyelids. One pupil was more dilated than the other. He needed medical attention quickly. We all did. Concern spurred me to hurry. I had enough guilt on my conscience without kicking myself for involving Brandt. I dragged the chain, about fifty pounds of it, out onto the deck, then began the laborious task of wrapping it around Culbertson's body. It wasn't easy as the boat pitched and rolled in the swells.

By the time I had Culbertson snugly wrapped like some ghoulish medieval birthday present, Reuben had pulled alongside the skiff and was securing it to the stern cleat. Then we dragged Culbertson to the side, and with grunting effort, rolled him up and over the gunwale and into the water with a splash. He faded from sight within seconds.

Reuben let me look at his shoulder wound, but wouldn't let me wrap it. The bullet had smacked into the meaty flesh, missing bone, making a very neat thumbnail-size exit hole. It wasn't bleeding much. Reuben rinsed down the deck with buckets of seawater, washing away all traces of Culbertson's demise. He drew one more bucket and poured it slowly over his bad shoulder, grimacing silently as the salt stung the wound. I went and fashioned myself a sling, gritting my teeth as I moved my arm to find the most comfortable position for it. I suddenly remembered that I had not untied Brandt, so I turned my attention to him for a minute. There was nothing I could do for him except cover him with a blanket. I found a bottle of whiskey in the galley and took it out to Reuben at the helm. I took a big belt and handed it to Reuben.

"How's your friend doin', mon?" he asked after a gulp.

"Not good. He needs a doctor."

Reuben replied by pushing the throttles until the boat was at its maximum. The skiff rode high, planing in our wake.

"So, what do you say?" I shouted over the revving engines.

Reuben flashed me a toothy grin. "Say, mon, I just took you and your friends fishin'. We be havin' a so-so day, and 'bout two hours out, the older man goes crazy, bustin' you two up good. First, he goes after your friend and lays him out. You try to stop him, mixing it up pretty good till he gets his mitts on dat billy club and busts you one. I be hearin' de commotion up on de bridge, and comes to put in my two bits. An' dat's when he pulls a pistol and plugs me. Then de crazy old goat be shoutin' and carryin' on, and lastly goes divin' over de side. I don' see him come up, but I gets de boat turned 'round to go lookin' for him. Dat mon was gone. I could go on all day talkin' 'bout dat crazy fool, 'bout de strange look in his eyes,'bout de fool things he be sayin'. Yep, I could bore you to tears talkin' 'bout him."

"Good. That fits in well with what I had in mind." I took another big swallow of whiskey, then gagged and ran for the rail to throw up over the side. I clutched the safety rail with my good hand and heaved until my eyes watered and my nose ran. It was not the whiskey that had made me vomit. It was the sickness I had seen and felt. It was people using and being used. It was Marty and what she had done and what had been done to her. It was Culbertson and what he had done. It was the bullet hole in Marty, the bullet hole in Reuben, Brandt's bloodied head, and the vision of Culbertson floating facedown with the gaffing hook waving like a pennant above him. And it was what I had done.

I had seen this sickness too many times. I had played this sort of game too often. But I was still bothered by it. It offended me and made me sick. The things people do to each other make me sick. What I had done made me sick. My consolation lay in the fact that there had been no alternative, and that I had killed an animal, a savage beast, not a man. I thought of Reuben ungaffing Culbertson as calmly and easily as he had the two fish earlier. Culbertson was like the unwanted shark greedily seeking prey. Instead of an unsuspecting innocent, he had found the fisherman's bait. We had cut off his tail and thrown him back. The necessity of what had been done did not lessen its distastefulness.

"Delayed reaction," I said when I rejoined Reuben.

He gave me another grin. "I won' tell no one, boss. But it's nothin' to be 'shamed of. It not be easy to gaff a mon like a fish. It take a powerful lot of hurt to make you want to do dat to somebody. An' I get de feeling dat mon caused a powerful lot of hurt. You be right to do what you did. You just lucky you got to him before me. Now you drink some more dis whiskey an' you be all right."

I took the bottle and we fell silent, listening to the throaty roar of the diesels that took us homeward.

XII

THERE WERE NO SIRENS, no flashing red lights, no white-suited attendants, no crowd of curious onlookers to greet us as Reuben laid it in close to the dock. I jumped awkwardly onto the pier, every movement causing pain to cut through the thin layer of anesthetic fuzz the booze had provided. I managed to get the stern line snubbed on a cleat, but Reuben spotted the trouble. He jabbered at a group of kids lounging in the shade of the customs shed, and two took off down the pier, while two others came to our aid. One took a running leap to land catlike on the bow, and threw the bowline to the other boy on the dock.

It was five minutes before a vintage VW bus, circa late nineteenth century, chugged haltingly down the pier, pulling to a stop with a screech of sand-filled brakes that woke up everything in a two-mile radius. Two women emerged from the rusting blue tin can, one in the white nurse's uniform, the other in civilian clothes. The nurse brought a black medical bag and her helper followed with a folded stretcher. Seeing that I was one of the walking wounded, they pushed past me without a second glance, stepping over the gunwale onto the boat. I followed.

The nurse was cool and efficient. She exchanged a quick verbal flurry with Reuben, who pointed to the cabin. Inside, she pulled a stethoscope and a penlight out of the bag, checked Brandt's pulse then his pupils with the penlight, then lightly probed the gash and lump over his ear with deft fingers. That finished, she and the other woman spread the stretcher on the deck next to the bunk. Reuben and I offered to help them move him, but the nurse looked pityingly at us and shooed us away. They lifted him with what looked like half the effort Reuben and I had expended getting him out of the skiff and gently lowered him onto the stretcher. Then the nurse let Reuben and me each take a corner, and they each took a corner, and we carried Brandt out onto the dock and into the VW bus. Reuben's shoulder had started to bleed again, and he and the nurse had a brief but heated argument to determine whether or not he was going to come with us. The nurse won, so Reuben shouted instructions to the boys who had helped us tie up, telling them to watch the boat. As we all climbed in, a crowd was already starting to gather, with more people walking down the pier toward us. We lurched away, spitting smoke.

The infirmary consisted of a tiny waiting room, two examination rooms, and a combination lab and storeroom. There was a connecting hallway to an adjoining house. It was small and bare, but immaculate. We carried Brandt inside and laid him on one of the examination tables. The nurse disappeared for a few minutes, while the older woman got warm water and a sponge and gently daubed away the dried blood from Brandt's head and face. She was a large, strong, black woman with snow-white hair and a face shriveled by sun and age, but her eyes were clear. She turned and saw me watching her, and gave me a small sad smile. The nurse came back, explaining that she had radioed the doctor on nearby Spanish Wells, and that he would arrive within half an hour. The nurse took over, carefully snipping hair away from Brandt's gash. She decided against stitches, instead using butterfly strips to close the wound, painted the whole area with merthiolate, and lightly taped some gauze over it. There was little else that could be done until the doctor arrived, but the nurse instructed the older woman to take his pulse every five minutes and let her know if there was any significant change.

Reuben was next, and he balked and fussed about being looked at. The nurse finally stamped her foot and gave him such a stern look that he quieted down, squirming meekly like a naughty schoolboy under the schoolmarm's hickory switch. She quickly cleaned his shoulder, painted him with the merthiolate, applied pressure bandages to both entrance and exit holes, and then wrapped gauze tightly and neatly over the shoulder and under the armpit and around his chest a few times, securing it with tape. For added measure, she made him sit still while she went to get a vial of penicillin. He almost bolted out the door when he saw the needle, but the three of us stood in his way and finally got him bent over the examination table with his pants loosened. The nurse swabbed his right cheek with alcohol and jabbed him expertly despite his quivering. He pulled up his pants with his back turned, gave us all a look that should have withered us on the spot, and went grumbling into the waiting room.

The nice nurse turned her attention to me, but there wasn't much she could do except clean up my face, dabbing at the small cuts with the merthiolate. She wanted to feel the break in the collarbone to see if she could set it straight, but I didn't want to go through it twice and told her I'd wait for the doctor. She gave me some Darvon, which I accepted gratefully, swallowing one to take the edge off the pain. I went outside and found Reuben talking to an officer of the law. The island has only one. I stood a few paces away and listened politely as Reuben finished telling the abridged and annotated version of what had happened. When he was done, the cop asked him a few questions, then sent him on his way.

"Mr. Ward, is it?" he said, turning to me.

I nodded.

"My name is Thomas Martin. Why don't we go inside and sit?"

We went inside and sat. I was humble, cooperative, eager

to please, and bewildered that such a thing could have happened. Martin was a handsome black in full dress uniform, and he seemed proud of it. He was in his late twenties, sharp, obviously well educated—the accent suggested he'd spent some time in England—and he asked the right questions. I refrained from making suggestions; they would have antagonized him, and he didn't appear to need any. He took out a pad and a pencil and took careful notes, first taking down names and addresses. Then I went into the song and dance I'd rehearsed on the boat—about how Brandt was a consultant, and how Culbertson had asked him down to proffer advice on development properties. I said that I had not known the specific nature of their business talks, that although I was Brandt's associate, I had come down for the sun and sea breezes more than anything else. I described the day's events, stressing the fact that Culbertson had seemed distraught and disturbed all morning. And I told him that although I did not know what Culbertson had been so upset about, I was absolutely sure that it could not have been the result of any provocation on Brandt's part, that the man apparently had been bent on self-destruction. I described our attempts to find him after he had gone over the side, and how we had been in too poor shape to conduct a proper search. Awfully sorry, but what else could we have done?

"I understand, Mr. Ward. And you were absolutely right to seek medical help. It's a wonder that you made it back, though Reuben is a pretty tough old goat." He paused, then sighed. "Culbertson was a wealthy, well-known, and influential man. Which means that he can't be presumed dead without a search. I'll get on that right away, though I don't think it will be organized until morning. It's too late to start today. On the other hand, it might behoove us at least to appear as though we'd done everything we could under the circumstances. What do you think?"

I was surprised he asked my advice, but his question was

valid—it would not do to create a diplomatic scene. "Send out two boats in a search pattern off the northeast end of the island until it gets dark, if you can spare them, and send up a plane tomorrow," I suggested.

"Mmm, yes, perhaps that would be best. Could you suggest whom you think I should notify about Culbertson's disappearance?"

It occurred to me that his questions were designed to trap me into revealing something he might consider incriminating. I would have to watch myself around this one. "I don't know that much about the man," I lied. "I guess the easiest thing would be to contact the home office in Chicago and let them handle it."

"I'll consider that, and I'll see what my superiors in Nassau suggest. I'm also going to suggest that the search be conducted for no more than two days. That's a big bloody ocean out there."

He at least knew the realistic possibility of finding anyone dumb enough to fall off a boat in the middle of the ocean, even if he didn't know that Culbertson lay weighted to the dark sandy bottom with only vagrant currents, fifty pounds of anchor chain, and all manner of swimmy, squiggly, crawly sea creatures to keep him company. The thought made me shiver.

"There will have to be an inquest, of course," he continued. "How is your friend?"

"I don't know. The doctor hasn't gotten here yet. He hasn't regained consciousness."

"I'm sorry. I know you're worried. I'll try not to take up too much more of your time. I'm going to push to hold the inquest in about three days, as soon as the search is over, assuming we don't find him. I don't want to inconvenience you and your friend any more than necessary. With your testimony and Reuben's, we probably won't need your friend's if he hasn't recovered. Of course, there's always the possibility that Mr. Culbertson wasn't hurt and will make it to shore. Or we may find him this evening."

"Thank you. I appreciate your concern."

"Thank you for your cooperation. If I have any further questions, I know where to find you."

The doctor arrived. He offered to give me a shot of Demerol before working on me. Since I had talked with the authorities, I could see no reason why I should prolong my agony under the pretense of keeping a clear head. So I rolled up my sleeve. He examined Brandt while I waited for the drug to take effect, then came out to talk to me a few minutes later.

"As you may have noticed, we do not have much in the way of sophisticated equipment here. I'd like to have an X-ray of your friend, but I don't think it's absolutely necessary. His pulse and blood pressure are good, and there's no skull fracture as far as I can tell. He most definitely has a concussion, and it may be more severe than I suspect. So I'll offer you a choice. Take him to Nassau or Miami for X-rays to determine possible fracture or hemorrhaging. Or trust my judgment and let him stay here."

"Let him stay."

He nodded. "He'll get good care, much less expensive care. And if there's any change in his condition, we can get him to a hospital quickly enough. In any event, when he gets better, he should be thoroughly checked by a neurologist just to be safe. Now, we come to you. Same problem—no X-rays. But I'll be able to tell soon enough if it's a clean break, and if it is, there won't be much trouble setting it. Are you game?"

"Sure, do your worst." I grinned wryly.

"All right. The Demerol will help, but I'm also going to give you a local anesthetic."

He had probably studied acupuncture in another life, pricking me with the needle three or four times to numb the whole area. In the few minutes it took for the anesthetic to catch, he pushed and prodded and thumped, giving me a thorough going over, asking me questions as he worked.

"How about the ribs? Any grinding feeling when you take a deep breath? No? Pretty sore, though? Bruised a bit, but, I think, nothing broken. Head feel okay? Any dizziness? How about the jaw? Any grinding when you yawn? No? Okay, I don't think there's anything wrong that a few days' rest won't cure. Except this collarbone, that is. Let's take a look, okay?"

He worked his fingers in around the two separated pieces of bone and brought them together, fitting the broken ends neatly with a barely audible click. He pulled my arm up across my chest and made me hold it there until he was satisfied with the way my arm hung and the bones set. Then he taped my arm to my ribs, and cut a new sling for me.

"Okay. Getting dressed, taking a shower, sleeping, and playing golf are all going to become challenging and exciting events in your life, but you'll get used to it. You have to be more careful, but in a lot of ways it's a hell of a sight better than being in a cast. That arm will have to stay taped to your side for a few weeks, and then the sling will stay for another six weeks or so. You may be able to stretch the sympathy out to three weeks, but don't count on it. I hope you're left-handed."

His cheerfulness made me smile. I assured him that I am among the fortunate few who are blessed with left-handedness. And he smiled. They moved Brandt into the adjoining house. It was large enough to double as a hospital when needed since it had four bedrooms and only the nurse lived there. The doctor assured me that he would spend the night. They were going to take shifts with Brandt, taking his pulse every fifteen minutes, making sure his condition didn't change. The Demerol was beginning to override my central nervous system in earnest, countering mental commands and slowly shutting down all functions. I left to look for a ride back to the hotel and my bed. I didn't care if I had forgotten to take care of something. I wouldn't have cared if they had come to arrest me. I cared only about putting an end to the day.

When my eyes fluttered open the next morning, blinking against the glare of light coming through the window, I wished fleetingly that Culbertson had put me out of my misery. I felt as though I'd been led into a boxing ring only to discover that my opponent was a runaway freight train. The doctor had been correct; it was nearly impossible to do anything with one arm, or so it seemed until I made a concerted effort to calm down and take everything slowly and carefully. My first task, after managing to roll into a sitting position, was to wash down one of the pain pills. I don't like taking drugs, don't like having the edge taken off mental and physical reflexes, but the pain was more distracting than the effects of the Darvon could have been. I took off the sling and stepped into the shower, unable to do much more than rinse off, then patted myself dry with a towel. The water hadn't loosened the tape, but I put the sling back on as soon as I was reasonably dry. Then I stepped in front of the mirror to shave. There were purplish bruises on my forehead and cheekbone, and a mouse on the right eye. A large area around the broken collarbone was blackened and swollen. I looked at the face again. The eyes that stared back at me were empty and haunted, as shallow as the light blue waters of the sand flats north of town, and I knew that beneath the reflective surface, ghostly visions darted to and fro like elusive silvery fish. It was not a good day to see what lay camouflaged in the depths.

I worked slowly and methodically, using the fingers of the bum arm to squirt shaving cream and unscrew the top to the toothpaste tube. I sat down on the bed to pull on a pair of pants, and found a shirt that buttoned up the front—getting a shirt on over my head would have been impossible even with help. And when I had made myself as presentable as possible, I went out to face the world. I was full of childlike reticence. The sunlight hurt my eyes. My head ached. My arm throbbed. Unexpected noises and people who came too close made me jump. I was full of apprehension. The lumps on my head and the drug in my system were causing funny things to happen inside my brain. Perspectives didn't seem right, and my arm made me feel clumsy. I didn't want to explain what had happened to me, and I knew that my appearance would raise questions. I didn't want to talk to anyone. I was grumpy and irritable. I had no more faith in the human race. I walked gingerly, carefully placing each foot in front of the other, a toddler taking his first steps. Somehow, I reached the infirmary without mishap.

Brandt had regained consciousness during the night, then had slept. A bone-weary nurse gave me a quick summary of his condition, saying that he had awakened again earlier in the morning and the doctor had spoken with him and had run tests. The doctor had left shortly before my arrival, confident that the concussion was much less serious than he had originally suspected, sure that all danger was past. Brandt had developed no suspicious symptoms, no signs of irreversible damage. He was still sleeping. I told the nurse that I would stay with him and would call her if she was needed. She was grateful for the chance to take a nap, and told me where I could find her. I pulled a chair up to Brandt's bedside and watched him, envious of his peacefulness. He looked like a small boy with a blanket pulled up to his chin. Now that he was out of physical danger, I worried about the emotional damage that might have been done. Even I had not been prepared for the violence Culbertson had wreaked. It was a long time before Brandt woke.

"Emerson?" he said in a small voice. I had slipped into a daydream, and was staring at the square of light coming through the window.

"I'm here," I said softly. He was looking peculiarly at me.

"You're hurt," he said, shifting position to get a better look at me.

"Not badly. How about you, old friend? How do you feel?"

"Like someone used my head to pound nails with. Other than that, everything seems to work. The doctor had me touching my fingertips together this morning, as I recall. Or was it yesterday? What day is this?"

I told him. And then I told him what had happened because I could see that it was the next question on his lips. He made me repeat parts of it, saying that he was having occasional trouble tracking, but he listened attentively and did not interrupt me often. He was silent for a long time when I had finished, and I thought he had gone back to sleep, but he suddenly opened his eyes to look at me. They were filled with tears.

"I'm sorry." His voice was husky.

"Don't go sentimental on me." I gave him a short smile. "It had to happen. I'm glad, in a way, that you missed the more unsavory moments. Listen, I don't want to tire you out. But before I leave, I want you to know what Reuben and I are saying about what happened out there." I explained the story we had concocted. He said he thought he had it straight, then gave a yawn that creaked his jaw. It was time to leave.

"I'll come back this afternoon and we can talk more then."

He closed his eyes, mumbled a reply, and was asleep within seconds. I tiptoed out. I found the older black woman in the house and told her I was leaving. She gave me one of her sad smiles and promised that she would look in on him.

The diamonds were in a paper bag nestled in the sling inside my shirt. I went to the bank and saw the officer I'd spoken to before. He expressed his regret for the misfortune of my friend and myself, and his condolences for Mr. Culbertson, who had been a great man, surely. I refrained from enlightening him. I gave polite responses, then asked for the key to the safety-deposit box. He produced it magically—

any way to be of assistance, Mr. Ward. I unlocked the box
and took out the briefcase, setting it on the floor. I crouched
on one knee and opened it with the good hand. The stacks
of banded money did not quite fill it. I took out five slim
stacks of hundreds, five thousand dollars, stuffed four into
the sling, replacing the paper bag, and unbanded one and
stuffed the bills into my pocket. I put the paper bag into the
briefcase and closed it, then locked it back up in the box. I
returned the key and left, followed by more regrets and condolences from the bank officer.

From there, I walked down to the pier to see if Reuben
was aboard his boat. He wouldn't be going out for awhile with
his bad shoulder, but I expected that he would be puttering
around on the boat. I attracted a number of curious stares,
and I guessed that the whole island probably had heard the
story by now. When Reuben saw me coming, he shooed away
the two kids who were scrubbing the decks. He dug in his
pocket and flipped each of them a quarter, and they scampered off in search of a soda machine. He waved to me to
come on board. We went into the cabin where it was cooler,
and Reuben got out a bottle of beer for each of us. His arm
was in a sling like mine, and he had to hold the bottles
between his knees to uncap them. He handed me one, and
I gratefully took a big swallow. I reached into my pocket,
pulling out the slim wad, and counted out five hundreds, then
handed them to Reuben. He looked at me and took them
without a word. We both sat back and settled in, silently
sipping our beers. I could hear the not-so-distant bumblebee
buzz of a light plane, the incessant drone drifting in and out
of earshot. The search for Culbertson had begun.

The AP and UPI reporters arrived late that afternoon. They
found me in a deck chair on the dock at the hotel. I told
them my story and answered their questions, eager to accom-
modate the press, but a little vague on specifics. No, I didn't
have any idea why Bertrand Culbertson would have wanted

to kill himself, or why he tried to kill us before leaping into the sea. No, I didn't think my friend Brandt Williams had any idea either, but maybe he could tell them something when he was able to have visitors. No, I'd never met Culbertson before. But, fellas, let me tell you about how Culbertson went absolutely berserk, and how I stepped in to save my friend but slipped on the deck and got clobbered before I had a chance to get on my feet. And how about the way Reuben came down to help and got shot. Or I could tell you about the fishing out there, what bait to use, how to tell what you've got on the line, how a good pilot uses the boat to play the fish, what it's like on the open water in the burning sun with a cooler full of beer.

They took all they could stand, then made polite excuses and thanked me for my help. They left with glazed eyes, yawning widely. More reporters arrived the next day. They, too, left with bored expressions and frustrated editors. They received the same treatment from Reuben, and Brandt was still unavailable for comment. We soon were of major disinterest to the press. Most stuck around until the official search was called off, and a number stayed for the inquest.

The inquest was held two mornings after that, and the reporters who stayed heard the official version of the same story we'd already told fifty times. Bahamian officials from Nassau presided, and there were some officials from the American consulate in attendance. Brandt took the stand and was marvelously vague about everything, protesting that he had been taken by surprise, knocked unconscious, and had missed the rest of the fireworks. They questioned me about possible motivation. They questioned Reuben about weather conditions and our distance from shore. The verdict was that Culbertson was missing, presumed dead through an unfortunate accident at sea. Reuben was held blameless; due to the extenuating circumstances, his decision to seek medical help on behalf of his passengers was sound. Brandt and I received the most sincere apologies for having been inconvenienced and regrets that the incident had caused us injury. And everyone went home.

XIII

"THIS IS NOT a neat package," I told Brandt. We sat on his bed in the infirmary, playing gin.

"Hmm, I'm not surprised." He picked up my discard. "Gin." He laid down his cards and smiled; the hand would put him over the five-hundred-point mark. "Your problem, Emerson, is that with only one hand you can't hold your cards properly, so it doesn't look neat."

"No, no," I said, exasperated by both his luck and lack of attention to my problem. "I mean this entire situation. I'm not comfortable with the way things have turned out."

"Why?" he asked, toting up the points in my hand. "I would think that this sort of resolution would be to your liking. Less publicity. With Culbertson dead, we won't have to testify against him and try to explain why we blackmailed him for fifty thousand dollars—or hadn't you thought of that?"

"I considered it." It had occurred to me that we were better off with Culbertson dead. It would have been difficult to put him in jail, and in any case would have required more explaining on our part than I would have liked. Brandt was right—a little publicity is one thing; ending up as a material witness in a grand jury investigation is quite another.

It occurred to me, too, that I liked my life of semi-obscurity. The writing I sold helped pay the bills—it did not make me famous. Even if it had, famous authors can still stroll down the street unnoticed unlike movie stars or politicians. It was all fine with me—the strange compulsion I have to live on the edge, to see how much I can get away with, is incompatible with being recognizable. It's hard enough for the average person to remain anonymous when computers everywhere have our names and vital statistics. All one has to do to "get to know" Mr. and Mrs. Average down the street is to run a credit check under one pretense or another. Being famous just exacerbates the problem; everyone seems to want a piece of you then.

But being more or less anonymous doesn't mean that your actions don't affect anyone else. I had played my own games by my own rules, thinking that that made everything all right. I realized with some chagrin that virtually every time I dropped a pebble in my pond, it caused ripples in someone else's. I had used people to gratify my own ego, to rationalize my romantic, semimacho self-image. I had spent my life looking for causes, waiting for someone to hand me an old parchment map so I could gallop off in the direction of the legend, "Here there be dragons." But this time I'd run out of luck. I'd forgotten my shield, my sword, and a trip to a wizard for a bag full of magic spells and potions. I was unprepared to protect those around me, and had barely succeeded in slaying the dragon. The dead and wounded lay strewn in my path—Jessica, Jack Saldi, Marty, Reuben, Brandt, Culbertson, even me—and it was still a long way home. The encounter with Culbertson made me seriously doubt my ability to play avenger.

"There's too much that's unresolved," I said finally. "Just because Culbertson's dead doesn't mean it's over, and that worries me."

"Why? What's to worry about?"

"Brandt, look at us! I'm not very happy about having gotten you into this."

"So, that's it. Feeling a bit guilty, are we?"

I stared at the cards between us, unable to meet his gaze.

"Emerson, I made the choice to get involved; you didn't

force me. And Martha was already involved. You have nothing to feel guilty about."

"What about Reuben? None of this had to happen. It was my brilliant plan that brought us to this damn island."

"*Our* brilliant plan."

"Well, I had no business interfering in Culbertson's affairs in the first place. He did nothing to me—why should I care what he does? Sooner or later, he probably would have been caught. Who am I to assume responsibility for pointing the finger at him?"

Brandt raised his hands to ward off my outburst. "Whoa. Culbertson used you, and you don't like being used—a natural reaction. And, more important, you had to strike back at somebody or something for losing Jessica." He said it hesitantly, even though he knew he was right.

"Aw, shit," I sighed, thinking about what he said. Knowing he was right didn't make me feel better. "Okay, I'll put aside these feeling of remorse—for the moment, at least."

"That's better. So, what else is bothering you?"

"Lots of little things that I can't put my finger on, and a few major questions that won't disappear as easily as Culbertson did. Here's a for-instance: at least three people knew about the diamonds—Marty, the late Bertrand, and Portolucci. What if someone else knew about them? He may be able to put two and two together and figure out we must have known about them, too. Then where will we be? The thought of a cold, dark, damp five-by-nine cell doesn't thrill me in the least, and the thought of a colder, darker, damper three-by-seven grave thrills me even less."

"The possibility is remote. It would have been too risky to let anyone else in on the payoff. I wouldn't worry about that one. What else?" Brandt shifted position and watched me with a look of earnest interest.

"Okay, here's another one. Culbertson said something on the boat that I found very strange, though it didn't register at the time. He said that Marty thought *I* was blackmailing *him*. Since she knew about the diamonds and the payoff to Portolucci, she knew it wasn't me who was blackmailing Culbertson, so what the hell did he mean by that? Was he being blackmailed for something else by someone else? Why would Marty even think that I was blackmailing her father?"

"Tell me exactly what Culbertson said, and how he said it."

I repeated as best I could Culbertson's words.

"Hmm, I'd say one of two things is going on. Either Culbertson led Martha to believe you were blackmailing him for some reason, or he just thought that's what she believed."

I didn't like his answer, but I had no better ones.

"Okay, how about this. We figured out why the diamonds were being smuggled, who they were being smuggled to, and by whom. But we still have no idea who tried to kidnap Marty, though we do know why—a ransom of a million dollars. Marty told me that she knew the men who took her out of the bar. They would have had to kill her or disappear after the ransom was paid to avoid being caught—they could have been identified too easily."

"I've thought about that ever since you told me about the attempt. Isn't it possible that the kidnapping was planned by someone else to happen later, and that those men really were taking Marty out for some fresh air because she wasn't feeling well?"

The simplicity of what he said stunned me. I had never seen the face of the man on the phone in her room, I had seen only the ransom note, and had assumed that what I witnessed in the hotel bar was a kidnapping attempt. They must have thought I was a crazed rapist or something when I grabbed Marty away from them, so one of them had taken a shot at me to protect her. Brandt's solution made a great deal of sense, but something still nagged at me.

"You don't buy it?" he asked, seeing my troubled look.

"Oh, I buy it all right. But we still don't know who may have tried to kidnap Marty."

"There's something else?"

"I don't know. Something just doesn't fit. Something in the back of my mind keeps telling me I'm forgetting a piece—something I've seen or heard." I frowned, trying to concentrate, but nothing surfaced.

"Okay," I sighed, "I'll buy your explanation. The other thing that bothers me is what Vince Johnston has to do with all this."

"Coincidence," Brandt said assuredly. "We already went through this."

"I know, but I can't dismiss it as coincidence. There's some tie between Culbertson and Vince Johnston, and whatever it is, or was, Culbertson didn't like it. In fact, he was vehement about it. 'I'll take care of that fucking bastard' is what he said. Sure, we all get the impression that Johnston rubs people the wrong way, but there's more to it than that."

"From everything I've heard, I have the feeling that Johnston is like a shark, a primordial creature that moves and acts on instinct, a beast that feeds indiscriminately on any prey that moves within range. It seems to me that Johnston saw some vulnerability in Culbertson and blindly moved in for a bite. Culbertson may have turned into more than a mouthful for Johnston—it sounds like Culbertson was about ready to shake him loose somehow."

It occurred to me that Brandt was coming up with some very plausible answers to what I thought were troubling questions. It also occurred to me that Brandt was trying to pacify me in some subtle way, and I couldn't tell if he fervently hoped everything was over for his own sake, or whether he thought I was in no condition to see this mess through to whatever end was in store. I knew only that that last rationalization was one I couldn't accept—Vince Johnston, I sensed, had more cunning than a shark. He did not simply

move in on his prey with open maw and ebony eyes; he used
guile and deceit first to get close to his prey and find a
vulnerable spot in its defense. A shark stands out in a school
of fish, and it swims for cover; the school would consider
Johnston one of its own until it was too late.

I turned to explain to Brandt that we would have to be
cautious until we discovered what Johnston's relationship to
Culbertson was, but he had closed his eyes. It was almost
cocktail hour, so I quietly got up, scooped the cards off the
bed, and tiptoed out, envious of the peaceful look on Brandt's
face.

I wandered down to the waterfront, shuffling along with
head bowed and shoulders bent. I felt old and tired. Shame
and remorse threatened to bring tears to my eyes. I was no
better than Culbertson. I had lied, cheated, extorted, and
killed under the guise of some indefinable sense of justice.
This quixotic impulse had led me to redefine my notions of
right and wrong, and I suddenly couldn't justify playing by
Culbertson's rules to satisfy my own needs, to appease my
sense of righteous indignation. I had taken a step too far this
time, an irretrievable one that stirred up clouds of doubt,
obscuring the tenuous moral code I had previously felt bound
by. The world around me seemed shadowy and insubstantial,
tinged with shades of gray. The vigilante tactics I'd used put
things into a different perspective, making me cynical and
sad about my childish whims and romantic daydreams. Above
all, I felt frightened and sorry for myself. I had lost a bit
more of my innocence, and wondered if in the process I had
lost a little piece of my soul. I wondered how close I was to
permanently crossing the line between my own definitions of
good and evil. And who would save me if I did?

I sought sanctuary from the nagging self-doubt on the veranda of the Coral Sands, the small bar on the waterfront. The
late-afternoon athletic set had not yet come in off the tennis
courts and beaches, so I had my pick of choice seats. I ordered

a beer and hunkered down in a corner with my feet up on the porch rail, and watched life go by. Two toothless old black men sat on the bench under a tree across the street. They played checkers, each of them cackling gleefully in turn as they jumped each other's men. The same two mangy dogs I'd seen before lay at their feet, lazily snapping at flies. A group of children splashed and romped at the water's edge, while two older kids buzzed around the small cove in a skiff. A crowd began to gather at the end of the main dock as the charter boats came in one after another with the day's catch. The babble and laughter grew louder as more people wandered down to the dock to see who'd had the best luck. Now a couple of wahoos were strung up on the scales to be weighed and measured, and then came the obligatory snapshots—Ma with the fish, Pa with the fish, Ma and the pilot with the fish, Ma and Pa and the pilot with the fish. . . . And afterward came the smack-smack sounds of fish being beheaded, cleaned, and cut into fillets and steaks. The babble grew louder as the pilots dickered for the fish their patrons didn't want, trading wahoo steaks for yellowtail fillets or grouper.

The veranda started to fill with freshly scrubbed sunburned faces and Izod shirts. The fishy odor from the dock was gone, overpowered by the scent of After Tan. I ordered a fresh drink—a Myers's and tonic this time—and listened to the conversations that bubbled around me. The sunlight danced and sparkled in reflections off the water and burned through the top branches of the trees across the street as its leaves fluttered in the light breeze. The street was busy with people walking or bicycling to cocktail parties or dinner, making way for the occasional scooter or Mini that puttered by. The effect was bedazzling—the people, the colors, the lights, the smells—and I found myself hypnotized, unable to do more than sip my drink and watch as though somehow detached from everything around me.

I ordered another drink and watched the sun slip toward

the ocean, down and sideways, bathing us all in a coppery glow that made the atmosphere even more surreal. The ultimate, I thought, staring into the sun's fiery glow, would be a "green flash." On clear days in the Caribbean, people say they've seen a brilliant emerald flash of light just as the sun disappears below the horizon. I watched in anticipation, wondering if it was true, and was strangely disappointed when the sun dropped behind the low, scrub-tufted hills of North Eleuthera across the bay.

The setting sun signaled the end of cocktail hour, and as the sky darkened, the veranda emptied. Finally, I was the only one left, watching the stars pop out one by one. The air grew cool, and the chill brought me out of my peculiar reverie. I was hungry. I got up slowly, nursing my bad arm, and started walking back to the hotel, hoping I could hitch a ride. Three or four steps convinced me that I was absolutely, delightfully hammered.

A Mini-Moke roared by trailing the sounds of laughter, then suddenly screeched to a halt in a cloud of dust. There was a brief grinding of gears, then a whirring sound like a wind-up toy as the little vehicle moved in reverse to stop a few feet away from me.

"Want a ride?" the driver called out. Four young, smiling, inquisitive faces peered out from under the fringed canvas top. Mini-Mokes have a strange identity crisis, not knowing whether to look like a jeep, a golf cart, or an old-time surrey-with-a-fringe-on-top, so they look like all three. The faces looked polite and expectant, while I dumbly pondered what I thought a Mini-Moke should look like.

"Sure," I said, grinning foolishly, now a little embarrassed that I was two sheets to the wind.

The jeep erupted into revelry again. "I'll get in back," said the girl in the front passenger seat, and there was laughter as she wedged herself in the back, half sitting on the laps of the couple already cramped in the small space. I eased into the front seat, trying not to bump my arm, and ended up with my knees jammed up between the windshield and my chest, holding on for dear life with my good hand as we roared off into the night. The headlights stabbed through the darkness, trying to cut a swathe through the jungle as we turned first left then right on the narrow, twisted road.

In the quick trip to the hotel, I didn't find out much more than that they all went to college together, but their youthful exuberance and carefree laughter lightened my mood and made me nostalgic at the same time. They would find out soon enough what a precious commodity youth is.

The "kids" dropped me off in the circular drive of the Tamarind Bay Club, then drove away, waving gaily, still laughing over some private joke. Their voices and the growl of the car faded in the distance, swallowed up by the dense undergrowth. I turned away from the visions of my own youth playing in the back of my mind and made my way to the restaurant.

I had one more Myers's and tonic waiting for a bowl of fish chowder that consisted mainly of sweet-tasting barracuda and grilled grouper with a cucumber dill sauce. By the time dinner arrived, I was feeling a little more hammered, a little less morose, and incredibly hungry. I devoured everything. There were only a few crumbs of homemade cheesecake on my plate when Roy stopped by the table to chat. We ordered coffee, and Roy ordered us two snifters of cognac, then magically produced two long, thin panatelas.

"Jamaican," he said, laughing, watching me sniff at it appreciatively. "Even here we don't get the legendary Cuban product."

"Roy," I said after a pause while a waitress served our coffee and brandy, "I hope we haven't caused you any trouble."

"Not at all." He looked surprised. "In fact, I came over to tell you how sorry we are that your stay has not been more

hospitable. You certainly haven't been any trouble to us—
the publicity will probably put this place on the map. I've
already gotten a call from a travel editor on one of the New
York papers asking about space next week—seems she needs
a break from the spring weather up there."

"It is nice down here, isn't it?" I leaned back in my chair,
puffing comfortably on the cigar, sipping cognac, and looked
out across the dining room veranda, down the slope to the
harbor. The lights of the guest cottages down the slope beckoned warmly, a few lights flickered faintly on Eleuthera across
the bay, and beyond, stars lit up the black velvet sky. Soft
breezes carrying gentle scents drifted in and out of the dining
room, and insect sounds created a quiet background symphony. It was more than pleasant, it was serene and tranquil.

"One other thing I wanted to mention," Roy said after a
moment's silence. "Some man was looking for you today. He
wouldn't leave his name or say what he wanted."

"Probably another reporter."

"I don't know. Maybe." He said it hesitantly, as though
something was on his mind. Whatever it was, he must have
decided it wasn't all that important. "Anyway, I thought you
should know."

"Thanks. And thanks for the cognac."

"Anytime. I'll see you around, okay?"

He had a troubled look on his face when he left, but I
shrugged it off, thinking he must have business on his mind.
I finished my cognac and took what was left of the cigar down
to the dock to look at the stars. It was after ten when I decided
to pack it in. I flicked away the cigar butt, watched it arc,
a glowing ember, out over the water, then land with a small
plop and sizzle. I walked back up the hill. Most of the lights
in the guest houses were now off; there is some nightlife on
the island, but people tend to turn in early. My own bungalow
was dark and still as I inserted the key in the lock. My
shoulder ached, my head hurt, and I was dog-tired. The

thought of slipping between cool sheets was inviting.

As soon as I stepped through the doorway, all the dread, the doubts, the nagging suspicions that had haunted me all day came rushing back. Something was wrong. Before I could take another step, something cold, black, and hard slashed at me from the corner of my vision and crashed against my right temple. A burst of light exploded in my brain, then everything went dark. I knew that I was falling, but didn't feel myself hit the floor. And now the dread roiled through my guts, leaden and burning, and I tasted bile and smelled my own fear. I knew who was in the room, and I was gripped with sudden terror.

Strong arms pulled me into a sitting position, then lifted me to my feet, causing lightning bolts of pain to shoot through my arm from fingertips to shoulder. My legs wouldn't hold me, and I began to topple, falling across a massive shoulder.

He carried me effortlessly. No one saw us as he quickly circled to the back of the bungalow, and I couldn't make a sound, as hard as I tried. Once out of sight of the main buildings, he broke into a slow trot, and I flopped up and down on his shoulder. My head was still in never-never land, and from my upside-down vantage point, the world bucked and swayed like some crazy carnival ride.

Vince Johnston unceremoniously dumped me in the back of a car. I lay in a heap and watched a small piece of sky shift and change patterns as we drove, winding down island roads to some unknown destination. It was difficult, under the circumstances, to regain any composure, but I mustered a bit of courage. I was not going to die, I told myself—he could have already killed me. He had surprised me, that's all, and when we got to where we were going, we would have a nice chat and clear up whatever was on his mind. Taking me by surprise in the dark and knocking me silly with a blackjack was simply Vince's way of saying hello. He was a violent person, I reminded myself, who didn't have time for the amenities of making friends. Despite that, I could reason with him. I could talk my way out of this dilemma. Maybe.

Every bump and turn that wedged my right shoulder toward the floorboards made it throb and ache. Oddly enough, the more pain I felt, the clearer my mind became, until finally I was able to wriggle my fingers, then my toes, lift my head, and untangle my legs. It was exhausting work. After a moment's rest, I slowly pulled myself up from between the seats. My muscles quivered, and I felt my strength beginning to fade. I managed to turn just enough so that when the arm gave out I flopped back into a position half reclining against the door. My butt was wedged in near the floor, but my shoulders were free. I could do nothing except wait for more feeling to come back and watch the stars bounce and spin as the car roared on through the night.

It seemed like hours before we got to our destination, but it couldn't have been more than a matter of minutes—it takes only ten minutes to get from one end of the island to the other. The silence was eerie when Vince shut off the engine. Then, far in the distance, I could hear the sound of surf breaking on shore, and after a moment, I heard the insect symphony that had seemed so pleasant a short time ago. All my feeling had returned, and what I felt most was pain, but everything seemed to be working except the useless right arm still taped to my chest. I began to think I just might be able to make a break for it if given a chance. The front car door opened, then chunked shut, and the door I was leaning against abruptly opened, and I half fell out of the car. Vince leaned over me, put his hands under my arms, and yanked me the rest of the way out. I stifled a scream and fought a wave of nausea. When I shook it off, I saw that Vince had me standing, albeit on rubbery legs, holding me up with my left arm draped around his neck and his around my waist.

He walked us to a building of some kind. We stopped for a moment just inside the door. It was black, and I looked around, hoping my eyes would adjust to the darkness, trying to get my bearings. I finally was able to discern a muted square off to one side a shade lighter than the rest of the darkness, and guessed it was a window. Then Vince pulled at me, and we shuffled a few steps to the left and stopped again. I heard more shuffling, then scraping, and Vince turned me around and lowered me into a chair. He moved away, and from the sounds I could tell he had crossed the room. My mind said it was time to go, and I hoped my legs had enough sense to follow. A match flared across the room just as I struggled to my feet and headed back the few steps to where I knew the door had to be. I willed my legs to move, first one step, then another, faster, and in the dim flare of the match I saw flickering images—Vince in profile bending over an oil lamp, the empty shell of the thatched hut, the black hole that was the doorway waiting to swallow me up. I took another step, sure that I must be running by now. I saw Vince's startled face across the room, then the beckoning doorway. He was too late! The next step would take me through the door to freedom.

This time I barely felt the blow, a light tap over the left ear that turned everything pillow-soft and the black night even blacker. I fell through the doorway and kept falling, tumbling slowly into an inky void until there was nothing.

I climbed slowly back to consciousness. I opened my eyes to the dim yellow glow of a kerosene lantern. It sat on an old wooden table in the middle of the room, and Vince sat in a chair on the other side of the table reading a magazine, his small eyes squinting in the dim light. We appeared to be in a one-room building, about twelve feet by twenty. The building was really more like a hut—someone had taken the trouble to construct a reasonably sturdy two-by-four frame, then had covered the whole thing with thatched palm fronds. Two largish windows were cut in one wall, but held no glass or screens, and there was no door hanging from the door frame.

In a far corner was a cot and what appeared to be a knapsack on the floor next to it. The only other furniture were the table and the chairs we sat on.

For some reason that I couldn't figure out, my head wouldn't move very far, but I managed to tuck in my chin and look down at the floor. It was dirt. My ankles were tied to the legs of the chair. I raised my head and looked out the nearest window, staring blankly into the dark, taking stock. My right arm was taped to my chest, and my left arm, I finally discovered, was tied behind my back to the chair. I began to feel pain again, a distant pounding in my head and throbbing in my shoulder that slowly grew. My neck felt stiff and constricted. I worked my head around to look up, and realized that a rope had been noosed around my neck then looped over a rafter and pulled tight, preventing me from any substantial movement. Suddenly, the idea of a friendly chat with Vince seemed remote, and I loosed an involuntary groan of pain and fear.

Vince glanced my way, then set down the magazine and stood up. In the glow of the single lamp, his bulk cast a huge, grotesque shadow up the wall and roof. He rummaged through the knapsack, then walked toward me. The lamplight cast a spectral halo around his head, casting his features in darkness. As he drew closer, I could finally see the face that had haunted me since that night in Chicago that seemed like aeons ago. He squatted in front of me, and now his features looked softer, almost feminine. My mind was playing tricks—he actually looked genuinely concerned.

"Here," he said quietly, "try some of this. It might make you feel better." He raised a bottle to my lips and gave me a big swallow.

It burned going down, and I coughed and spluttered. "What the hell is it?"

"One-fifty-one-proof rum." He grinned. "Your shoulder hurt?" I nodded. "Looks like a broken collarbone. Culbertson do that?" I nodded again, curious. "He was a tough old bird, no doubt about that. You killed him, didn't you?"

His eyes searched my face, but I said nothing.

"It doesn't matter." He reached and untied my left hand, giving me a little freedom of movement. I looked curiously at him—maybe I had been wrong about him. "I brought your pain pills. I thought you might need them." He opened the prescription bottle and handed me one, then poured some of the rum into a plastic cup. "I'm sorry I don't have any water— I'll remember to bring a canteen," he said, handing me the cup. I was stupefied and confused, but gratefully swallowed the pill.

Vince took a swig of rum from the bottle, then stood up and walked to the table to get the other chair. He brought it back and swung it around so the back faced me, straddling it.

"I'm sorry I treated you so rough," he said gently. "I had to talk to you privately, and I didn't think you'd come willingly."

"You're damn right I wouldn't have," I said belligerently. "And what makes you think I'll talk to you now?"

"Hey, take it easy. Here, have another snort." He handed me the bottle and I took another pull, letting the liquor slide down slowly, warming my insides. "Let's just have a belt and a nice friendly chat, okay?"

"Fine." The rum had already hit me, fuzzing the edges of my mind, reducing the pain in my shoulder to a dull ache, making me forget, strangely, the fact that I was tied to a chair in a shack in the middle of nowhere.

"All I want, Ward, is a little of what's coming to me. No one has to get hurt, no one's nose has to get out of joint. Just give me what I want, and I'll slip away quietly, no muss, no fuss."

"Sounds reasonable," I said, taking another swallow of rum. The effect of the pill was kicking in, amplifying my

dreamy state. I was beginning to feel positively chummy—
Vince wasn't such a bad guy after all. "What is it you want?"

"I want the diamonds and whatever else you took Culbertson for."

"Diamonds?"

"Sure," he said, seeing my incredulous look. "It wasn't
hard to figure out. I knew Culbertson was trying to cut a deal
with Portolucci. I read the papers. When I saw that Portolucci
had stopped work on the Sandbeach, and then read that
Culbertson had been lost at sea while on a fishing trip with
one Emerson Ward, it didn't take me long to figure out that
you'd somehow managed to foul up Culbertson's deal. So,
where are they?"

"Why should I tell you?" I said smugly, taking another
pull from the bottle.

His reply was a backhanded blow to my face that whipped
my head around. The rope around my neck caught me up
short, keeping me from being knocked off the chair. The
sudden violence put the fear of God back in me and confused
me even more—we had just been such pals. "A friendly
chat," he'd said—what had I done to anger him?

"Twice now you've gotten in my way and messed things
up," Vince said, and struck me again across the other side
of the face. Now I tasted blood, and sudden nausea. I choked
it down and blinked back the tears the blow brought to my
eyes.

"You should tell me," he said, hitting me, "for the simple
reason," and again, "that I'll kill you," and again, "if you
don't."

"Wait," I managed to mumble through a split lip, feebly
holding up my left arm to ward off the next blow. It sounded
like a hell of a good reason to talk, and part of me pleaded,
"Tell him, tell him." But some other small voice told me that
I couldn't give up yet. Vince had answers that I had to have.
If I gave him what he wanted, I'd never find out what I needed

to know. I tried to pull myself together, tried to uncross my eyes so I could focus on his face. Three images merged, blipped, then merged again into one reasonably focused image.

"You can't kill me," I croaked. The noose felt tighter, making me rasp for breath. Vince looked at me dispassionately.

"Why not? If you won't tell me, I'm sure I can get your friend to talk."

"Leave him out of this. He can't help you. I'm the only one who knows where the diamonds are and how to get them." Talking was difficult. My throat felt raw and dry, and my mouth was puffy and swollen.

"Then tell me—now!" he barked.

"No." I was afraid not to, but I couldn't.

"Bastard." Rage filled his eyes, and they turned smaller and meaner, closing into slits like a cat's eyes.

I'd bought it now. I saw his arm swing, and was filled with familiar dread when I saw the black object in his hand. I tried to turn my head away, wincing with anticipation. My head exploded into bolts of multicolored lightning that ricocheted off the inside of my skull like speeding bullets, then gradually faded away until there was nothing but cavernous darkness everywhere.

The shack looked different when I woke, and it took me a while to realize that it was filled with a faint pink pallor instead of lamp glow. It was almost dawn, and I shifted uncomfortably in the chair, trying to stimulate some circulation. My legs were cramped with the chill, and everything else just plain hurt. I had apparently found a position in which I wouldn't choke when I was unconscious—my neck was stiff and tender from leaning my head back against a two-by-four frame all night. My head was splitting, no doubt due to the rum, so I ignored it. I peered through the gloom and listened intently, trying to determine if Vince was nearby, but I appeared to be alone.

Sleep was out of the question—I was too uncomfortable. With Vince gone, I had plenty of time to think. My headache didn't go away, and it slowly dawned on me that Vince had used the blackjack on me three times the night before. I tried not to think about the possibility that there might be a slow leak of blood into the brain case that could build up and create so much pressure on the brain that I would simply stop thinking, breathing, living, at any moment. Instead, I tried to think of ways to get myself out of this mess. Things looked bleak. Vince was being overcautious with me for some reason. How much trouble could a one-armed man be? I would somehow have to put him at ease. The man frightened me, no doubt about that. He had used the good guy—bad guy routine on me with startlingly effective results. I had *wanted* to be pals with Vince, knowing that he was the key to whether or not I felt pain. I read somewhere that the relationship between someone like Vince and his victims is like that of lovers. My pain evoked a kind of tenderness from Vince, a feeling akin to love, at least as close to love as Vince would ever experience. I was not happy to be the source of this wonderful feeling. I didn't want to be a warm and cuddly teddy bear for Vince, the kind he would rip the ears off and stuffing out of. I wasn't sure I could hold up for long. I was full of pain, and I was rapidly losing strength and resolve. I was inclined just to end it all. I would tell Vince what he wanted to know and be rid of him. Then I would tuck my tail between my legs and go hide somewhere for the rest of my days.

I thought about Brandt. I would have to come up with a way to protect him from Vince. It was the least I could do. I'd have to convince him that Brandt was untouchable as long as he was still in the infirmary. That would buy Brandt a few days, assuming I figured out a way to help myself in those few days. In a few days, I could easily be dead.

The air grew noisier as the world began to wake up. A breeze rustled the thatch outside the hut. The sounds of surf on the beach carried on the wind, and suddenly the sun popped over the horizon, casting flickering orange-tinted shadows throughout the shack. I sat and waited, not knowing for what.

I must have dozed off. When I opened my eyes again, the light was brighter. Sunlight streamed through the door at an angle off to my right. I heard the sound of a car door clunking shut—the noise of its engine must have awakened me. I knew better than to get my hopes up, and wasn't disappointed when Vince stepped through the doorway. He barely glanced my way and strode to the other side of the room without a word. He set a paper bag on the table. Then he sat down and pulled out what looked like sweet rolls and a thermos. The smell of coffee filled the room when he opened the thermos, making my stomach rumble in anticipation. I tried to lick my lips—my mouth was bruised and caked with dried blood. He watched me with a curious look as he munched on his breakfast, as though wondering what to do with me. The smell of food was driving me crazy, but I said nothing. When he had finished, he came toward me with a canteen and a small paper sack. He squatted and set them on the dirt floor while he untied my left hand. I shook it, trying to restore some circulation, then took the canteen he offered. I drank slowly, carefully, but some of the water dribbled out of my swollen mouth and down my chin. I never knew water could taste so good, even tepid, tinny-tasting water from a canteen. When I was done, he handed me the sack. I reached in and pulled out a piece of some kind of fried dough, like a fritter.

"What is it?" I mumbled, taking a bite.

"Conch fritters," he replied.

I turned my head and spit out the piece in my mouth.

"What did you go and do that for?" He sounded annoyed.

"Conch makes me sick."

"Then I guess you'll just have to go hungry."

"I'm sorry. I just can't eat it." My voice sounded whiny, like a bratty child's, and I wondered why I was apologizing to him.

"Suit yourself." He shrugged, then began untying my ankles.

"What are you doing?"

"Taking you for a little walk. Fresh air will do you good."

He helped me to my feet. For a moment I didn't think my legs would hold me, then they began tingling and feeling prickly as some of the feeling started coming back. He gathered up the ropes and the chair in one hand, and held the rope around my neck in the other and led me outside like a dog on a leash. He set down the chair outside the door, and walked me around a few paces from the shack. I stopped to urinate against the side of the shack, grateful that my bladder hadn't burst while I was still sitting in the chair. He watched indifferently, standing a step or two away, loosely holding the rope. I walked around some more, shaking the cramps out of my legs and stretching to pull out some of the kinks in my back and neck.

"That's enough," he said after a few minutes. "Strip down to your shorts." I looked curiously at him but obeyed, careful not to antagonize him. He led me over to the chair and sat me down, then tied the end of the rope around my neck to the back of the chair, leaving only an inch or two of slack. He roped my ankles to the chair legs again, and finally tied my hand behind my back. He looked up at the sun and back at me, then reached over me, grabbed the seat of the chair and picked it up with me in it and repositioned it more to his liking. Then he stood in front of me. I squinted up at him, half blinded by the glare of the sun peeking over his shoulder.

"The diamonds weren't in your room. But I guess I didn't

really expect to find them there. I did find this, however."
He reached into his pocket and pulled out a wad of bills—
the cash I'd taken out of the briefcase. "I figure there has to
be more, and I can wait until you tell me where it is."

I said nothing, deciding, stupidly, to be brave.

"You can sit out here and think about it," he said after a
moment. "I'm going to take a nap—trashing your hotel room
was tiring. I wouldn't advise yelling for help or anything like
that unless you want to annoy me. No one will hear you
anyway. Have a nice day—looks like it's going to be a warm
one." He disappeared into the shack.

It was pleasant at first. The sun baked some of the stiffness
out of my sore muscles. The breeze was gentle and refreshing.
I could see a patch of black around the corner of the shack,
maybe fifty yards away. It made me curious. I looked to my
right. There was the car, parked on a dirt road that led into
the underbrush. Why was the car there when there was a
perfectly good blacktop road on the other side? The breeze
was coming from the east, and since it had picked up some,
now I could hear the surf more plainly, and occasionally the
sound of faint shouts and laughter. Some children playing on
the beach? The beach, then, could not be far away. But when
the breeze died down, I could hear water sounds even closer,
a gentle lapping of water on shore. We must be on the harbor
side of the island. And the island must be narrow at this
point to hear sounds from the beach in the distance. At last
I had it. The patch of asphalt had to be the old airstrip, and
the shack had been the ticket office and departure lounge.
Vince was right. No one would think to look for me here. In
fact, Brandt probably figured I was pouting for some reason
and just hadn't come to visit. He wouldn't start to worry for
a day at least.

The sun grew hotter, and the day became less pleasant.
My throat was parched, and my eyes felt gritty and dry as I

squinted against the glare. I could smell salt and dried sea-weed and the pungency of the island underbrush on the air, and it made me hungry first, then nauseated because my stomach was empty. I tried to think of something else. I watched intently as a scorpion, its tail quivering like a nose sniffing the air, scuttled crablike in my direction, leaving a squiggly trail in the brown sandy soil. Another of the green-brown creatures scurried out of a shadow to meet the first, and the two stopped, poised like bizarre war machines in the desert, waiting for the order to attack. They approached each other, stalking slowly, until they were inches apart, then they locked pincers and danced, back and forth, side to side, a grotesque, primordial rumba.

Vince had said I'd messed up his plans twice. We'd never ever been formally introduced. How could I have become such an integral part of his life, and he of mine? Okay, count the fact that he hadn't gotten his hands on the suitcase Jessica had brought with her from New York as one time. How else had I managed to get in his way? I wanted nothing to do with this man, yet each of us sought something from the other. Why couldn't he just leave me alone?

The sun climbed higher and grew hotter. Despite the color I already had, my skin was beginning to dry and burn. Small blisters were forming where the skin was most tender, in the crook of my elbow, at the top of my thighs where my shorts rode above the tan line. I could feel my lips cracking, and as I worked my tongue over the sore spots trying to moisten them, I tasted blood. A fly hovered around my head, attracted by the bright red trickle, and finally landed near the corner of my mouth. I shook my head violently to chase it away, but it kept coming back.

The heat shimmered in waves off the ground, the trees, the car, the strip of asphalt, making everything appear blurred and unfocused. The sun pounded down, a massive weight that pressed me deeper into the chair. Reality just sort of slipped away. I was alone in a huge, brightly lit theater, and entire scenes suddenly appeared out of the shimmering haze as though laser-holographed. There were faces I knew and ones I didn't, visions of tranquil beauty and ones that terrified, and they all whirled around me in a confusing array.

Finally, one sensation overwhelmed the rest: it was cool. My skin was on fire, but the weight of the sun had been lifted and little puffs of breeze felt like icicles pricking my skin. I reluctantly opened my eyes. It was dusk, and I had somehow been transported back inside the shack. Vince watched me as I looked around, confused, then he got up and walked toward me. I cringed. He poured water over my head from the canteen, a small trickle that hit me like an electric shock then turned into an exquisite pleasure. I turned my face up to let the water trickle down my face. Vince held the canteen to my lips and let me take a few sips. I pleaded for more, but he walked away, and I felt like dying. He was back in a moment with a cup full of water and one of the pain pills. He put the pill between my lips, then held the cup so I could drink. I slurped it greedily, and he brought me another cup. I drank this one more slowly. When I was through, he untied my hand from the back of the chair and offered me the bottle of rum. The alcohol stung my lips and burned my throat, but I didn't care.

"How did you know Culbertson was smuggling diamonds?" I croaked when I was able to talk.

Vince looked at me in surprise. "Marty told me, of course. Yeah, she told me a lot of things she probably shouldn't have."

"Like what?" I tried to think, to stall for time.

"Oh, this and that. Little things about her daddy, for example. She didn't even realize what she was telling me half the time."

"Oh, come on. Marty isn't that stupid. You mean things you could blackmail Culbertson with?" I couldn't believe

Marty would have knowingly done that, but something in his voice told me I was right.

"Shit, her old man was into me so deep, I arranged to kidnap Marty so he could pay me off with the ransom money the company was going to cough up." He sounded pleased with himself.

I was stunned. "You arranged it? And Culbertson knew about it?" Culbertson must have known, I realized; he had been too unconcerned on the boat over Marty's whereabouts.

"Yes, I arranged it," he said, mimicking my voice. He was angry now. "And you fucked it all up."

"Why would Marty tell you those things?" I was desperately trying to distract him, to keep him talking. I strained against the ropes.

"It's this power I have over women. She did what I told her to. Why do you think she slept with you? Because you're irresistible?" He chuckled. "She was watching you, keeping tabs on you for me."

"Why? Why would she do that?" I was confused, and I felt betrayed.

"Because I told her you were blackmailing her father. She would have killed for Culbertson. She had no idea what a crook he was, but she knew he was ruthless, and she's as ruthless as he was. She's just not as smart." He paused. "You see, you had two hundred and fifty thousand dollars that belonged to me, and I thought you might be lying when you said you'd sent it back to New York. I wanted that money, so I told Marty you and Jessica had set up that stock scam, and had blackmailed Culbertson for the quarter-million. I told her that I was trying to help out her old man and get back the money. She was eager to help."

"But Marty said Jessica was her friend. She never would have believed that." I couldn't believe my ears.

"You're a fool, Ward, just like Jessica was. Marty has no friends. She's interested in two things—herself and the power she could get from 'Uncle Bertrand.'"

"Oh, God," I moaned. "You know about that, too?"

"Of course." He snorted with derision. "My relationship with Jessica led me straight to Marty, and once I saw how much money there was to be had, I looked for the skeletons in Culbertson's closet. It wasn't hard. Then you popped up."

He was pacing the floor like a caged tiger. "Jessica's scam was pretty good. She knew just how to get me to bite, I'll give her that much. I never intended to let that money out of my sight. But you really didn't have the money. You actually sent it back to that ass Pearson, you fucking do-gooder.

"That was the first time you messed things up. Now I want retribution. I want what you stole from Culbertson. Tell me where it is." There was menace in his voice now, and I was scared. I knew my stall tactics weren't going to work any longer.

I suddenly saw a flash of light sweep across the wall of the hut. The sound of a car outside registered a moment later, but in that instant Vince had moved quickly as a cat. Before I could cry out, Vince had clapped a huge paw over my mouth and had doused the lantern. I heard a small scuffling in the dark, and Vince suddenly took his hand away from my mouth. I took a breath and was about to yell when a ball of greasy, foul-smelling paper was stuffed in my mouth. It was the crumpled paper bag that had contained the conch fritters, and I nearly retched. Vince whipped a piece of rope around my head and tied the gag securely. I grunted muffled squeals through the gag, and Vince slapped me hard.

"Shut up, or you're a dead man."

I grunted again, feeling I had nothing else to lose. He smashed a fist into the back of my head, and I slumped into half-consciousness. I dimly heard more scuffling, then nothing for what seemed an eternity, and the dim, dark shapes in the hut blurred into darkness as reality slipped away.

I woke up sputtering. Vince had thrown a bucket of seawater on me. I was beaten and exhausted, and chilled to the bone with fear.

"Some kids necking in the brush," he said. "They're gone, didn't even suspect someone was here." Vince paused. "Where are the diamonds?" he asked gently, almost tenderly. Then he hit me twice in the face with an open-handed slap that numbed me.

Unable to recapture whatever bravado I'd had earlier, I gave in. "I'll tell you."

He backed off, and I took great breaths, trying to get a grip on myself.

"They're in the bank vault, here on the island," I said calmer now. "Only Brandt Williams and I can get them out."

"I guess I'll just have to enlist his aid if you won't get them for me."

"No. Look, I'd do it, but I'm not in any shape to walk into the bank. They'd know something was wrong. Brandt will help you, but you don't have to hurt him. Just tell him you're holding me, and he'll do what you want."

"Wonderful. I can have the diamonds and be out of here by tomorrow morning."

"Wait," I pleaded, hoping to reason with him. "You can't pull Brandt out of the hospital and drag him to the bank. Are you crazy? He's supposed to be checking out the day after tomorrow," I lied. "Wait until he's back at the hotel, then get him to help you."

"You may be right," he mused. "I guess another day won't hurt. No one knows you're missing, so it wouldn't hurt to wait. Well, now that's settled, I think I'll go have some dinner. I've really worked up an appetite."

I watched Vince leave, then quietly cried myself to sleep. I was beyond hurting or even caring.

XIV

I SLEPT FITFULLY, waking often during the night. Each time, I listened intently for the sound of Vince's breathing, but I seemed to be alone. He had neglected to put the noose back around my neck, but I was uncomfortable anyway. When dawn finally came, I didn't think I would ever be able to move again. My joints were frozen stiff, and my legs were numb. My strength was almost gone, and I wondered how long I could keep going. There didn't seem to be much left to want to live for.

Vince returned about two hours later. It must have been around eight o'clock. He had undoubtedly spent the night in a warm, comfortable hotel bed, but I was too tired to care. He was humming cheerfully—probably the thought of all that money sitting in a safety-deposit box had brightened his spirits considerably. He had brought a thermos with him—for me this time. He untied my hand and helped me drink a cup of cinnamon coffee with lots of milk and sugar and laced with rum. Then he untied my feet and helped me up. He took most of my weight while he walked me around until the numbness in my legs started to go away, then held me up while I took a few tentative steps of my own. I didn't care that Vince watched while I picked the same spot on the wall of the shack to urinate; I didn't care about the grinding pain in my shoulder that meant the collarbone would probably have to be reset. I felt marginally better, and wanted some more coffee.

Vince led me back inside and let me stay untied while I finished the whole thermos of coffee. When it was gone, I asked him if there was any rum left in the bottle. I wanted to get drunk, to obliterate the present with a thick alcoholic fuzz. While I nursed the bottle, Vince tied me back into the chair.

"I don't think we need to put you outside today," he said with a grin. "No need to overdo it. But I am going to have to tie you up. I'm spending the day at the beach, and I wouldn't want you to get ideas about going anywhere."

I chugged the last two inches of rum and handed him the empty bottle, then put my hand behind my back to be tied. The coffee had revived me some, but the rum was beginning to kick. My head started feeling a little loose on my shoulders, and my vision was just beginning to blur. I waved good-bye to Vince, giggling at his admonition to be good.

The rum loosened my tongue, and I started talking to myself, arguing with an alter ego about my lot in life. Then I talked to the room, seeking advice from unseen bystanders, and finally I bitched to the world at large. After I got all that out of my system, it occurred to me that I had killed the goose that laid Vince's golden eggs. He'd had some kind of dirt on Culbertson, and I had stopped him from collecting on it. Even with the diamonds, Vince would not take kindly to that fact. Indeed, knowing the kind of vindictive guy he was, I didn't think much of my chances for survival, and I had a sudden interest in living. I was not as afraid of death as I had been only two days before, but I wanted a nobler death than at the hands of Vince Johnston. I thought of Brandt and the friends who had seen me through when Jessica had died, and discovered that I wasn't ready to check out yet. I wanted more.

Another realization slowly reached out and slapped me in the face. My mind had wandered to thoughts of Jessica, and things gradually began to make a horrible kind of sense. I thought back to a night in Chicago months before: Vince hadn't asked to speak to Jessica; he had asked only for the money. He'd known that she had brought it to my house, and he must have known that she was dead. Jessica had not been careful enough.

And Jack Saldi, I thought, had been found in the park with a broken neck and an unexplained bruise over his left ear. I hadn't given him that bruise. I thought about our struggle; he hadn't hit his head against anything. A sudden chill ran through me. Vince—Vince and his trusty sap. Who else could it have been? Witnesses had seen a big man about my size at the scene, Lanahan had said.

I felt anguish and pain and anger. It had all been a setup! It hadn't been a freak accident. Vince had had Jessica deliberately killed, and then had silenced the man who'd done it. I rocked back and forth in the chair, trying to hold on to reality, trying to control the pent-up fury and searing emotional pain that threatened to overwhelm me.

I would stop him, I vowed. I knew, now, what he had done to Jessica, all the hurt he had caused her, and my heart felt like breaking. Now I could empathize. Vince had come damn close to destroying me in two short days—Jessica had never had a chance. But she had struggled to come back, to become a whole person again, and Vince had taken that away from her, too. No, I wasn't ready to die. First, I would stop Vince.

I was only semiconscious when he returned at dusk. I had slipped into a twilight fantasy world around midafternoon. A kind of numbness had set in, and all the pain had slowly melted away. It belonged to someone else now. It had detached itself from me—or I from it—and I could see myself, a poor, miserable wretch, tied to a chair in a thatched hut. Vince couldn't cause me any more pain. The burning thirst and gnawing hunger had disappeared. I was free, and in that strange dream world I had been able to get up out of the chair and frolic away the afternoon outside. I had taken a fantasy walk around the shack and up and down the airstrip, and had lain in the sun for a time, all the while relishing the thought of how mad Vince would be if he had known I was free to come and go as I pleased. When I had seen his car coming up the dirt road, I had slipped back into the shack and into my chair, so he wouldn't know what I had been doing.

When Vince actually walked through the door, I couldn't tell what had been fact and what fantasy. I couldn't remember what I had done that day, or the day before. I was barely conscious of Vince's presence, unaware that he untied me, forced me to sip water from the canteen, and carried me out of the shack to walk me around. Pain began to bring me back to reality and I became more and more aware of my body. As that awareness grew, the hunger and thirst *and rage* came rushing back. I focused on the rage and let it push the pain aside, clearing my mind. I stopped, sniffing the clean sweet night air, and looked around, letting reality sink in. My legs were a little wobbly, but they worked. I turned to Vince and pointed to my mouth. It was so dry I couldn't talk. He understood my request and led me inside. I felt strong enough to walk by myself, but I leaned against Vince and let him carry most of my weight.

He handed me the canteen, then helped me raise it to my lips when I pretended to be too weak. My rage tapped some inner reserve of strength and pumped adrenaline through my system. I emptied the canteen with Vince's help.

"Are you going to starve me to death?" I managed to rasp.

"As a matter of fact, I brought you some dinner," he said, grinning. "I have something much better in mind for you than letting you starve. Sit down at the table."

"My, my, so formal this evening." I plunked myself into the chair. Daylight was almost gone, and Vince lit the kerosene lamp. Then he came around to my side and began tying me to the chair, starting with my ankles.

"Not so damn tight," I snapped. "I'm not going anywhere."

He laughed, but didn't pull the ropes as taut as they had been. I could actually move my feet. He left my good arm untied, but put the noose around my neck and tied it to the back of the chair, giving me just enough slack so I could lean over to eat. Then he went over to the cot and brought a paper bag back to the table. He set it down and pulled out two foil packages, unwrapped them, and presented me with a cold, soggy cheeseburger and greasy french fries. He stepped back to the cot and retrieved a new bottle of rum and two plastic cups from the knapsack, and sat down across from me. I bit ravenously into the congealed cheeseburger. Vince poured rum into both cups and pushed one over to me.

"Here's to tomorrow." He raised his glass. "It's going to be a big day." He smiled and drank.

I picked up my glass, staring into the rum's amber depths for a long moment. The oil lamp flickered in refracted tongues of color through the liquid. And I suddenly began to get the beginnings of an idea.

I took a sip of rum and set the glass down, then put my hand against the edge of the table and slowly pushed.

"The chair is uncomfortable," I told Vince by the way of explanation. I managed to tip the chair back as though simply pushing away from the table a bit, raising the front legs off the ground. I locked my elbow and held the chair there while discreetly wriggling my feet and pushing my legs toward the floor. If it worked, I could work the ropes loose of the chair legs.

"You had Jessica killed, didn't you?" I said to distract Vince.

He looked startled, then smiled. "Yeah, but I wish I could have done it myself. She deserved it. I should have done it myself. I had something really special in mind."

His voice had taken on some of that sick, dreamy quality

again, and for a moment his eyes were far away. Now I had one leg free.

"Where did you come up with the money to settle up after you sold short?" I worked feverishly on freeing the other leg.

"I told you—Culbertson. He was into me deep. The thing is, I never expected to lose that two hundred and fifty thousand. I had the broker followed from the minute he left my office, and I had Jessica followed just to see what she was up to. Of course, when I found out that she had been the one behind my misfortune, I had to kill her." He said it matter-of-factly. He would feel no more remorse about breaking someone's neck than he would about accidentally stepping on an ant.

I had freed my other leg, and now I gently lowered the chair until I was again sitting upright at the table. I picked up my glass and raised it.

"Here's to your good fortune," I said, taking a mouthful.

"Too bad you won't live to see it," he replied.

I threw my glass at him, then called on all the reserves I could muster and scrambled to my feet. I had to bend over to keep from choking on the noose, but I was comparatively free. I grabbed the back of the chair with my free hand and swung it across the table. Vince sat with his mouth open in surprise and disbelief as my first swipe smashed the oil lamp, sending shards of glass flying across the room. The room went momentarily dark, then immediately brightened with a strange flickering of light as the kerosene on the table ignited. Vince quickly got to his feet and reached across the table for me. It was a mistake. The moment he leaned over the table, the front of his rum-soaked shirt burst into flame, and I hit him with a second swing of the chair, breaking it across his hunched shoulders. He staggered, then struck again. I reached for the rum bottle, miraculously unbroken, and as Vince charged, I tipped over the table in front of him. He crashed into it and stumbled, but kept coming. I moved in and smashed the bottle over his head. The blow brought him to his knees, and suddenly his head erupted in flames. The stench of burning hair filled the hut. Vince staggered to his feet, flailing his arms, trying to swat out the fire. I stood mesmerized as he stumbled around blindly, making a strange whimpering sound as his clothes burned and melted against his skin.

Abruptly, he turned in my direction and attacked wildly. I still held the neck of the broken bottle and managed to plunge it into his upper arm as he pawed at me. I collapsed in a heap, then realized with horror that the thatch behind me had caught fire. I rolled away, and saw flames flickering up the opposite wall. They spread with astonishing speed, fiercely consuming a spot almost four feet wide from the floor to the roof. Blind now, Vince crashed through the burning hole, screaming as the thatch sparked and smoldered around him, and ran out into the night.

I managed to get to my feet and followed him out onto the airstrip, the remains of the broken chair dangling from the noose around my neck. He drew closer to the end of the runway, and I followed, drawn like a moth to the flames that still licked up and down his body. The short runway juts out into the harbor, built up on an artificial spit of land. Vince ran close to the edge of the steep embankment that led down to the deep water of the harbor. His macabre gyrations were lit by another flickering glow that grew even brighter, and I turned to see the hut awash in leaping columns of fire. I turned back just in time to see Vince pitch headlong over the edge of the embankment and tumble down out of sight.

I hobbled to the end of the runway and peered into the darkness. Vince was floating in deep water about fifteen or twenty feet out. He was moaning softly, crooning to himself, when suddenly there was a loud splash of water next to him and he disappeared under the surface. He bobbed up a moment later with an inhuman shriek that split the night air.

The horrible sound faded to a low gurgling, and I thought I would be sick. I watched with horrified fascination, rooted to the spot, as he went down again. The water around him churned and bubbled. When he came up this time, he made a retching sound, then his body was viciously yanked to one side, and he was silent. He floated facedown, his body occasionally jerking as the sharks lurking beneath the water's surface ripped away another piece of flesh.

I fell to my hands and knees on the asphalt and threw up, then sat back on my haunches and stared up at the stars, trying not to look back down into the water. I heard the occasional splash below me, and the crackling of the burning hut behind me. I heard cars honking and engines moving closer. Then I heard shouting voices. I turned back toward the shack, and saw three, four, five sets of headlights swarm up to it, then saw lots of running bodies silhouetted in the flames. More men ran shouting to the little strip of beach off to my left down the embankment from the airstrip. They filled buckets with water and ran back with them. The shack was almost completely consumed, so I guessed they must be concerned about the possibility of a brushfire. I watched them curiously, in a strange fog. They paid no attention to me. Finally, through the din, I heard another voice shouting my name, over and over.

"Hello?" I tried to shout it, but it came out more like a high-pitched squeak.

"Over there," I heard the voice shout, and a figure came running toward me. I waited unmoving, wondering who was looking for me. It was Brandt. I looked up at him in disbelief, not sure if he was real.

"Oh, my God," he said, looking with horror at my bruised and bloody face, the burns and blisters, fingering the noose around my neck. "What happened to you? Emerson, I'm sorry, I'm so sorry. Roy said that he hadn't seen you, and the maid told him your room had been ripped apart. We've been looking for you since yesterday morning. What in God's name happened to you?"

He cradled me gently in his arms, pulling my head to his chest, and I began to cry big wet warm tears.

XV

WE STAYED another two weeks, lounging around the Tamarind Bay Club, resting and recuperating. The doctor from Spanish Wells finally gave Brandt the okay to go to Nassau to get clearance from a neurologist to fly home in the pressurized cabin of a commercial jet. I packed him off and stayed on an extra few days to attend to details and to be alone. The burns were superficial and had healed in a few days; the face had healed within a week. The doctor had reset the collarbone and had managed to stop the hemorrhaging, but it was a mess, and would take longer to heal this time. I had not yet been able to talk to Brandt about what had happened. I had bottled it up, refusing to think about it, but I knew I would have to face it if that part of me was to begin healing, too. I needed some time to survey the internal, psychological damage.

I retrieved the briefcase from the bank the second day after Brandt left, and settled up with Roy at the hotel. I kept five thousand in cash and converted what was left—just over thirty-five thousand—into a cashier's check. When I had packed and double-checked my list to be sure I hadn't forgotten anything, I went down to the yacht club dock in the midafternoon to catch the seaplane I had chartered to Governor's Harbour.

I had called ahead, so Dr. Gilbert was expecting me. He met me at the landing, and we drove into town for a drink. I had mixed emotions about the meeting. I had been emphatic that Marty was not to know I was there. I didn't want to see her. But I did ask about her. Gilbert informed me that she was up and around for short periods of time, and that she would be fully recovered in another two weeks or so. I expressed relief, forcing sincerity.

Over a drink, I told Gilbert essentially the same story about Culbertson he had probably read in the newspapers. Then we discussed his fee, he wanting much less than I thought his services were worth. We finally arrived at a satisfactory compromise, and I gave him an additional sum to hold until Marty was ready to leave, so she could buy clothes and an airplane ticket. On the way back to the seaplane landing, Gilbert remarked that Marty had not yet learned of her father's death, suggesting that he would try to keep her uniformed until she was stronger. The man's compassion and composure were astounding. Without regard for possible danger, he had agreed to care for a fugitive with a bullet in her back, and when I had returned to tell him why he had been nursing said fugitive, he had listened calmly, without questions. His trust was remarkable. I told him so.

"Look at it this way, Mr. Ward. Living on a tropical island has its advantages. It's warm, peaceful, pretty. But ever since my tour of duty in Korea, life has not been so adventuresome. Twice now you have burst into my life, and both times you've brought a measure of, shall I say, intrigue into an otherwise mundane existence. You presented me with a challenge I had to accept. A man needs to be challenged." He looked as though he wanted to say more, but he remained silent, thoughtful. I understood his need, guessed his unspoken thoughts, and when he gave me an uncomfortable glance, I nodded knowingly.

We arrived at the landing. I scribbled a hasty note to Marty telling her to contact me in Chicago as soon as she was able, and gave it to Gilbert. He assured me that if anyone came looking for Marty he would put him off with a plausible story.

We shook hands, and I climbed into the waiting seaplane. As we took off, I looked back and saw Gilbert's dwindling figure still standing motionless on the landing. As much as he might wish it, I decided, he would not want to trade places with me.

Towering thunderheads were gathering in the west as we approached Nassau, and the sky changed colors dramatically as the sun sank into the sea. It was a peanut-butter-and-jelly sunset, all deep purples and burnt umber, dark and ominous. This awesome sight made me feel small and insignificant and gave me a queasy stomach. I was relieved when we touched down in calm water off Paradise Island and taxied in toward shore. The landing was not far from the hotel Marty and I had stayed in, so I shouldered my bag and walked. I had called the hotel from Harbour Island two weeks before to ask them to hold my luggage for me, and I went to pick it up. The sky darkened rapidly, strangely affecting my mood. My bad shoulder throbbed, and a gnome was hard at work inside my head, methodically tap-tap-tapping away at my skull with a tiny tack hammer. I didn't want to go to the hotel. The gnome gleefully flipped switches at random as he tapped, turning on projectors in my mind that flashed conflicting images against the back of my eyes. Paranoia set in. Someone could be waiting for me to collect my belongings from the hotel. The gnome laughed at my discomfort, a malevolent chortle. I mustered all the bravado I could, gradually pushing the paranoia back to the far edges of consciousness. Jumpy and suspicious, trying not to attract attention, I collected my bag from the bell captain, then, at the front desk, I presented the claim check that I had so carefully put in my wallet weeks before. The desk clerk retrieved the camera case from the hotel safe while I nervously glanced around the lobby to see if I was being watched. I grabbed all my belongings and beat a hasty retreat. The experience left me shaking with fright, and outside the hotel I leaned against a wall until my knees stopped quivering.

I checked into another hotel for the night, hoping I could catch a flight to New York in the morning. I ordered food from room service, afraid to go out. I found myself double-locking the door, closing the curtains, checking the window locks, peering into the closet, and talking to myself. I stopped short as I dropped to one knee to look under the bed, recognizing how foolish I was being but unable to squelch the impulse. There was nothing beneath the bed.

Room service knocked on the door. I jumped like a rabbit evading buckshot. I tipped the boy and bolted the door behind him, then poured three fingers of Scotch into a glass and drank it neat. Warmth spread through my belly. I poured another, but added ice this time, and sipped. I took the drink and the sandwich and set them on the nightstand, then got the camera case and dumped its contents on bed. The Scotch was beginning to loosen tense muscles and soothe twanging nerves. I plopped down on the bed, and while I munched my sandwich, I tried to make sense out of the pieces of camera lens strewn on the bed. Finally, I got it back together with the diamonds inside snuggled in cotton, satisfied that it would pass a cursory inspection. I left a wake-up call with the front desk, and climbed into bed, wishing with childlike longing that it was my own.

I took a taxi straight from Kennedy Airport to midtown Manhattan in a bleak, gray drizzle. I did not call ahead. I did not even announce myself when I got to the small suite of offices in the building on Third Avenue. I marched past the receptionist into the office with John Pearson's name on the door.

John looked up from the papers on his desk when he heard the door close.

"Emerson! This is a surprise." He peered over half-frame

glasses, then leaned back and motioned toward an empty chair. "Come in and sit down. What are you doing in town? What happened to your arm?"

I ignored the chair and stood in front of his desk, staring down at him.

"Read the papers lately, John?" My voice was controlled. "Bertrand Culbertson is dead."

"Yes, missing at sea, I heard. I wouldn't put it past someone like Bert to reappear suddenly one of these days." He said it with a forced smile, then looked at me perplexed.

"So, you wouldn't put it past 'old Bert,' huh? Know him pretty well, John?"

"No, I, uh, that is . . ." He spluttered in embarrassment.

"He's dead. So's Vince Johnston. I bet you haven't heard about that. It wouldn't make the news up here. So I guess all your troubles are over."

"Johnston's dead? What happened?" He looked even more confused.

"You tell me. Wasn't it Vince who blackmailed you for some terrible family secret? Wasn't it Vince who found out—rather easily, I might add—that your wife's maiden name was Cranston?"

John paled, and seemed to shrink in his chair. I paced across the room, trying to work off some of the anger, and leaned against an oak filing cabinet.

"You see, I talked with Marian Culbertson shortly after you came to Chicago. Some of the things she told me didn't register at first, but later they made sense. She said that her daughter—Martha Culbertson—was adopted. She said that Martha was her sister's daughter, and that her sister had died when Marty was very young. She also said that she and her sister had inherited a great deal of money.

"You didn't know that I'd been seeing Marty Culbertson, did you? No, of course not," I answered for him. "I never told you, and you never asked. Well, it suddenly occurred to me that your wife and Marian Culbertson's sister sounded an awful lot like one and the same person. And I realized why Marty Culbertson seemed so damn familiar to me.

"Do you know where Marty Culbertson is now? Do you know where *your* daughter is?" I nearly shouted the questions, hurling my anger across the room at him.

John looked at me emptily, forlorn and gray, as though Death had just touched him.

"My daughter is dead," he said in a cold, hollow voice.

"Jessica is dead. Your *other* daughter, Martha, is lying in a bed with a bullet hole in her side!"

"Martha is not my daughter," he shouted back at me. "Not anymore. Not since she decided—at five years old, for God's sake—that Bertrand Culbertson was her real father! You have no idea how much that hurt me." He was close to tears.

"So you just let her go and disavowed that she'd ever been your daughter. And you never told Jessica." I paused, watching him reach for a handkerchief to wipe his eyes. "How old was Jessica when your wife died?"

"She was a baby, just a year old," he sobbed. "Martha was almost six, and when Maudie died, something in her just snapped. She turned on me like it was all my fault, and said she wanted to live with her 'real' father, Uncle Bert. It broke my heart, but it was all I could do to take care of Jessica. So I sent Marty off to Chicago."

"And Culbertson?"

"Bertrand and Marian couldn't have children. Marian was delighted at first, and Culbertson was even happier. He knew that Marty took after him, and he never liked me. He saw it as a chance to put me in my place, show me what a nothing I was as far as he was concerned." He blew his nose.

"John, do you have any idea what kind of hell Brandt and I have been through in the past few weeks? You knew when we had lunch in Chicago that I'd gotten involved with some of Culbertson's dirty dealings. You knew that Vince Johnston was still involved. Yet you didn't say a word! You could have saved us all a lot of trouble. Your terrible family secret didn't make a damn bit of difference anymore. Jessica was *dead*! Johnston had her murdered, damn you! And you just sat here in your office pretending to be important while Johnston and Culbertson went on their merry way, destroying people's lives."

"Oh, God, no," he groaned. "Don't tell me any more. Maybe Culbertson was right. Maybe I am a nothing."

"Jesus. Stuff it, John," I said disgustedly. His self-pity reminded me too much of my own. I walked around his office, looking at the knickknacks and paintings, while he pulled himself together. Rain pattered against his window, driven sideways by the wind swirling in random eddies around the Manhattan skyline.

"I can't believe it," John said quietly after a long moment of silence. "Vince killed Jessica?"

"Had her killed," I corrected him.

"Why? Good Lord, why? He'd already taken everything she had."

"Because she managed to get even. He took the last thing she had—her life."

"How did you find out?"

"He told me. We had a little run-in down in the Bahamas two weeks ago."

"You killed him?"

"Let's just say he had a tragic accident."

"What was he after this time?"

"Something that belonged to Culbertson. And that's what really burns me, John. You probably know Culbertson as well as anyone—"

"Not true," he interrupted, raising his head sharply to look at me. "I've stayed as far away from that man as possible."

"Right. You sit here in your protected little fantasy world, and pay no attention to what's going on around you," I said sarcastically. "Simply by virtue of the fact that you're family to Culbertson means that you probably know him instinctively. You may not know specifics, but you must know how he thinks, what makes him tick. And that's what I want from you."

"You mean you still want me to help?" There was a glint of hope in his eyes, a sudden belief that perhaps somehow he could redeem himself.

"Yes, I do. And I'm not asking you, I'm telling you. I know now why Jessica died, and I got my retribution. Vince died as he deserved to die. Badly. But he had some hold over Culbertson that not even Marty knew about. He blackmailed Culbertson to get the two hundred and fifty thousand that he used to pay off Jessica. I want to know what he had on Culbertson that was worth that much money."

It was more than a desire to tie up the loose ends, I knew. Though I didn't want to admit it, my conscience needed to be salved. Some piece of me needed further justification for killing Culbertson. I had rationalized the killing five different ways, but a nagging voice inside had to be assured that Culbertson had not deserved to live, that he had committed enough heinous crimes to warrant the sentence I'd meted out.

John had turned to look out at the rain that smeared the window. Now he swiveled to face me.

"I haven't got anything left, have I?" He said it softly, but there was no despair in the words. "Finding out what Bertrand was into is the least I can do."

"You *do* have a daughter, John," I said gently. "When she finds out what happened, she just might come to you for support, for help. Especially if she's convinced about Culbertson's guilt."

"I'll find you the answers." He said it with quiet determination.

"Thank you." I picked up my bags and left without a backward glance.

*   *   *

Chicago welcomed me with a warm, soft breeze, green budding trees, and new spring flowers. It was good to be home. The house sme
lled musty from disuse, and I opened all the windows to air it. Brandt came over while I was unpacking, bringing a stack of newspaper that had collected on his porch while we were gone. I was not yet ready to find out what had gone on in the world in my absence. But over the course of the next weeks, Brandt and I avidly pored over all the stories having anything to do with Culbertson or the hotel chain, catching up on all the news since his death.

It was a strange time. We spent most days together, potting about in his yard or lounging on my patio like two old men, lifetime companions, each afraid to leave the other alone for fear he might up and die. The outside world did not exist for us—we were still somehow lost in a small world created by the experience we'd been through, and we clung to each other, bonded by that experience. We shared a secret, a secret that haunted us, always in the back of our minds, yet one that we could not voice even to each other. We talked about what had happened only indirectly, comparing notes on newspaper articles, discussing the stories as though we were following a soap opera, catching each other up on the latest developments in the Culbertson saga with a mixture of morbid curiosity and mock disgust.

Culbertson's disappearance had been news for three days, and after that the stories had changed focus and had concentrated on the upheaval within the Culbertson empire. The major question had been, of course, how the empire was to be divided, and whether it *could* be divided without proof of his death. And then it had become clear that Culbertson's only daughter and heir was more than "unavailable for comment." She had mysteriously dropped out of sight, according to the press. Culbertson Hotel officials had vigorously denied all rumors of foul play, but after another week had passed, a massive search had been ordered, with no results. Until finally it was learned that Martha Cranston Culbertson had gone into seclusion in the Bahamas following her father's death and would return to Chicago when she was good and ready. And by the time Martha had returned, a new scandal had hit the papers. Somehow, news had been leaked to the press that Culbertson had left virtually no personal estate. The only thing left, apparently, was stock in the hotel chain that was frozen in a trust account. The rest—and everybody assumed there must be a good deal more—was gone, and nobody knew where.

The spring days passed, each one bringing less rain and more sunshine. My nightmares were less frequent. The funny things that had been happening inside my head were going away, too. The gnome had not put in an appearance for a while. But I was still moody and irritable. It wasn't over yet.

I kept myself occupied repainting the patio furniture, cleaning the windows, fixing the leaky faucet in the kitchen, wallpapering the bathroom. Someone offered to buy the house for an outrageous sum of money. Brandt's tulips blossomed satisfactorily. The stock market seesawed predictably. The lakefront beaches unofficially opened for the season. The price of milk rose six cents per gallon, contributing to a point-oh-four percent increase in the wholesale price index. City firefighters negotiated a new contract.

It was a hot day in late May when I finally heard from John Pearson. I was on my knees, pulling weeds from the cracks in between the patio bricks. It had not rained for a week, so I had hosed down the patio to soften the dirt. Even so, the stubborn rascals clung tenaciously to the little bits of soil. I stabbed at them with a kitchen knife, trying to pry them loose, frustrated by the lack of two good hands, sweating with the effort. There seemed to be no end to the task, and my

knife-wielding had taken a savage turn when Brandt let himself in my back gate.

"I intercepted this at your front door," he said, waving a
Federal Express package. "You must not have heard the
doorbell."

"You're right," I said, glad for the excuse to get up and
stretch. "All I can hear are these damn weeds taunting me,
daring me to try and pull them up." I took the package from
his outstretched hand.

"You're in a good mood today."

"Next time I'm going to hire someone to napalm the damn
things." I lowered myself into a patio chair, still stiff from
spending half the morning on my knees.

"Come on, open it," Brandt said eagerly, perching on a
chair opposite mine.

I grasped the cardboard envelope with the fingers of my
bad arm, and struggled to tear it open with my other hand.
Inside was a white #10 envelope. I pulled it out and ripped
open an end with my teeth, then shook the contents onto my
lap. All that slid out were a newspaper clipping and a piece
of memo paper folded once. I picked up the clipping, swiped
at the sweat running down my nose so it wouldn't drip on the
newsprint, and read.

The article was brief and vague, only hinting at some
investigation of two officials at a construction company for
alleged kickbacks to clients. But the name of the construction
company was startlingly familiar. I passed the clipping to
Brandt, and unfolded the memo. It had just a few words
scrawled across it.

"Emerson," the note said, "B.C. owned Drescher (barely)
through a dummy corporation. You take it from there. Best,
John."

I read it twice, then stared at it while thoughts ran through
my brain. When I looked up, Brandt had finished reading
the newspaper clipping and was staring at me.

"Well?"

"Why don't you get us a couple of beers." He looked at me curiously, then went into the house. I reread the note while he was gone, and when he came back I exchanged the piece of paper for the bottle he had in his hand. He stared at it for a long time, then raised his head to give me a quizzical look.

"I think it all makes sense now," I said with a small smile.

"I'm not sure I get it. Tell me."

"Drescher Construction was the company that was rebuilding the Sandbeach and actually building other Culbertson properties." I started slowly, picking my way through the pieces of the puzzle that were starting to click together in my mind. "John's note says that Culbertson had a controlling interest in the company through a dummy corporation. Why a dummy corporation?"

"Conflict of interest," Brandt said immediately. "He was obviously giving construction contracts to his own company."

"And that's also where he was probably taking in most of his cash, but he was having so many problems with his personal investments that he was spending the money as fast as he was taking it in from Drescher. Enter Vince Johnston— and Jessica. Jessica, by sheerest coincidence, picked Drescher stock to play with, and started driving up the price. Vince somehow found out about Culbertson's conflict of interest, and when he saw the stock price going up, saw an opportunity to make a killing. He couldn't lose, even by selling short, because he knew he could blackmail Culbertson into *giving* him a thousand shares to sell.

"But Culbertson refused to give him the thousand shares because that would have meant losing controlling interest and possible exposure to the other stockholders. So he had to come up with the quarter million when Vince got caught in Jessica's squeeze."

"Very neat," Brandt said admiringly.

"Yeah, but it doesn't end there. Vince kept putting the squeeze on Culbertson, but Culbertson was tapped. He had virtually nothing left. So Vince came up with the idea of kidnapping Marty. As distasteful as the idea was to Culbertson, he went for it like a starving dog. Culbertson Hotels' insurance policy would have covered the ransom, and both Vince and Culbertson would have come out of it ahead. Culbertson assumed that by arranging the kidnapping himself, Marty would come to no harm, and no one would be the wiser.

"It fits. It all falls neatly into place now, doesn't it?" I fell silent, remembering the frightened look on Marty's face as she lay in the bunk of Derek's trimaran, the worried look on Culbertson's face on the boat, and Vince's look of smug satisfaction when he told me he had Culbertson by the balls. So it was all wrapped up, a tidy solution neatly sealed and topped with a bright bow. I felt strangely dissatisfied, as though I'd eaten Chinese food an hour earlier. I frowned, searching for the source of my discomfort, looking around to see if I'd missed a course.

"Something still bothers you," Brandt said softly. "What is it?"

"I don't know. I keep having these nightmares. . . ."

"Culbertson and Vince are gone. They won't be coming back. You said yourself that it had to be done. No, it's more than nightmares."

I thought a long time before the words came to me.

"I lost a part of myself when Jessica died. A big piece of me." Brandt started to speak, but I knew what he was going to say and I cut him off. "No, listen. You couldn't help me. No one could. I had to find out by myself what I had lost. And I did. It took a long time, but down there on Eleuthera I found what I was looking for. I found myself. And I found that part of that self is a little boy who is afraid of just about everything. I became determined to stop being so afraid.

"When I finally admitted to myself what was wrong and

got back in touch with me, with my feelings, I thought that everything would be back to normal. I had confidence in the Emerson who had been lost all those months. Having found that piece of me, I got cocky and daring, and challenged the big bad man. I underestimated Culbertson, and I underestimated Vince. Or I overestimated my ability to play in their league, the games Emerson would play only when the deck is stacked in his favor. Sure, I took precautions, but Culbertson still almost managed to mess everything up. He almost killed *all* of us. He shouldn't have been able to hurt us that badly, but he did. The man scared me. And Vince scared me even more. And for the past month I've been trying to convince myself—and that little boy—that as frightened as I was, I stood up to them. I grossly misjudged my abilities, but somehow it all turned out okay."

I paused to swallow some beer. Brandt was looking intently at me, waiting for me to continue.

"At least it turned out okay in the sense that we're all alive and Culbertson didn't get away. But too many people got hurt. There was no reason to take on Culbertson; I had no business taking him on. I was going to let it drop. I had already messed up the payoff to Portolucci and I'd busted up the kidnapping attempt. There was a point where I could have—should have—dumped the whole affair back into Marty's lap. But I was angry, angry at myself, at Marty, at Culbertson. And I felt I had to prove something to myself. But more important, I realize now, I had to finish the whole thing to hide the hurt I felt. I lost Jessica, and seeing this through to the end was a way of keeping myself occupied, a way of delaying the pain."

My voice broke, and I hoped that Brandt wouldn't notice the wetness that brimmed in my eyes, the embarrassment I felt. But he had turned his back and was too busy honking into a handkerchief to notice.

"You know something funny?" Brandt said, taking a self-conscious swipe at his eyes with the handkerchief. "That female cur was asking about you the night of the yacht club party. She was setting you up. I heard her casually ask three or four people who you were, what kind of guy, and why you were so hangdog dismal. I thought of warning you, but you obviously didn't want company, and I was sure that you would see through her act."

"All because she thought I was blackmailing her so-called father."

"More than that. Martha Cranston Culbertson was Bertrand's only child, and she is accustomed to getting what she wants and to having her own way. She's an aggressive, dominating, forward woman. She needs to control situations. She needs to dominate in a relationship. You were a prime candidate for her needs—a good-looking, single, rugged, but *malleable* male.

"In spite of your other shortcomings," he continued after a pause, "you are not the sort of fellow who allows himself to be dominated. Though you don't require control over situations, you do expect to have control over yourself and your emotions in most situations. I could see what was happening, but I couldn't do anything about it."

"I know," I said quietly. Brandt missed his calling; he should have been a psychologist. We both fell silent, and in a moment I got up to get us both another beer.

"The problem," I said when I returned, "is that I still don't feel comfortable with myself. It's time to reassess, to reexamine. Why did I challenge Culbertson at his own game? It isn't fear itself that motivates—though it helps—nor is it the ability to conquer fear or channel it into positive energies. The motivation and reward, I think, lie in righting a wrong, correcting an injustice, surmounting seemingly impossible odds to reproportion an imbalance. Sheep have little chance against a pack of wolves, but the presence of a shepherd or a good sheepdog in the flock helps even the odds."

I spoke hesitantly, choosing my words carefully.

"Do I take on too much? Do I play judge and jury? By what right do I give myself the power to determine right from wrong, to arbitrate ethical questions, to judge a morality fitting for others? What is this compulsion?" I paused, searching for the answer to my questions. "Is it an instinctive reaction to the unfairness of the world? Am I uniquely and predeterminedly suited to the task of protecting innocents, like the sheepdog who knows nothing other than its life purpose of keeping the wolves away from the flock?

"I don't think so." I shook my head. "As hard as I try to fool myself, I'm *not* clever and crafty and quick. There are a lot of people who are better qualified for the job. So why do I continue to play avenger, beating my chest and leaping half-assed into the fray? Maybe it's some deep psychological need to prove my own goodness, my own selfworth, an attempt to solidify my own sand-castle virtues. Perhaps it is guilt that motivates me, and not any moralistic sense of indignation. I don't know."

Brandt didn't reply. I didn't expect him to. He couldn't answer my questions, though I knew he would try in time. We had both skirted emotionally charged issues for a long time, especially ones that had concerned my lifestyle. It felt good to get some of it off my chest, to voice some of the concerns and put them in perspective. The air around me seemed to clear as I verbalized and loosed the anxieties, shrugging off my grisly preoccupation with the deaths of Bertrand Culbertson and Vince Johnston. The world brightened perceptibly, and the day came alive. The air smelled sweet, scented with newly blossomed flowers and fresh-cut grass. The sun stood almost directly overhead, shining with the intensity of summer. The world whirred busily by, cheered by the bright freshness of it all.

I stood up, smiling, then was startled by the tinkle of the bell. Brandt and I looked at each other, hesitating, then I went to open the gate. Standing there, looking as beautiful as ever, was Marty. Surprise took my breath away for a moment, and without being aware of it, I stared at her with slack jaw and open mouth. I had expected her at some point, and yet I hadn't. She looked well, though thin and pale, not quite filling out the bust and hips of her dress. There was an unusual quality about her, and I finally put my finger on it: she looked vulnerable, like a small girl in dress-up clothes.

"Come in," I said when I regained my composure. She hesitantly stepped through the gate and looked around. "Marty, this is my friend Brandt Williams," I said to introduce them. Brandt beamed at her.

"Would you like to come into the house?" I asked. She nodded and Brandt silently indicated that he would wait on the patio. I led the way into the living room.

"How's your arm?" Marty asked softly.

"Troublesome, but healing," I replied. I didn't take the trouble to ask her how she was. She was alive, and should have been thankful for that. I sensed that she was uncomfortable, not really interested in small talk, but she was being polite. I asked her to wait a moment while I got the camera case. I handed it to her.

"I replaced the diamonds just as they were," I said. "It seemed the easiest way to get them into the country. What you do with them is none of my business. I'm sure you'll find someone who will cut and appraise them, or perhaps you'd like to let Mr. Portolucci take care of that?"

Her eyebrows rose half a centimeter, and momentary surprise flashed in her eyes.

"You used me to deliver the diamonds in the first place, so I used them to find out what Culbertson was up to." I shrugged. I saw no reason to tell her about the money we'd taken from Culbertson. Her overall calm puzzled me. She seemed almost humble, and her lack of questions was odd under the circumstances.

"I guess that's it," I said, turning toward the door.

"Emerson," she said, causing me to turn back. "I don't want to know what happened down there—Roland Gilbert told me enough to piece together most of it—but obviously it was messy and painful." She hesitated, then spoke in a small voice. "You killed him, didn't you?"

"Yes. I killed Culbertson before he killed us. And I killed Vince because he murdered your sister." I said it firmly but quietly, looking her dead in the eye. She turned white as a sheet, but said nothing. "You signed Jessica's death warrant by throwing in with Vince, by believing his lies. And for what? To protect a man who never even truly loved you?"

"No, God, no," she said in a small, choked voice. "I had nothing to do with Jessica's death. It was an accident."

"Vince had her killed!"

"I never meant her any harm," she cried, her voice getting shrill. "But I wouldn't let anyone try to take advantage of my father, not even Jessica!"

Her eyes searched my face. When she didn't say anything more, I turned to leave, but she called me back again, her voice calm now.

"Emerson, I guess I should thank you for saving my life. I know you don't think much of me after what's happened, and I know you can't forgive me, just as I can't forgive you for what you've done. But I want you to know that I understand."

"You still don't get it, do you? You've got nothing left. Your so-called father pissed it all away with his greed and his hate. He used you, just as he used everyone else in his life. And you've spent a lifetime emulating the man. Do you think you'll end up any better off? If I were you, I'd think seriously about asking John Pearson's forgiveness, because he's about all you've got."

I don't think she was capable of understanding the hurt and pain, the anguish, the guilt, the sweaty nightmares, but after seeing the sudden confusion in her face I mentally conceded that in her own way, in her own time, perhaps she would understand some of it. It was no longer important.

She turned abruptly and preceded me out the door. I saw Brandt watch us curiously as we came out. I lengthened my stride to reach the gate ahead of her, lifting the latch and swinging it open with mock gallantry. Martha Cranston Culbertson cruised right on out without a backward glance, camera case in hand swinging at her side as she disappeared down the alley to the street.

MICHAEL SHERER is a marketing communications consultant and freelance writer. A contributing editor of several trade magazines, Mr. Sherer was the recipient of the 1989 Cahner's Publishing Company's "Award of Excellence." He resides in Chicago with his family and is currently at work on his fourth novel featuring Emerson Ward.

■ HarperPaperbacks *By Mail*

LISTENING WOMAN.
An incredible murder investigation carries the Navajo Tribal Police from a dead man's secret to a kidnap scheme, to a conspiracy that stretches back more than one hundred years.

THE DARK WIND.
Sgt. Jim Chee is trapped in the deadly web of a cunningly spun plot driven by Navajo sorcery and white man's greed.

A THIEF OF TIME.
Lt. Joe Leaphorn and Officer Jim Chee must plunge into the past to unearth the astonishing truth behind a mystifying series of horrific murders.

DANCE HALL OF THE DEAD. Compelling, terrifying and highly suspenseful, DANCE HALL OF THE DEAD never relents from first page till last.

THE BLESSING WAY.
When Lt. Joe Leaphorn of the Navajo Tribal Police discovers a corpse with a mouthful of sand at a crime scene seemingly without tracks or clues, he is ready to suspect a supernatural killer.

SKINWALKERS.
Brimming with Navajo lore and sizzling with suspense, SKINWALKERS brings Chee and Leaphorn together for the first time.

THE FLY ON THE WALL. A dead reporters secret notebook tell of a scandel involving a senatorial candidate, a million-dollar scam and murder. Soon John Cotton hears the deadly footsteps of powerful people with something to hide

SEVEN TONY HILLERMAN

M Y S T E R I E S

YOU WON'T BE ABLE TO PUT DOWN

Tony Hillerman's novels are all best sellers. All his books are unique, riveting and highly suspenseful. Be sure not to miss any of these brilliant and original mysteries filled with Navajo lore sizzling suspense.

Buy 4 or More and $ave

When you buy 4 or more books from Harper Paperbacks, the Postage and Handling is FREE.

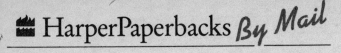